STILL WATERS

STILL WATERS

A Lake District Mystery

E. C. R. Lorac

with an introduction by
MARTIN EDWARDS

This edition first published in 2025 by
The British Library
96 Euston Road
London NW1 2DB
bl.uk

1 3 5 7 9 10 8 6 4 2

Still Waters was first published in 1949 by
The Collins Crime Club, London.

Introduction © 2025 Martin Edwards
Still Waters © 1949 The Estate of E. C. R. Lorac
Volume copyright © 2025 The British Library Board

Represented in the EU by Authorised Rep Compliance
Ltd., Ground Floor, 71 Lower Baggot Street, Dublin,
D02 P593, Ireland. arccompliance.com

Cataloguing in Publication Data
A catalogue record for this publication is
available from the British Library

ISBN 978 0 7123 5534 6
e-ISBN 978 0 7123 6220 7

Cover Illustration © Private Collection
Christie's Images / Bridgeman Images.
Text design and typesetting by Tetragon, London
Printed in England by CPI Group (UK) Ltd, Croydon, CR0 4YY

CONTENTS

INTRODUCTION 7
A NOTE FROM THE PUBLISHER 13

Still Waters 15

INTRODUCTION

Still Waters, an unusual and atmospheric novel of detection, is an excellent example of E. C. R. Lorac's ability to blend people, place, and plot. First published in 1949, this was the third Lorac novel to be set in the relatively unfamiliar (at least as a setting for mystery fiction) area of Lunesdale in north Lancashire. Although it was the thirty-second book to feature Chief Inspector Robert Macdonald, there is no hint of staleness or reliance on formula. On the contrary, this is the work of an author on top form, juggling the disparate elements of her story with quiet confidence. There is a great deal to enjoy here, including the clever title, the full significance of which is only revealed at the end of the book. Above all what stays in the memory is the evocation of the landscape and the lives of the characters who inhabit it. This may be a work of fiction, but its strength lies in its authenticity. No one who reads this book, even if they skipped the author's foreword, could doubt that Lorac was writing about somewhere she knew well—and loved.

The story opens with Caroline Bourne coming to live in Lunesdale, in order to be close to her cousin Kate Hoggett and her husband Giles, a former bookseller who comes from a family with a long tradition of farming in the locality. Caroline has been "racketing around in London and on the Continent for the greater part of her life", but as her half-century approaches, she wants to settle down: "In these days of atomic potentialities and food shortages there was a lot to be said for striking roots in the remote peacefulness of northern fell country."

Her "escape to the country" is no whim. She likes Kate and Giles very much, and recognises "that their vigorous practical lives endowed them with something which she was in danger of missing... they belonged to a stable environment, and stability was becoming rarer and rarer."

Caroline sets her heart on a smallholding called Broadgarth and a nearby area of woodland that includes a ruined cottage and a deep quarry pool: "I've always wanted a lake... you can see the sea from the cottage, and the Morecambe sands."

Broadgarth is up for auction, and Caroline finds herself in competition to buy, which pushes the price up as far as she is prepared to go. Luckily, her final bid (of two thousand pounds; property prices in 1949 bore no resemblance to those of today!) is successful, and she is so thrilled that she doesn't mind the fact that the auctioneer seemed reluctant to hear her bid. Nor is she overly curious when someone immediately tries to offer her one hundred pounds more for Broadgarth than the purchase price she has agreed. Caroline suspects he may be "a black market racketeer", and this is one of the many period touches that make books from this era a mine of fascinating detail about post-war English society.

She consults an architect friend, Francis Rolph, for advice about renovations, and he is involved in another strange incident while looking at the quarry pool in the moonlight. He thinks that someone has attacked him and knocked him down, but since he did not see his assailant, he admits that it's possible he simply tripped over a bramble. When the matter is reported to the local police, Inspector Bord is sceptical about Giles Hoggett's attempts to play the amateur detective, and in particular his theory about a dead body (that of a local man who has recently gone missing). Is it really possible that the corpse is concealed beneath the still waters of the quarry pool?

Matters take a fresh turn when Kate receives an unexpected but welcome visitor: Chief Inspector Macdonald. The policeman, who got to know the Hoggetts during the events described in *The Theft of the Iron Dogs*, suddenly turns up on their doorstep. He has been up to Ulverston (on the other side of Morecambe Bay) and Heysham while investigating a case of Customs evasion and has decided to call on his friends while in the neighbourhood. Macdonald is sufficiently intrigued by the Hoggetts' account of events to visit the quarry pool himself, where he finds a familiar face emerging from the water "marred with black mud stains and clinging slime". Meanwhile, Caroline—who is an artist and writer by profession—has been invited to stay at a luxurious new hotel some miles away to undertake an artistic commission, but some aspects of the arrangement seem puzzling, and the plot continues to thicken.

At one point, Inspector Bord ruminates on the "rum days" they are living in: "When I was first in the force, there was virtually no crime in this area. Occasional drunks, occasional tramps, some petty larceny... To-day, with black market and deserters and maniacs and perverts—well by gum, anything might happen anywhere." Readers may be reassured, however, that Lorac's interest as a crime writer was not in chronicling the activities of maniacs and perverts.

This is not, however, to say that this is a book that can helpfully be described as "cosy crime", a hackneyed term beloved of publicists with limited imagination. Lorac never wallows in gore, but much as she delights in rural England, she does not romanticise it, often reminding us of the tough nature of farm work and the tensions that can brew within small, enclosed communities. Her attitude towards sudden and violent death is reflected in the words of one character towards the end of the story: "You thought you'd found a corpse and you didn't enjoy it. Decent blokes never do enjoy it. That's why some detective novels drive me mad. Bloody corpses aren't funny."

The appeal of *Still Waters* derives in part from the fact that it was a deeply personal book. Lorac's foreword is addressed to Kate and Giles, but in reality to their real-life counterparts, namely her sister Maud and her husband John Howson. The foreword gives clues to the real-life locations featured in the story, which are "marked on the Ordnance Survey map", and the accuracy with which she captures the topography is crucial to the storyline, as when Macdonald reflects that "if a man wanted to play hide-and-seek in this little known area of England… he might do worse than learn about the old wool-pack routes that avoided the main roads". Lorac also makes clear that she had done her homework on police procedure, consulting an expert "who assured me that some of my flights of fancy were not more wild than was commensurate with possibilities. He even accepted the donkey which Giles refused to believe in." As a result, the descriptions of the activities of the detectives Walsh and Bateson as events approach an exciting climax in the latter stages of the book are as convincing as they are vivid.

Caroline Bourne is a rather charming self-portrait of the author, whose real name was Edith Caroline Rivett (1894–1958). She used the pen-name Mary Le Bourne for a late novel, *Two-Way Murder*, that did not appear in her lifetime but was published as a British Library Crime Classic in 2021. Not only was the real-life Caroline (or Carol, as she was generally known) also a writer and artist, she too came to Lunesdale at about the same age as her fictional alter ego, and for much the same reason, to be close to Maud and John.

The overlap between fact and fiction didn't stop there. There are, for instance, cameo roles for a neighbour of the Hoggetts, Mrs. Beck, and her small daughter Lena. These characters were based on Lizzie Clark (who became her housekeeper) and her daughter Lena, now Lena Whiteley, whose home happened to be called Beck Cottage.

Over the past decade, I have had the great pleasure of getting to know Lena and her family, particularly her son David and her daughter Helen, and they have supplied me with a great deal of information about Carol Rivett and her work. David tells me that, for instance, "The route that Walsh took by bike to the sands at Bolton-le-sands (Western-le-sands in the book) is via Nether Kellet and is an accurate description of the route." Pleasingly, an exhibition about Lorac's life and work was held at Bolton-le-Sands library in 2024 before transferring to the library at nearby Halton (known as Hulton in this book).

I find it especially fascinating that Lena was present at the event which became the starting point for the story of *Still Waters*. She and her mother attended a sale of a smallholding called Sidegarth (the model for Broadgarth) in the company of Carol Rivett. At that time, the Clarks were hoping to buy the property, but the total cost of the purchase price together with equipping and stocking the smallholding proved to be out of reach. I gather from David Whiteley that over the years, the house has been extended and modified, but the barn remains very much as described in the book; he believes the ruined cottage in the story was originally an old ruined smithy built during the packhorse era which was demolished by the landowner in the 1980s.

There is one final reason why it gives me enormous pleasure to see this book back in print. It was a favourite of my parents, who often visited Morecambe and the Bay, as my grandmother lived there for many years. This was the novel that prompted them to introduce me to Lorac's detective fiction, and I'm sure they'd be as thrilled to see it enjoying a fresh life in the twenty-first century as I am.

MARTIN EDWARDS
www.martinedwardsbooks.com

A NOTE FROM THE PUBLISHER

The original novels and short stories reprinted in the British Library Crime Classics series were written and published in a period ranging, for the most part, from the 1890s to the 1960s. There are many elements of these stories which continue to entertain modern readers; however, in some cases there are also uses of language, instances of stereotyping and some attitudes expressed by narrators or characters which may not be endorsed by the publishing standards of today. We acknowledge therefore that some elements in the works selected for reprinting may continue to make uncomfortable reading for some of our audience. With this series British Library Publishing aims to offer a new readership a chance to read some of the rare books of the British Library's collections in an affordable paperback format, to enjoy their merits and to look back into the world of the twentieth century as portrayed by its writers. It is not possible to separate these stories from the history of their writing and therefore the following novel is presented as it was originally published with minor edits only made for consistency of style and sense. We welcome feedback from our readers, which can be sent to the following address:

> British Library Publishing
> The British Library
> 96 Euston Road
> London, NW1 2DB
> United Kingdom

STILL WATERS

FOREWORD

DEAR KATE AND GILES,

When I had finished writing *The Theft of the Iron Dogs*, I felt more than a little apprehensive. Was it possible that this story about a tiny hamlet in Lunesdale, with its authentic description of Wenningby Barns and its owners, could interest anybody "from away"? Apparently it was possible, for I am still surprised at the number of people who have read the book, and have written to me to tell me they have enjoyed it.

Here is another story about Lunesdale. As you both know, the quarry pool, the derelict cottage and the ruins of one ancient small holding exist in fact. They are, indeed, marked on the Ordnance Survey, though the place names I have used are fictitious. If anybody wants to employ the detective method to locate them, I will say this to assist their researches: I have given the real names of the fells and limestone heights which can be seen from "Broadgarth" and "Wenningby." Some of my kind correspondents have assumed that "Wenningby" is the little town of Wennington. That is not so. Looking south from "Wenningby" we see the fells from Claughton Moor to Clougha: our eastern skyline is the Pennines—Ingleborough, Pen-y-ghent and Whernside. To our north, we can see Scafell and the Langdale Pikes if the day be clear.

From the cottage in the copse can be seen Warton Crag and Morecambe Sands. The pack-horse bridge and the bridle-paths exist, too, as does "Merchant's Corner"—a free rendering of its ancient and honourable name. The great mass of masonry carrying and abutting the canal aqueduct, and the stone arches of the railway viaduct are not difficult to locate—but the quarry pool itself is hidden so well that it would take ardent detective work to find it.

The one place which has no foundation in fact is "Hauxhead Castle." When I asked Kate Hoggett for a possible place-name which did not exist, she said "Call it Hauxhead. It's the ancient way of spelling a name common in the north-west—Hawkshead."

Again I acknowledge my indebtedness to you both; also to one of His Majesty's Inspectors whom I may not more closely specify: it was he who assured me that some of my flights of fancy were not more wild than was commensurate with possibilities. He even accepted the donkey which Giles refused to believe in.

Yours, in all gratitude,

E. C. R. LORAC.

LUNESALDE, 1948.

ONE

I

"IS THAT THE PLACE, GILES?"

Caroline Bourne spoke eagerly, leaning forward in the car as it bumped and lurched over the woodland track.

"That? Of course not. That's only an old ruin of no interest to anybody."

Giles Hoggett spoke in what Caroline described as "His Landowning Voice." It was not sharp, only terse and authoritarian, and, as he always pointed out, it was *not* the voice he reserved for his tenants. Giles was always even-tempered and easy-going, but he did think that on this occasion Caroline was showing less than her usual intelligence. He had been in the midst of a cogent description of the advantages of the Broadgarth shippons, capable of accommodating six milking cows and several stirks or heifers, and Caroline must have been wool-gathering to imagine that he was taking her to view an ancient ruin with intent to purchase it as her home.

"Broadgarth is a good house, sound and weather-worthy, conveniently placed with easy access to its own land," he said cheerfully.

Caroline sat back and wondered if she was being really unwise. She wanted to live in the Lunesdale district, she was quite certain about that. To herself she would have described the hill country between Lancaster and the Pennines as enchanting: with Giles she would have observed a more becoming reticence and would merely have said it was "good country." She also wanted to live near Giles and Kate Hoggett. After racketing around in London and on the Continent for the greater part of her life, she had come to the conclusion "when her half-century stared her in the face" that it was desirable to strike roots and look forward to a serene old age. In these days of atomic potentialities and food shortages there was a lot to be said for striking roots in the remote peacefulness of northern fell country, but, since she was a sociable and talkative soul, Caroline wanted company in her riper years. To Caroline's mind, her cousin Kate Hoggett, plus that philosophic husband of hers, were ideal companions. They talked, very vigorously, on every topic from nuclear fission to manure (called "muck" in Lunesdale), but apart from their conversation they possessed the tranquillity of people living in peace in their own environment. Caroline liked them both very much, and she had the sense to see that their vigorous practical lives endowed them with something she was in danger of missing. In short, they belonged to a stable environment, and stability was becoming rarer and rarer.

The car bumped clear of the woodland track and lurched yet more violently as it drew nearer to Broadgarth, "that valuable small holding" which Giles advised Caroline to buy.

"You wouldn't really call this a road, would you, Giles?" she inquired. "At least, it might be a road if I could get a steam roller. Would it be my road?"

"This section would be yours—and the approach, too, if you buy that bit of woodland as I advise," said Giles. "There's some useful timber in it. I dare say you could approach the authorities on the matter of the steam roller, but that's a minor point. Those are the pigsties; they're the finest sties around here."

Caroline was getting more and more frightened. She was prepared to cope with a couple of cows, and even a bunch of stirks, but pigs plus a steam roller daunted her. Giles pulled the car up in the open space in front of the farm-house and Caroline got out and looked around her, bracing herself against a wind which whipped through her tweeds as though they were non-existent. It was an ancient stone house on an eminence, standing without any trees or other windbreaks among green pastures and greener meadows: a house with no nonsense about it, it could not be called picturesque even by the most ardent amateur sketcher, but it was sturdy, and it belonged to its environment. "It must have grown there," thought Caroline.

"You had better inspect the house yourself," said Giles firmly. "I want to have another look at those shippons—ah, there's a good muck-heap, and a pump for the liquid manure... That muck should be put on the land at once..."

Caroline went in at the little gate, up a short flagged path, and knocked on the front door. Her hair was blown to the golliwog type of coiffure, her tweed skirt ballooned violently and her jacket felt miserably inadequate—but this *might* be her own front door—and there were some daffodils: they were not exactly "taking the winds of March with beauty," but they were fighting vigorously to keep their roots in the soil.

"Mrs. Brough?" inquired Caroline, when the door was opened.

"Yes. Miss Bourne, isn't it?" inquired the representative of the executors who were putting Broadgarth on the market. "It's a good air up here," observed Mrs. Brough, and Caroline shivered as she stepped thankfully into the still air of the ancient house. As she followed her guide through kitchen and dairy and parlour Caroline recovered her balance.

"Kate is perfectly right," she thought. "Of course I shan't attempt to farm this land. I shall let it to the Bromsgrove farmer, and the shippons and pigsties as well. Giles is quite mad to encourage me to farm it. It's not a bad house, and anyway it'll be a good investment. Land always is, especially now..."

"The well is just close by the back door," said Mrs. Brough. "It's lovely water. I never fancy water out of a tap myself."

"There's plenty of it," murmured Caroline inadequately. There was. The well was full.

"Does it ever overflow?" she asked weakly.

"That's very good water," said Mrs. Brough firmly. "Here, shoo! get along with you," she shouted to some inquiring lambs. "That's just a gap in the hedge, a bit of wire will put that right," she said encouragingly. "It's a nice garden."

Caroline did not argue. It *might* be a nice garden… The lambs and ewes had seen to it that nothing succulent remained. "It's convenient for blackberries," she said pleasantly.

"Oh, them. I take no count of them," said Mrs. Brough. "Now you've seen the house, you'll be wanting to see the land."

"Yes. Mr. Hoggett is here and he will go over the land with me," said Caroline firmly.

"Mr. Hoggett? Hoggetts have never farmed here," said Mrs. Brough suspiciously.

"No, but perhaps they will now," said Caroline sweetly. "Mr. Hoggett is advising me, you see. Thank you very much for showing me the house. It's a very interesting house."

"Well, she thinks I'm plain bats anyway," said Caroline to herself, and went out into the good air again. She found Giles in the barn. It was a lovely barn, and its spacious emptiness appealed to Caroline.

"Why, this could be turned into a glorious studio," she exclaimed unguardedly.

Giles dealt firmly with this outrageous suggestion.

"The barn is essential to the farm," he said: "it was the first consideration of the builders. They paid no heed to the inhabitants of the house, they planned the whole structure according to the number of beasts to be accommodated. This is a six-cow shippon. The six cows determined the size of the house." He leant against the boostings (the wooden partition between the stalls and the threshing-floor). "You don't know how lucky you are," he said firmly. "This farm is only twenty acres, and yet you have this fine barn to house six head of cattle, and standing for two calves, and plenty of room for your hay and oats. I hope you won't mention this studio idea again. The proprietors would be quite justified in refusing to sell the place to you if you did."

"I'll remember," said Caroline. "Do you think it's necessary for me to see the land? I'm quite willing to take your word for it."

"Of course you must see the land," replied Giles. "I gather the present arrangement gives you six acres of meadow, two of arable and twelve of pasture. The main pasture lies to the south—" He strode resolutely into the wind and Caroline followed him meekly. He was very thorough and they had a long walk, because he insisted on examining the state of hedges, dry-stone walls, gates and ditches.

"Twenty acres seems much bigger than I thought," panted Caroline when they reached the fold yard again, and Giles said:

"Now the pigsties—" But at last Caroline rebelled.

"I'll take them as read," she said. "You say they're fine pigsties and you know much more about the needs of pigs than I do. I want to see that bit of woodland; you've advised me to buy it and I want to consider it."

"But you *ought* to see the pigsties," insisted Giles. "The drainage is particularly good. The pig—"

"Is a very clean animal," cut in Caroline. "I know that, and I'm glad the drainage is satisfactory, but if we examine both the sties *and* the woodland we shall certainly be late for tea, and the last thing Kate said was 'Be sure you are back in time for tea,' and you promised we would be."

"Did I?" asked Giles, rather apprehensively, and Caroline made for the car.

"You did," she said firmly. "Giles, if I buy this place I shall buy a jeep. No car would stand this track for long. Now come on, and pull up when we're level with that ruin."

"If you buy a jeep you'll need another garage," he argued, and Caroline just stopped herself saying "I shall keep it in the barn…" She was beginning to realise that Giles had deep-seated convictions on the subject of barns.

They bumped slowly past the meadow and ploughland and came level with the coppice. It was mostly beech trees, observed Caroline, who loved trees: it was open coppice, with occasional ash and thorn; the beeches were young trees, with fine slender trunks, upright and well grown. Giles pulled up, saying: "I think I saw a very fair oak in the hollow yonder. I could do with some oak myself, it's very hard to come by."

"Go and look at it, but come back when I sound the horn," said Caroline, who had plenty of practical common sense, apart from barns. She knew that Giles had no sense of time and once he got interested in timber he might wander for hours. Left to herself, Caroline made a bee-line for the ruin.

"*This*," she said to herself, "is where I should like to live. It's a heavenly position."

She scrambled through the undergrowth to the little eminence where the old cottage stood, and gazed around. To the south she could see the line of the fells across the Lune: to the east the limestone crags of Warton shone in the pale sunlight, to the north-west a shining line puzzled her until she realised she could see Morecambe Bay, and the lakeland hills beyond. "It's perfect!" she exclaimed, delighting in the slender trees and the long buds which were just beginning to swell.

The cottage was not really a ruin. Its stone walls and roof and mullions were intact, though the doors and windows had gone, and, as she walked gingerly over the ground-floor, Caroline discovered that every bit of woodwork had been stripped away from the interior—doors, window-frames, skirting-boards, shelves, dresser, all had been looted.

"Sign of military occupation in the twentieth century," she murmured to herself. "All woodwork looted to light arm-fires... The same thing has happened all over the country. Ah, but this could be a lovely house if I could get an architect on to it..."

She went outside again to explore the back of the cottage, and found signs of a track leading farther into the wood. The sun was shining, the birds singing, the willow catkins were golden. Caroline came to another small clearing and found some yet more ancient remains: there were the great stone uprights from which gateposts had been swung, and some stone flags which indicated a fold yard or barn floor, as well as some walls and a section of flagged roof. "Possible garage," she murmured. "This must once have been a small holding all on its own, before the plantation was planted. There must be water somewhere. They never built a farmstead where there wasn't a water supply."

She soon found the water, and once again stood and stared, more convinced than ever that this was to be the site of her future home. "Is it a lake or a tarn or a pool or a mere?" she asked herself, walking along the border of the still waters which stretched away under the beech trees. She found she was walking on a stone ridge, with the lake some feet below her.

"Of course it's a quarry pool!" she exclaimed. "That explains everything. The stone for all the Broadgarth buildings was quarried from here, that's why they're so big. Plenty of building stone available. And my cottage, and the little old farmstead, were quarried from here, too. Then the spring found its way into the quarry and gradually filled it. Of course the water flows down to the Broadgarth beck... This must be the site of an ancient settlement. Heaven knows what we shall find if we dig..."

"Caroline! Where are you, Caroline?"

Giles Hoggett's deep voice had a note of anxiety, and she called back hastily:

"I'm here, Giles. Come and look, it's marvellous."

"I thought you'd fallen in," he said, as he strode through the undergrowth. "I'd forgotten about that black hole. There's more water there than I remembered, but there's no need to worry. You can fence it off, but, better still, never come near it."

"But I like it!" she protested. "I think it's lovely beyond words. I've always wanted a lake. And Giles, you can see the sea from the cottage, and the Morecambe sands."

"You needn't look at them," said Giles. "In any case, you can't see them from Broadgarth. We'd better get back, Caroline. We shall be late for tea."

"Yes. All right, but Kate will be awfully interested. I don't believe she's ever been here," said Caroline, as she turned regretfully away from her lake (tarn? pool? mere?) and walked back along the track.

"Giles, isn't this a marvellous position for a house?" she exclaimed, as they passed the cottage.

"This?" exclaimed Giles contemptuously. "In a wood, dark and shut in, with that black hole beyond? I don't wonder the place has become ruinous. It's no fit place for any one to live."

Caroline refrained from arguing: she remembered now—Giles was one of those queer people who mistrusted woods. He liked open spaces; a house set on a hillside with a wide prospect of field and fell and dale. Also he did not love the sea. He was a countryman, derived from farming stock, and love of the land was in his bones.

Caroline glanced at him with affectionate respect tinged with amusement as he swung on ahead of her through the coppice. He still moved like a young man, rhythmically, with the balance of finely co-ordinated muscles, though his hair was grey. His old russet tweeds harmonised with the undergrowth, and he looked part of the landscape. "It's a pity he doesn't like trees, he's such a sensible creature otherwise," said Caroline.

All the way back to the Hoggetts' house at Wenningby, Giles kept up an enthusiastic flow of information about Broadgarth, and its possibilities if properly farmed. He knew the late owner, and the owner before that, right back to his own childhood, and he began to assess the possible income to be won from those twenty acres, if they were farmed according to his advice.

Just before they got out of the car, Caroline said: "Look here, Giles. I'd like to buy Broadgarth and that coppice as well, but I'm not going to farm it. You say Bromsgrove Farm would be glad to hire the land and the farm buildings, and that would leave me the house. If I tried to farm, and 'made a mulock of it' as you say up here, I should have to leave the district because everybody would laugh at me."

Giles scratched his head thoughtfully. He was obviously disappointed at such pusillanimity: then he brightened up.

"You could let the land to Bromsgrove for a term of years, while you are gaining experience. You're quite intelligent, Caroline, and I think you'd soon learn enough to enable you to farm with a competent hired man. I was thinking. You might get a licence to repair the quarry cottage if it's to be inhabited by a farm worker. Yes, you'd certainly better buy that coppice. It's probable the ruined cottage will hardly affect the price. It's quite useless as it is."

"Yes, Giles," said Caroline meekly. ("That's gone rather well," she thought to herself.)

2

Kate Hoggett was waiting for them when they got back to Wenningby: the kettle was boiling, the newly lighted log fire crackling and spluttering between the hobs of the ample fireplace, and a grand spread of sandwiches and scones and home-made cakes and jam welcomed them. Kate had been gardening, and she was hungry.

"Are we late?" asked Caroline anxiously. She knew that her cousin hated being kept waiting for tea after a long afternoon in the garden.

"Not very. Come along and tell me all about it," said Kate. "What sort of house is it?"

"It's quite a decent house. I'm going to buy it if it's not run up to too high a price at the auction," said Caroline. "Giles thinks it's worth buying."

She left it at that, knowing that Giles would have plenty to say on this topic. Sandwich in hand, Giles weighed in on the excellence of the property, leaving Caroline to study Kate's thoughtful countenance. "What an unexpected creature to find in a north country farm-house," she thought to herself. Giles, for all his university background and philosophical mind, was derived from one of the oldest families in this valley. Despite his bookishness, farming was in his bones, but Kate was a Londoner born. She, also, had an academic background, and the habit of mind developed in her scientific training was just as acute as ever. She was a woman of wide interests: poetry and painting, science and sociology, politics and agriculture, she could talk and ponder over them all. "She's the most intelligent woman I know," pondered Caroline to herself, "and she likes living here, in this tiny village... she's happy here. Much happier than most of the woolly intellectuals who lay down the law in London restaurants and clubs. I'd rather be like Kate than any woman I know, but I don't think I can farm Broadgarth. But I *could* restore that cottage and make a garden there..."

Giles paused in his dissertation to consume another scone and Caroline put in:

"Have you ever seen the quarry pool, Kate?"

"No. Where is it? I didn't know there was one," replied Kate.

Caroline detailed the result of her researches in the coppice, including the more ancient of the two ruins, with its surviving stone "stoops" for hanging the gate of the fold yard, and the rough timbering of the lean-to. She knew that Kate would be interested, and she was. Giles refused to express any enthusiasm about the ruins and was most unencouraging about the quarry pool, but he admitted that there was some good timber in the coppice, including two valuable oak trees.

"I would be quite prepared to buy those trees from you, Caroline," he said judiciously. "They may be worth ten to twelve pounds. I could get some good planks out of them when they're seasoned."

"Good!" said Caroline. "Now look here, Giles. You know about the owners of that copse. Couldn't you phone them up and ask if they're willing to sell? You'll know how to approach them much better than I should, and you're a responsible landowner. They'll take much more notice of you than of me. For one thing, I'm a single woman, and I've noticed that single women are regarded as less than the dust in these parts. 'She's no' but a single woman,' they say, and that's that."

"Well, they might prefer to do business with someone known to them. I'll think about it. There's no immediate hurry."

"Ask him again when he's finished milking," put in Kate, *sotto voce*. "It's never any use asking him to do anything just before milking."

Caroline saw the sense of this; far be it from her to intrude herself between a farmer and his milking herd; but when Giles had gone out to the shippon, she turned to Kate again.

"You see, I want to know if I can buy the coppice and Quarry Pool *before* I go and bid at the Broadgarth auction," she said. "If I can buy the coppice, I'm prepared to put my shirt on it. If not, I won't bid so high."

Kate nodded sagaciously. "Don't you worry, lovey. Giles'll see about the coppice for you, he wants those oak trees, but you must remember the tempo of life is different up here. It's no use trying to hustle people in Lunesdale. They just put up a defence mechanism at once."

Caroline nodded thoughtfully. "Yes. I see. But I *do* want that coppice. It'd be a heavenly place to live. I'm going to help bring the cows in. The more I learn about cows the better."

"Don't steal my last apples to feed to the cows," called Kate peremptorily. "You ought to realise that cows are not domestic pets, and there are hardly any apples left. If you must feed them, give them an old broccoli. They adore these."

3

While Caroline and Kate and Giles had been enjoying discussing the buying of Broadgarth, the stout Mrs. Brough, in charge of the house, had also derived quite a lot of entertainment value from the afternoon, though she would not have used that phrase herself. "That's rum, that is," was more her own idiom.

Giles and Caroline had not been the only persons to view Broadgarth that afternoon. About an hour before their arrival a stout young fellow, in farming clothes and clogs, had knocked on the door, and asked laconically to see the house and buildings. Mrs. Brough was a shrewd soul, and she had a shrewd tongue. Standing with her hands on her hips, she surveyed the young man, and recognised him as a tractor driver who worked for local farmers. "Reckon he's not got the brass," was her unspoken comment. Aloud she said:

"Tha's goin' to try farming thiself, then?"

"Maybe—and not so much 'thy,'" he retorted, resenting the local familiarity. "'Tis for sale I'm told."

"Aye, 'tis for sale, by auction. Reckon you're wasting your time. Prices are up," she replied. "Wipe thi boots—I scrubbed t' flags and I don't want 'em mucked up."

She led him round the house, and then over the farm buildings, conscientiously, though she had no belief in him as a buyer. She tried to find out, indirectly, if he were going to get married, where he lived, who his people were, but she got no satisfaction. He stared solidly at the house and the barn and pigsties, and went off leaving her puzzled.

"That's a rum go, that is," she said to herself.

After Giles and Caroline had gone, another visitor appeared just as Mrs. Brough was deciding to shut the house and go home. This visitor was a prosperous-looking, well-built man of about fifty—good clothes, good shoes, good hat—but not a countryman, very definitely not a countryman.

"Now what's he about?" wondered Mrs. Brough.

"I'm told this place is for sale. It's a good bit of land," he observed. "Are you the owner?"

"No. I'm not. I'm in charge while the farm is on view, to-day and to-morrow. 'Tis up for auction. Do you want to see t' house?"

"The house? I'll just take a look round," he said. "I should like to deal direct with the owner—I've taken a fancy to the land and I'm prepared to buy."

"Oh, you are, are you. A mighty hurry you're in," she thought. "Not much of the farmer about *you*."

"'Tis up for auction," she said stolidly. "If you want it, you must bid for it."

She led him round the house, and he scarcely bothered to look at it.

"It's the land I'm interested in," he repeated; "there's good grazing and the outbuildings could be used as stables," he said. "Now I want to know the owners. As I say, I'd rather deal direct."

She studied him with a calmly calculating stare.

"If you like to give me your name and address, I'll pass it on to the executors," she replied, "but 'tis up for auction."

He took out a card, inscribed Mr. John Wilson. "I'm staying at Hauxhead Castle. Ask them to write to me there—no object in paying auctioneer's fees when I'm prepared to agree to the price, within reason."

When Mrs. Brough got home, she went to see her cousin, old Polly Makin. Polly had the largest share in Broadgarth, and though she was crippled by rheumatism, Polly had the strength of mind to dominate her fellow beneficiaries. Mrs. Brough told the wizened old lady of her various "viewers," with particular comment on Mr. John Wilson and Miss Caroline Bourne.

"Came with Mr. Hoggett of Wenningby, she did," said Mrs. Brough. "Got more money than sense, I reckon, but she'll likely bid up."

"Hoggetts is aw'reet. Farmed in Lunesdale generations past. He'll see she don't play ducks and drakes wi' good land."

"Aye, maybe he will. Looked at things proper, he did. Then there was a real watch-and-chain chap—posh. Name o' Wilson, staying at Hauxhead. Said he wanted to buy direct and he'd pay your price."

"Eh... did he? What *is* our price? Nay, reckon he can bid like the rest, and if Hoggetts run him up, us'll be none the worse off. Who was he?"

"I don't know, Polly. Not the sort to live at Broadgarth. Said he wanted grazing for his horses."

"Horses, eh? That'd be fancy stock. I don't like that. Been farmed well once, that land has. Reckon it can go by auction, and let 'em all bid up, eh?"

"Tha's right," agreed Mrs. Brough.

TWO

I

"We'll leave the car here. I'm not going to risk my tyres on that so-called road," said Caroline, backing her car neatly into the Broadgarth turning at the junction with the main road.

It was a glorious sunny morning, crystal-clear, and the birds were all "shouting their heads off," as Caroline put it. She had prevailed upon Kate Hoggett to leave house and garden in order to inspect the coppice and quarry pool.

"Of course, if I *do* take to farming, I shall be allowed new tyres: farmers can get anything," said Caroline, as she hastened along the track. "There it is. Isn't it a marvellous possibility?" she asked.

Kate looked carefully around: she always considered deeply before supporting Caroline's enthusiasms.

"It's a good site... and the view is beautiful, all round," agreed Kate, when she had climbed the small eminence on which the cottage stood.

"You can't see all of Ingleborough, but you can see Warton Crag and the sea. Goodness, it *is* clear this morning. That must be the Langdale Pikes; you can't mistake them." She went into the doorless house. "You're quite right, this isn't really a ruin, because the walls and roof are intact," she said. "The stripping of all the woodwork was deliberate... they've even taken the floorboards. This must have been the parlour, it had a wooden floor, the kitchen's got a flagged floor... Look, the Tommies left their cigarette cartons and tins... and chewing-gum wrappers—they always do. I'm surprised the place isn't damper... but of course it's built right on to the solid rock, and it's open to all the winds. Yes. I think I agree with you. It would be worth restoring. It's still beautiful in its own way—but it's very lonely."

"It's less than a hundred yards from the main road and telegraph wires," said Caroline. "It's not nearly so isolated as Broadgarth—that's nearly a quarter of a mile from any road. Come and see the real ruin; it's fascinating."

Kate followed her to the back of the cottage.

"Why, how odd, there's quite a track here," she said. "I wonder who uses it? Is there a hull or a shippon to house some stock?"

"Well, there *was* a shippon, but there's not much of it left," said Caroline. "It must have been a small stone house with a barn and lean-to, but the roof's come down. Here it is."

Again Kate stood still and considered. "Oh, yes. It was a small holding all right; that was the fold yard. I suppose it was left derelict when the landowner planted the coppice for the shooting—that'd be about seventy or eighty years ago judging by the size of the trees. Rather a shame, it must have been a nice little farm-house. Of course there was once quite a settlement around Broadgarth, going back to the thirteenth or fourteenth century, and Hulton, the nearest village, was named in Domesday Book. Caroline, I wonder who uses this track?"

"Well, *does* anybody use it? It's quite hard. I suppose it's just survived."

"If nobody used it, it wouldn't be quite hard," said Kate patiently. "It would have disappeared under leaf-mould long since. Besides, the bluebells have been trodden down at sometime. I saw several which had been bent and twisted when they first came through the soil."

"Oh, of course, you and Giles are hot on detection, I'd forgotten that," laughed Caroline. "The track leads to the quarry pool, Kate, my mere, tarn, or water. I expect someone has been watering their cattle in *my* lake. Look, isn't it lovely?"

Kate clambered up on to the ridge and looked at the dappled sunlit water.

"I'd no idea there was a pool of this size here," she said, following the curving ridge to the narrower end of the water. "It must be eighty yards long."

"But don't you think it's beautiful?"

"Yes, of course it's beautiful, especially on a day like this one. It'd be pretty grim at night, it looks deep... You can be quite certain of one thing, Caroline. No countryman would ever bring his beasts here to water them. Look at the steep sides! The cattle would risk breaking their legs every time they came near. No. If anybody comes here it's probably to fish. It's extraordinary how fish always appear in any water. There'll be eels, certainly, and probably perch—"

"All the better, perhaps I shall get some fishing birds—kingfishers and herons and wild duck."

"Not herons," said Kate, "and not wild duck. They prefer the river. Kingfishers? Well, possibly, but they're not very common up here. You'll get water-wagtails, and there'll be a lot of birds nesting in the coppice—warblers and finches and yellowhammers. I've heard some of them already." She began to walk round the sheet of water. "What exactly *is* your idea, now you've seen both Broadgarth and the quarry buildings?" she asked.

"I'm going to buy Broadgarth and this coppice. I shall live at Broadgarth *pro tem.* and let off the land. Then I shall look out for a promising married couple who would be competent to farm Broadgarth, and I shall apply for a licence to restore the cottage and add to it, on the grounds that I shall free Broadgarth farm-house for a married couple when the alterations are complete."

"That sounds perfectly reasonable," said Kate. "I should think you'd get the licence to rebuild all right. I agree with you it's a lovely site. Giles is quite incapable of appreciating it, because he's got a prejudice against living in a woodland. Look, there's a whole clump of wild arum, and some wood muscatel. It'll be a lovely sight when the bluebells are out."

They retraced their steps round the pool, and Kate said: "You'll have to fence the coppice and put up a notice-board sometime. It's obvious that people *do* come here, fishing or poaching or something. There may be some pheasants nesting here, there are generally a few about. I saw a cartridge-case just now."

They left the quarry pool and made their way back to the car. Caroline walked into the middle of the road and said:

"You can see the cottage from the road. It isn't really isolated at all, just nicely set back. How I shall enjoy seeing wood smoke coming out of my own chimneys!"

As she turned back towards the car a young man walked past along the road, and Caroline gave him "Good day" in the country manner. He replied: "Good morning, miss," and touched his cap.

"Now who on earth was that?" demanded Caroline. "He doesn't sound like these parts."

"He doesn't belong hereabouts, you can tell that from his voice. By his clothes he's a townsman, and he comes from the Midlands or the south," replied Kate. "Perhaps he's the poacher; you'll certainly have to fence the coppice if you buy it, or nobody will know it's private property. There's been no game preserving here for years. Now let's get home, I've got the dinner to cook. I like your site, it's full of possibilities."

2

Caroline went to the Broadgarth auction sale by herself. She asked Giles not to come, saying she would feel less self-conscious by herself.

The auction was being held in the King's Arms Hotel at Carnton, and Caroline set out in her own small car. About two miles from Wenningby she saw two figures ahead of her, and recognised a Wenningby neighbour, Mrs. Beck, with her small daughter, Lena. Pulling up, Caroline called:

"Would you like a lift, Mrs. Beck? I'm going to Carnton."

"Thank you very much, Miss Bourne. I'm going in for the Broadgarth auction, at the King's Arms."

"How funny! I'm going there, too," said Caroline when Lena and Mrs. Beck had got in the car. "Are you going to bid?"

In her own heart Caroline said to herself: "Well, that settles my hash. I can't bid against the Becks. They're farming folk and they ought to have it if they want it."

Mrs. Beck, who was a cheerful, practical young woman, answered quite readily:

"Well, I'm just going to see. We do want a small farm, but we're not going to bid high for it. My husband thinks a thousand pounds is the most we'll go to. It's only a small place."

Caroline nodded. "Yes, only twenty acres. I hope you get it if you really want it."

"Well, I'm not counting on it," replied Mrs. Beck philosophically. "I hear there's quite a number of folks from away who're after it. Emma Brough—who looked after the house—says any number of people have been making offers for it already, but that may be just her way of talking."

"Well, it'd surprise me if there are many strangers at the auction," said Caroline. "Broadgarth is so isolated, so tucked away, how can people get to know about it? Do I turn right here? Goodness, what a bend—and the camber's all wrong."

She swung her little car neatly round the sharp bend, changing down for the hump-backed hill which came unexpectedly.

"You've got to expect anything in these parts, but that was a steep one," she said. "Hallo! What an opulent car, and what a silly place to leave it."

She sounded her horn and swung wide to avoid the stationary vehicle. It was pouring in torrents now, and Caroline's attention was concentrated on the road. It wasn't until she had passed the other car that she realised that somebody had signalled to her from the hedge, but she did not pull up.

"I know it seems mean not to stop, but it would have been dangerous to stop there and I'm not going back," she said. "If that stream goes on rising we might get bogged down."

"I'm glad you didn't stop. I didn't like the look of him," said Mrs. Beck. "He looked real bad-tempered. Perhaps *he* was going to the auction, too."

Caroline laughed. "If he was, I'm all the more glad I didn't pull up," she said. "You and I couldn't bid against the owner of a car like that. Besides, I don't think it's fair for wealthy townsfolk to buy up small country properties. I believe some big firms are doing it, just to get the country produce—cream and butter and eggs and bacon."

"That doesn't seem fair, does it?" agreed Mrs. Beck. "It's very hard for a farm worker to get started on a small farm, and with prices going so high, it'll soon be impossible."

Caroline nodded. "I quite agree. But perhaps we've stopped our wealthy bidder, anyway. He's got about five miles to walk and twenty minutes to do it in."

3

Caroline and Mrs. Beck had been quite right in their guess. The owner of the beautiful car which had its near front wheel in the ditch was the Mr. Wilson who had viewed Broadgarth after Giles and Caroline had left. A less careful driver than Caroline, he had taken the turn and the hill too fast in his powerful car, and had landed himself in the ditch. When Caroline drove on, disregarding his belated signal, Mr. Wilson swore, long and loud.

"Devil take the bitch! That's torn it," he said bitterly. He knew quite well that his chances of getting to Carnton in time for the auction were pretty remote, and Mr. Wilson was no pedestrian.

Meanwhile, Caroline drove on sedately until the little stone town of Carnton came into view. "I'll drop you and Lena at the hotel, and go and park round the corner," she said.

When Caroline parked the car, she found she had a few minutes to spare and went in search of cigarettes, and thus entered the auction-room by herself. It was an ordinary hotel sitting-room, and on the chairs round the walls about twenty people were sitting in solemn silence. They were mostly farmers, and Caroline was aware that her own entry caused a slight sensation, though no word was said. Some of those assembled would know her as Mrs. Hoggett's cousin, but several obviously wondered who this alien creature was. Sitting discreetly by Mrs. Beck, listening to the subdued conversation, Caroline learned that there was to be a strange auctioneer, unknown to those present, the old auctioneer being ill.

She had time to have a look at this new auctioneer when he began his routine eulogy of "this valuable small holding." He was a big man, very stout, and Caroline took a dislike to him. While the auctioneer said his "blurb," Caroline tried to assess probable bidders. Mr. Harrow, a retired farmer, was the most probable buyer, but there was also a man in a dark lounge suit, an obvious townsman, who might be the representative of some long-pursed bidder.

"Now, who'll give me an offer for this excellent little property?" began the auctioneer. "Will you start me at £1000? £900?... £800?

Come, gentlemen! A valuable small holding. £500? Thank you, sir. £500 I'm bid... £600... £700. Thank you. £750..."

How on earth did he recognise the bids, wondered Caroline. No word was uttered: occasionally somebody nodded: one farmer bid by an upward jerk of his thumb, one by raising the stem of his pipe.

"£1000 I'm bid. £1000 for this unique small holding. Come, it's worth more than that. Land to-day is the finest investment... £1000... Thank you, sir, one thousand and fifty I'm bid, one thousand and fifty..."

That was Mr. Harrow's bid, and feeling that she had played fair by Mrs. Beck, Caroline took a deep breath.

"£1200," she said clearly, her audible voice causing something like a gasp of consternation, while the auctioneer looked as though his eyes would pop out. Her unexpected bid seemed to have paralysed him.

"£1050 I'm bid," he reiterated, as though Caroline did not exist.

"£1200," she repeated, even more loudly than before.

The auctioneer took notice at last and the company seemed to recover from the shock of this unorthodox audible bidding.

"£1250," panted the auctioneer, looking round hopefully. "It's against you, madam, twelve fifty I'm bid..."

"£1350," said Caroline. At £1500 Mr. Harrow had dropped out. So far as Caroline could see, the sallow-faced "townee" was her only opponent. For some reason she had taken a dislike to him. "I'll give you a run for your money," she said to herself.

"£1700," she declared, beginning to feel really excited.

The stout farmer who had dropped out at £1400 gave a deep breath, and the townee scratched his head and nodded.

"£1750 I'm bid," said the auctioneer exultingly. "£1750. Now you're not going to let this valuable... thank you, madam, £1800. Some of the finest meadowland in Lunesdale, a wonderful property—£1850! Thank you, sir."

"Two thousand pounds," said Caroline. Her voice was quite casual: she wasn't going to let them know this was her limit—her final bid. She sounded exactly as though she were prepared to go on bidding indefinitely, leant back in her chair and smiled across at the disgruntled townee. With a scowl he left his place and walked out of the room.

A moment later Caroline was sitting at the auctioneer's desk writing out a cheque for her deposit and receiving the congratulations of the auctioneer, who had every reason to feel satisfied with his afternoon's work.

"I'll go and bring the car round, Mrs. Beck," said Caroline. "It's raining rather hard."

As she passed the telephone box in the hall the sallow-faced man emerged.

"Pardon me, madam. I wonder if you would care to do a deal? I am authorised to offer you another £100 beyond the purchase price..."

"Are you, indeed?" said Caroline. "I have bought Broadgarth for myself and I have no intention of selling it again. I am *not* a speculator. You might assure your principal about that. Good afternoon."

"I bet he's an agent for some of the black market crowd," she said to herself as she went out and eased her small Ford clear of the cars packed round it.

4

"Well, Caroline, how did you get on?" inquired Giles benevolently when she returned to Wenningby. Caroline tilted her chin up and stood squarely, her back to the fire.

"I got on very well, thank you," she responded. "You now have to regard me as a fellow landowner. I am the owner of the land, buildings, messuage or tenement with appurtenances, situate lying and being in Broadgarth in the Hundred of Lonsdale in the County of

Lancaster, together with all stables, orchards, gardinges, meadows, pastures, woods, moors, mosses, brackens and brackendales, together with delves, mines, quarries, waters, and fishing, whatever to the said messuage appertaineth... I can't remember any more but it's quite considerable."

"Squire," said Giles, striking an attitude, "I hope you will notice me when next you pass me on the road."

"Come off it, both of you," said Kate. "How much did you pay for it?"

"I paid two thousand pounds, and before either of you tell me it's more than Broadgarth is worth, let me tell *you* that I was offered £100 over and above the purchase price before I left the King's Head," replied Caroline, and then burst out: "Whoopee! How marvellous it all is! I never expected to own a messuage with all that to the tenement appertaineth. Giles, what *is* a messuage?"

Giles gaped, but Kate responded:

"The word is derived from the same root as the French 'ménage,' in brief, all that to a household appertaineth. Now tell us about the bidding."

Over many cups of tea, Caroline gave a lively résumé of her observations, ending up with a description of the final scene outside the telephone box.

"Now *that*," said Giles weightily, "is a most unusual occurrence. Do you know who the man was?"

"I've no idea, but I bet he was an agent for one of these black market racketeers. Their latest stunt is to buy up small holdings and put a man in to farm it to cover the possession of poultry and stock. However, I pipped him at the post. His instructions must have limited him to two thousand, until he phoned through and got further powers. By the way, I saw Mr. Harrow as I got the car out. He looked highly amused. 'So you'll be turning farmer, Miss Bourne,' he said, and I answered: 'Not just yet, Mr. Harrow. I'm too ignorant. I'm going to live in the house and let the land until I know a bit more about things.'"

Giles looked somewhat dubious, and Caroline went on: "What's the matter with that? I thought he might like the land himself to amuse him in his retirement. They say he wants a few head of cattle to keep him happy now he's let his son John take over at Thornhill."

"Well," said Giles, "you have your own way of doing things. We're not disposed to rush at things quite so much up here. What did Mr. Harrow say?"

"Oh, he just grinned and said: 'You'll have a lot to be learning like.' Giles, when you've finished milking, *quite* finished, could you ring up the agent again and try to click over my coppice? Or may I ring up myself?"

"No, I will do that," said Giles firmly.

"Very well. Then may I come and milk the nice quiet Ayrshire? She didn't mind me last time, and I do need practice."

Rather sadly, Giles agreed. It was he who had encouraged Caroline to learn to milk, and the Ayrshire was a very sweet-tempered cow—but novices were not good for milk production.

5

It was after supper that the trio settled down by the fire at Wenningby, all the work on the farm finished for the day. Giles, after a chat with a neighbour over the fold yard gate, and a long conversation over the telephone, told Caroline that Mr. Waine, the agent for the owner of the property adjoining Broadgarth, had agreed to sell her the four acres of coppice including the quarry pool for £400, and that he would have a deed prepared for her to sign.

"It's a curious thing, but Waine has had other inquiries about that coppice," said Giles. "However, he kept his word, and said that you had been the first to bid for it and you could have it."

"Good for him! One thing about folk up here, they *do* stick to their word!" said Caroline. "Of course the other bidder for the coppice is my black market racketeer. What a good thing I hustled you, Giles. If I'd agreed with you and said: 'There's plenty of time, we'll consider it next week,' I should never have got it. You ought to be very pleased. I have been the instrument which prevented a possible black market malefactor settling in your midst, cornering your eggs and cockerels, bidding for your bacon, skimming your cream, poaching your trout and salmon..."

"That is an unwarrantable assumption," said Giles solemnly, and Kate put in:

"Well, I think Caroline will make a responsible landowner and a good neighbour, so every one ought to be satisfied. Giles, what was that story that Edward Troutbeck was telling you in the shippon just now? He sounded very solemn."

Giles scratched his head. "He was telling me about Alice Wynne. Her husband has left her. I never liked him, he's got Welsh blood in him."

"That's not a reason, it's sheer prejudice," said Kate. "I never liked him either, but I dislike him because he's lazy and quarrelsome and unreliable. I should think she's well rid of him."

"Well, that's what I meant," said Giles. "He's been keeping bad company, too, with those fellows who tried to get a dog-racing track at Strand. There was a youngish fellow going about with David Wynne lately, and they had a row over something—a proper scrap, so Edward says. David came home with a black eye and his front teeth knocked out."

"Yes, I heard about that," said Kate. "David had the nerve to tell Mrs. Clough that Alice had been too free with his friend. It's a lie, because she's a very decent girl and she's done her best to keep David straight."

"Well, you *do* surprise me!" exclaimed Caroline. "I never thought that matrimonial troubles existed in Lunesdale. It's a place where every one lives happily ever after... What are the immortal lines? 'The women there do all they ought: the men observe the rules of thought. They love the good, they worship truth'..."

"You must remember that David Wynne came from away," said Giles solemnly. "I always said—"

"You are conservative to a degree which is inconsistent with both reason and experience, Giles," said Kate.

He smiled tolerantly, quite unoffended with his wife's vigorous attack.

"Yes, Kate, I am. Please note that the matrimonial infelicity to which Caroline alludes is caused by the bad behaviour of a husband who, on your own admission, is lazy, unreliable and generally worthless. Also he is from away. I know of no marriage between the natives of Wenningby which has resulted in other than a lifetime of mutual respect and affection."

"'... and when they get to feeling old,
They up and shoot themselves I'm told,'"

murmured Caroline. "I'm going to bed to dream of my messuage and all that to the tenement appertaineth... When next I travel to these parts with my goods and chattels, I shall no longer be living under the shadow of going away again in the immediate future. I shall be living in Lunesdale! Wonderful thought!"

6

If Caroline Bourne went contentedly to bed that night, happy in the thought of her new property, it was very otherwise with Mr. John Wilson, who had also wanted to buy that desirable small holding known as Broadgarth. After Caroline's car had passed him, it was nearly an hour before any other vehicle came by, and Mr. Wilson did not arrive at the Carnton Hotel where the auction was held until after the bidding was over, and the deposit paid by Caroline.

Mr. Wilson made a few inquiries from one or two people who were still hanging about after the sale. He then had to go to a garage to arrange about the towing of his car and the repair of a twisted axle. He then betook himself to the railway station and after some delay succeeded in getting a call through to the Adelphi Hotel in Liverpool.

"That you, Dick? John here."

"Good. I was expecting a call. Did that little business go through all right?"

"No, devil take it! I got bogged in a ditch on one of these infernal roads. Never got there until the auction was over and the place sold. Some infernal woman ran the bidding up. She'd evidently made up her mind to go on until she got it, so rather than draw attention to the sale he let her have it."

"Hm... That's a pity. Still, it's a nice point, y'know. I don't know that I was altogether in favour of buying. Country people are so damned inquisitive. Of course, if your scheme had gone through, it might have worked—stables and kennels and that... but all these controls play Old Harry with private enterprise..."

"You're telling me! And there's another point I want to discuss sometime. Looks as though our simple rustic thinks he can be a clever dick and do the dirty on us behind our backs. There was another bidder I'm very suspicious about."

There was a grunt from the other end, and then Dick replied:

"He'd better not try to be funny. That quarry pool has possibilities..."

"Shut up and don't be a damned fool. I'm fed up with to-day, everything gone wrong, and I nearly burst my innards trying to lift the car out of a ditch. I'm going on to Sholto's, you can ring me there."

"Right. Sorry about the hitch. I must think things over. So long."

Mr. Wilson sat and waited for a train which was already very late. He was rather a noticeable figure at that north country junction. He was tall, a man of about fifty, well built, well poised: his clothes were notably well-cut tweeds, and his raincoat contrived to look like the advertisements of expensive waterproofs. He was too much immersed in his own thoughts to notice those around him; "country bumpkins" he would have called them, probably adding "and damned ugly at that." The sodden evening made the waiting passengers look a dreary crowd, and their faces were dour. One stout body, in bulging mac and shapeless hat, stared across at Mr. Wilson.

"Him and his 'buy direct.' Wanted something for nothing—never even made a bid," said Mrs. Brough to herself. "All his money on his back like... Well, 'twas a good auction and Polly can't grumble. Two thousand pounds; that's a tidy sum, that is."

THREE

I

"It's a trunk call, so it must be for Caroline," said Kate. "Call her, Giles. I can't understand why all her London friends prefer to spend fortunes on trunk calls instead of twopence halfpenny on a sensible letter."

"Caroline! Hurry up! It's your picture gallery agent again, or else it's your publisher or else it's the B.B.C.," roared Giles.

Caroline came running: it was only nine o'clock in the morning and most of her London friends would be still in bed.

"Hallo... Yes. It's Wenningby 92. Yes? Good gracious! When? To-day? Heavens, let me think... Yes. I could meet you in Lancaster..."

"The way people do talk over the telephone, I think it's an exhausting habit shouting yourself hoarse because some scatterbrained Londoner keeps on saying 'I can't hear,'" said Kate. "Caroline won't have a telephone at Broadgarth, so her friends will have to learn to write letters."

"That was Francis Rolph," said Caroline, when she had finished telephoning. "He's in Manchester, where he's been surveying a site for a factory. He is taking a busman's holiday and coming to Lunesdale to survey my ruin. He's a very good architect, Giles, and he's a feeling for the stone of the district."

"Yes, I remember that," said Giles. Rolph had stayed at Wenningby a year or so back, and had proved a valuable visitor, with an almost uncanny knack for improvising methods of repair to old stone houses. "I shall be very glad to see him here again."

"I'm not so sure that you *will* see him," said Caroline. "I'm going to meet him in Lancaster, and I shall take him straight out to Broadgarth. If Kate will let me have some eggs and butter, I'll buy bread and coffee in Lancaster and we can picnic in *my* kitchen. Once he comes to Wenningby he'll never get on to my plans, he'll just start playing around with Giles. I know there's a wall down by Lamb's Intak, but I'm not letting Francis anywhere near it. If I take him to Broadgarth, he can concentrate on my problems."

"I see your point," agreed Kate, "and of course you can have eggs, and milk and bacon too. But surely you'll bring him here to sleep. He doesn't want to go back by the night train, does he?"

"No, but he can camp out at Broadgarth," replied Caroline firmly. "I've got a camp-bed in the car and a sleeping-bag and plenty of rugs, and there's a magnificent lot of logs left at Broadgarth. He'll enjoy it no end. He never gets a chance of an evening to himself, and there's a table for him to draw on. If I only leave him to it, he can survey my ruin and work out plans and estimates, and tell me where I can put a bath in Broadgarth, and if I can get that hideous fireplace out and have an open chimney like the Wenningby Barns one, big enough to hide a corpse or roast an ox, or whatever it was you did down there when you got matey with the C.I.D."

"But I do think that's rather the limit, putting a London architect to camp out in an empty farm-house," protested Kate. "He'll think we don't want him here, and we *do*. I've always looked forward to seeing him again."

Even as she spoke Giles was rumbling on in his "Landowning Voice"—"We did *not* hide a corpse in the Wenningby Barns chimney, the corpse was in the river, and we didn't roast an ox either. The law wouldn't allow it."

"Never mind—but you *did* have a chief inspector of Scotland Yard camping out at Wenningby Barns, so I see no reason why I shouldn't have an F.R.I.B.A. camping out at Broadgarth," said Caroline cheerfully. "I'll say Kate sends her love—plus the eggs and bacon—and that she was very indignant with me for not bringing him here to sleep. In any case, if he doesn't fancy my camping-out idea he'll come here of his own volition. He'll probably come anyway, because he doted on this place, but I shall prevent him if I can. I want him to *concentrate*. And now I've only just got time to collect food and plates and all that... No, of course he won't want sheets, and yes please, he'd love some cream, and may I borrow the small frying-pan and a saucepan?"

"I suppose so," said Kate resignedly, "but I disapprove of the whole thing. It'd be much more sensible to bring him back here and give him a comfortable bed to sleep in—"

"'Like a Christian,' as the saying goes," said Caroline flippantly. "Only I don't think Francis Rolph *is* a Christian, not in the sense of enjoying conventional creature comforts. He's much more like a pagan: anyway, if he doesn't like the idea of camping out, he won't hesitate to say so."

2

But Francis Rolph did like the idea of camping out. He had stood for a long time staring at Caroline's "ruin," his obstinate jaw jutting out, his brows frowning above long-sighted, observant blue eyes. There was no need for her to ask if he liked it, one glance had been enough to settle that. He had walked round it and scrambled through it and clambered up it. He had tapped it and measured it and plumbed it, and Caroline had considerable difficulty in persuading him to leave the cottage and come down to Broadgarth for a picnic lunch.

"What do you think of it?" she asked, as they walked towards the farm.

"That?" he jerked his chin towards the cottage. "It's a fine job of work—built to last for centuries. The fabric's virtually intact, the woodwork's all been looted. How on earth did that happen?"

"Troops, I suppose. They did the same thing everywhere."

"Maybe. The W.D. supplies coal and expects them to ignite it by faith; but what were troops doing there?"

"Goodness knows. They had O.C.T.U.s and Combat Schools and Searchlight Stations all along the bay. I suppose it was easier to loot timber from an empty cottage than to cut down trees. Will it be very difficult to get the necessary timber to restore it?"

"It'd be a job to get new timber, but one can scrounge a lot of old stuff, doors and panelling and what-not. I'll look out for you, I'm always getting stuff when old houses are being altered. I don't think you can do much in the way of additions, unless I come up here and turn mason. You've got stone enough on the spot to build a castle, it's the labour that's short. So that's your farm house, is it? Plain and sensible—but the roof's good, they knew how to pitch a roof in the days when this place was built. It's a lost art. Look at the pitch of the roofs in any of the modern houses around Carnton. They damn the houses at the first glance."

He growled on to himself while Caroline unlocked her own front door and admitted Rolph to the uncompromising kitchen. He grinned at her.

"It's a good kitchen," she said defensively.

He grinned the more. "You'll be telling me it's functional next—of all the idiotic words ever coined by clever dicks. Of course it's a good kitchen, but I can't see you living in it. I know you can cook and scrub, but you're one of those creatures who ask for something else in addition to necessities. You'll always be aware that this room is ugly and that the window's too small and badly placed. Here, give me those..."

"Those" were kindling and logs, and the next half-hour was occupied with fire-making and cooking. It was not until they had consumed the eggs and bacon, plus Kate Hoggett's apple cake and Giles's cream, that Rolph said: "To get down to brass tacks. You're going to live here at Broadgarth until the cottage is restored. Don't think it can be done quickly. It can't. If you're lucky it may be ready next Lady Day, not before. So I'd better look around and decide just what you need here. Then you can ask for a licence for this little lot, and we'll see about your ruin after that." He got up, in his abrupt, purposeful way, and then said: "We'd better wash up, and then you can leave me alone to consider what needs doing, and what it's possible to get done."

"Kate would like you to come to supper at Wenningby, and she did say that it'd be much more sensible for you to sleep there, like a Christian," murmured Caroline.

He laughed. "Will you thank Mrs. Hoggett for me, but say I'd like to stay here to-night? If I'm to make out reasonable plans it means a lot of work. After dark I can work at that table—all night, if I choose. So you'd better leave me to it. I'll come over to Wenningby in the morning if you can fetch me."

"Of course we'll fetch you, but can't I do anything to help here?"

"No, lady, nothing. If you stay here, we shall waste time talking. Oh, yes, I know I talk as much as you do—or nearly as much—but if you're not here, I can have a chat with myself about the matter in hand."

Caroline laughed. "As you will. I'm very grateful; I know you've got quite enough work already without surveying my ruin. And there's plenty of food here, and logs... Don't fall in the well after dark, will you, I'm sure the cover is rotten..."

He took her firmly by the arm and marched her to the door.

"I know you think I'm a lunatic," he said, "but I know more about wells than you do, Miss Caroline Bourne. Off you trot, and I'll see you in the morning."

3

Giles Hoggett was somewhat troubled in his mind over the scant hospitality shown to Francis Rolph. Giles was by nature hospitable, and though he lived by choice in the remote countryside, he enjoyed an occasional guest "from away," with whom he and Kate could discuss the "isms" which plagued the busy world beyond the peaceful confines of Lunesdale and its sheltering fells. It struck him as being casual behaviour to house a guest in an empty house, and Caroline's assurances that Rolph had liked the idea of staying at Broadgarth by himself did not quite convince Giles that the arrangement was desirable. The following morning, therefore, as soon as the routine of milking and "mucking out" were finished, Giles set off in his long-suffering car and drove the four miles to the Broadgarth turning at something more than his usual conservative speed. As the car bucketed over the woodland track after leaving the high road, Giles had to admit that Caroline's suggestion of a steam roller seemed cogent, and he began to consider the best person to approach among local authorities in order to get the idea carried out. He had just come to the conclusion that the first requirements were a tractor and some loads of stone from his own shilla beds in the river when he reached the Broadgarth entrance and saw Francis Rolph leaning over the gate, a very disillusioned expression on his face. Giles scrambled out of his car in great concern. An expression of disillusionment might not be unexpected, but to find the architect with his head cut and bruised and his face the colour of an indifferent potato was the last thing Giles had expected.

"What on earth has happened to you... had a tumble?" he called, in great concern, as he strode up to the gate.

"I suppose you could call it a tumble," said the architect resignedly. "Personally, I should call it a good attempt at murder. Come inside for a minute."

Giles said nothing. When he was really startled he seldom said anything, he reverted to the taciturnity of his forebears. As he entered the house, he said: "I'm sorry, Rolph," and his voice conveyed a lot more than the simple words.

"Oh, it's all right. I was lucky, and I've got a thick skull," rejoined the other resignedly. "Caroline will say it was my own fault—you see if she doesn't. I suppose it was, in a way. Have you seen that quarry pool she's so taken with?"

"Yes. I have! I don't like it," replied Giles promptly.

"Like it? Well, it may have its points so far as natural beauty goes, but there's some damned funny games being played there, Hoggett," rejoined the other, sitting down on the kitchen table. "I worked in here until well after midnight—thought I might as well get all the paper work done while I was here—and then I thought I'd go up the fields and have a look at that water in the moonlight. It was a grand night, and I thought I should sleep better after some fresh air. Well—say if we go up the way I went last night and have a look at it."

"But hadn't you better come straight back with me and get that cut dressed?" asked Giles.

"That can wait, it's nothing—it's the bruise that hurts," rejoined Rolph. "I'm all right. Come on."

He led the way to the back door of the house and across the garden. "I went this way, through the hedge and up the bank," he said. "It's only a few hundred yards to the wood. I made for that big ash; I could see it against the sky."

The two men went up the sharply sloping pasture until they reached the coppice. The fence was broken, and Rolph scrambled through the gap and up the rocky bank to the edge of the quarry pool.

"Looks peaceful, doesn't it?" he observed. "It did last night, with the moon shining across it. I followed round the ridge about twenty yards, to about here."

Hoggett stood beside the other and noted the lie of the ground. They stood on a ridge, as Rolph had said, and the bare rock sloped away on every side. To their right, they could just see the stonework of the ruined shippon which Caroline thought she could have converted as a garage.

Rolph stood still and fingered his confused brow tenderly. "I stood here and thought about whatever gods there be," he said in his abrupt, gruff way. "It was incredibly beautiful with the moon shining between the beeches and the stars shivering with their own brightness. It was very silent, too—no wind, no birds. And then I heard footsteps along the path there. Slow, careful footsteps. I think there were two men. I swear I heard a man panting, as a chap does pant if he's carrying a heavy burden. I wondered. I couldn't see anything, the moon was in the south, and that ruin was a black shadow. I knew something was wrong." He paused, still fingering his bruised head. "I realised I was standing against the sky," he went on, "and I moved a step down and dislodged a stone. It fell in the water—splash. I waited then, expecting to hear a voice or commotion or something. I didn't hear anything at all. I was just going to move again when I was tackled below the knees. That's all I remember. It was dawn when I recovered my wits. I was lying on the rock there—damned cold, too. I was lucky I didn't break both my legs—and get drowned into the bargain. It was sheer chance I didn't fall in the water."

Giles Hoggett stared at the place where Rolph stood. "You were tackled from behind, then?" he asked.

The other nodded. "Yes. The chap must have crept behind me—you can see there's soft ground from the old shippon to behind where I was standing. I thought there'd be some footprints, but I can't see any. It's all covered in fallen leaves."

Hoggett looked at the ground, covered in last year's damp beech leaves, and then back at Francis Rolph's face.

"Look here," said Giles firmly, "I'm going to take you back in the car to Wenningby. My wife will see to that wound for you, it needs bathing."

"It's all right," protested Rolph. "The graze is nothing. I've got to catch the midday train; that's essential. I've an appointment in town this evening."

"I'll see you catch the train all right," said Hoggett, "but you'd better come straight back with me. I'll come back here later, just in case there's anything to be seen."

They turned back towards the gap in the fence.

"A rum go, wasn't it?" said Rolph, a grin twisting his mobile lips.

"Rum it was. I can't tell you how sorry I am," replied Giles.

As they went down the sloping pasture towards Broadgarth, Giles Hoggett found one sentence repeating itself in his mind: "I heard a man panting, as a chap does pant when he's carrying a heavy burden."

"A heavy burden." Giles Hoggett pondered over the words, and the more he pondered, the less he liked them.

4

"Look here, Giles," said Rolph, when they were in the car, "this is a damned silly story, I know that. Looking at it one way, I've been a victim of a murderous assault. Looking at it another way, I caught my foot in a briar and knocked my head on those qualified rocks. I think I prefer the second way of looking at it."

"But you believe the first to be true?" replied Hoggett.

"Well, that's as may be," said Rolph. "What I'm getting at is this. A case of assault should be reported to the police: tripping over a briar shouldn't. The last thing I want to do is to involve myself in giving evidence to the police in Lunesdale when I'm up to the eyes in work in London."

"I quite see that," replied Hoggett, "but this thing's got to be investigated. It's all very well for you to go off at a tangent and say you tripped over a briar—"

"I didn't say so. I only said the evidence could be taken to indicate that I did. I'm quite sure you'll investigate, and you'll find out if there's any funny stuff much quicker than the police would, because you know local conditions so well. I'm also quite sure that you'll see to it that Caroline doesn't go and live in Broadgarth by herself, as she's quite capable of doing."

"She can't do that," replied Giles firmly. "The feeling in these parts is all against a single woman living alone in an isolated house. I've been considering that point, but I assure you she shall not move into Broadgarth by herself."

"Well, that's all right; and it'll be some time before the house is ready for her," said Rolph. "Now as to my own position. I've told you what I feel about it. I don't want to be bothered with reporting to the police and all that."

Giles Hoggett shook his head. "Sorry, Francis, I can see it's a nuisance for you, and I'm very sorry that it ever happened, but we're not justified in taking no steps to report such a happening. You say you *heard* the men—heard them moving—and you thought they were carrying something. Also, however much you try to minimise it, you're really quite certain that you were attacked. A thing like that can't be ignored."

Rolph grinned. "Oh, devil take it... I suppose you're right, and there's this to it. If Caroline means to live in that farm-house, it's desirable to get the business cleared up. So what do we do about it?"

Giles Hoggett looked worried. Although he would not have admitted it, he tended to think more slowly now that he had become part and parcel of the countryside. Rolph, with his quick speech and his tendency to jump from one side to another in an argument, seemed lacking in proper seriousness in a very serious situation. Then Giles had an idea, reverting perhaps to the quicker decision of his once urban environment.

"After Kate's looked to that head wound of yours, I could drive you into Carnton to see the inspector. Carnton is a railway junction, and the London trains stop there. You could get a fast train there as easily as at Lancaster."

"All right. Have it your own way," said Rolph resignedly.

FOUR

I

"WHAT DID THE INSPECTOR SAY?" DEMANDED KATE.

Giles Hoggett came and sat down by the fire with a profoundly thoughtful face. He had just come back from Carnton, whither he had driven with Rolph to report the matter of assault to the police, after which Giles had duly seen the architect into the London train as he had promised to do. Giles took his time before replying. To Caroline's eye he looked portentous and a thought gloomy: to his wife's more experienced eye Giles looked portentous but not dissatisfied.

"I don't regard Inspector Bord as a man of any great acumen," he began.

Caroline chuckled. "That means the inspector didn't believe a word of it," she put in.

Giles rubbed his head. "Bord was very polite, and he listened attentively. He asked a number of questions. Had Rolph *seen* his attackers? Had he been robbed? Did Rolph realise what a surprising number of noises there are in any wood at night, especially to a townsman unaccustomed to the sibilance of owls and the creaking of trees and the lapping of water?"

"Did he really say sibilance," asked Kate.

"No, but he meant it," replied Giles. "Bord then went on to ask whether there were any long brambles or briars close to the spot where Rolph was standing. Of course there were briars *and* brambles," said Giles, "and they can trip you up on occasion, because they're very strong. Bord then turned to me. He spoke very handsomely of my extensive local knowledge, and asked me if I had ever considered that Garth coppice and the quarry pool were visited by undesirable people. Of course I said no, that I had always found the coppice a most peaceful spot, that I had never seen any intruders there, and that the previous tenants of Broadgarth had said they never saw a tramp during their whole tenancy and had no complaints about the solitary position of the farm-house. I added that I had advised my wife's cousin to buy Broadgarth."

"I bet he knew all about that," said Kate. "The whole of Lunesdale knows about that auction sale by now."

"Oh, yes, he knew about Caroline," agreed Giles. "He added that the police would pay particular attention to the matter, as a lady was going to live at Broadgarth. He also inquired if any of us had walked along the track to the quarry pool recently. I had to tell him that we had all walked that way—Kate and Caroline and Rolph and myself—"

"And of course the inspector implied that with all the hoofing about we had done, it would be only natural if there were a few footsteps," murmured Caroline.

Giles nodded. "The real fact was that Bord didn't know what to make of Rolph," he said. "I couldn't blame him. Bord's a countryman, and Rolph's quick speech and flippant way of talking didn't impress Bord. I could almost see his mind working. Bord said to himself, 'This chap's a Londoner. He's not used to the country, he's a nervy type and he's imaginative. That wood rattled him up. I've met the same thing before. Townsmen coming along and telling us about troubles like this. I've got to listen to him, but no need to take his story too seriously.'"

Kate nodded. "Yes. I think you're right about Inspector Bord, Giles, but all the same, Bord is wrong if that's his judgment about Francis Rolph. He may be nervy, but he's very observant."

"Oh, dear," said Caroline. "How tiresome the whole thing is. Poor Francis, he *liked* my ruin, and he's got an awful bump on his head just because he was so interested. He's one of the ablest men I know: he's got brains and imagination and artistry, and I'm perfectly certain he *did* trip over a briar and imagined someone had grabbed his ankles."

"I don't agree," said Giles. "Francis has played rugger. He knows perfectly well what it feels like to be tackled. It's not in the least like a bramble."

Caroline began to laugh, and Kate put in indignantly:

"Considering he's your friend, and it was really your fault he stopped by himself at Broadgarth, I think you're very unsympathetic. I told you I disapproved of him camping out there."

"I'm *not* unsympathetic," said Caroline. "I'm very sorry about him being hurt, but why was he ass enough to go up to that dangerous place by moonlight, when his head was wuzzy through working too hard and smoking too much? Of course he was just in the state when he *would* take a header and imagine he'd been attacked. He was excited, as he always is after he's done a good job of work, and the wood and the pool in the moonlight were intoxicating to an artist's mentality. He's done me some lovely drawings for my cottage," she concluded.

Kate refused to be sidetracked by the mention of drawings. "What do you think the inspector will do, Giles?" she asked, "or won't he do anything at all?"

"Of course he will do something," said Giles. "He will go and inspect the quarry pool, and the bank up from Broadgarth. He will notice it's a dangerous spot where Rolph stood, and he'll probably get an attendant constable to trip over a bramble. After that he will observe our footprints along the track, ask a few questions at Bromsgrove and from such police patrols as have been along the main road at nights, write a nice report, and leave it at that. He will also probably indulge in a few pleasantries about amateur detectives."

"That's what I mean by doing nothing," said Kate, whose practical common sense often led her into giving voice to abrupt judgments, "but I suppose there isn't very much he *could* do."

Giles made no reply, and Caroline took up the issue again. "Giles, don't you think the probability is that Francis just tripped up himself?" she asked insistently. "Do you really imagine that anybody in these parts would make a murderous assault on a complete stranger? It's so utterly crazy. If you argue that it wasn't a local inhabitant who attacked him, how do you account for the presence of strangers in that coppice? It's right off the road, and nobody passing along the main road would ever notice the old cottage, or guess at the existence of the quarry pool."

"You've got to admit that Kate noticed that the track past the cottage had been used of recent months," insisted Giles gravely.

"Did you tell the inspector that fact, Giles?" demanded Kate promptly. "If not, why not?"

Giles did not reply immediately, and Kate went on trenchantly:

"You didn't tell him because you want to go detecting on your own. I could tell from your face when you came into the room that you were pleased about something."

"Why, I thought how gloomy he looked," said Caroline, and Kate retorted:

"I know him. You don't. He put that gloomy face on to cover his own satisfaction at the way things are going. Giles, it's your duty to report to the inspector that somebody—probably a poacher—has been using that path."

"What corroboration can you offer him?" asked Giles, for the first time allowing a grin to lighten his solemn face. "If Bord didn't accept poor Rolph's broken crown as evidence of assault, he's not going to accept our unsupported testimony about footsteps you noticed before we'd trampled them out. And talking about duty, I think I ought to get the soil in the greenhouse ready for your tomatoes. We mustn't neglect our work on account of all these extraneous excitements."

He got up and made for the door, while Kate muttered:

"Clever, aren't you? My tomatoes are only an excuse for guillotining the argument."

Caroline stood and examined a fine white *Primula obconica* on the window seat. "Kate," she inquired, "do you think Giles has got a theory of his own about last night?"

"Of course he's got a theory," said Kate, folding up her needlework. "You remember he's been absorbing all the local gossip about Alice Wynne's husband, and the rumpus with Tom Field? Giles is building an elaborate theory about murder and corpses and quarry pools for hiding them in. He's determined to have a mystery. Oh, I know Giles is quite astute over putting one and one together and making a sum of it," she added, "but although he's good at observing things, he's not good at making right deductions from his observations. We both learnt that when Macdonald was up here about that Wenningby Barns business. Giles and I had all the facts, but we made nothing of them. Untrained minds can't really deduce properly."

She put her needlework neatly into the basket and added: "I might as well get something out of the situation myself. If Giles is going to get new soil into the greenhouse, I'll get busy with those tomatoes. Do you want something to do, or are you quite happy on your own?"

"I think I'll go and sketch in your gill. The blackthorn is coming out round the beck," said Caroline.

"All right. You'll be safe enough there; but for goodness' sake don't go tripping over a bramble. The gill's very steep and quite slippery."

"I don't trip over brambles," said Caroline indignantly. "The only time I ever tumbled was when I tried to round the cows up."

"Don't do it again. We've had quite enough tumbling for one day," said Kate.

2

"A deep depression covers the British Isles."

Kate Hoggett switched off the radio impatiently. She knew all about that depression. The halcyon weather of the past fortnight had vanished in the night; the moan of a west wind at sunset had heralded the mist of rain which swept up Lunesdale, obscuring the fells, blanketing the Pennine Chain, reducing visibility to the home pastures and the sodden wallflowers in the garden. Giles had come into dinner at twelve sharp: he had helped with the washing up, as he always did, and had then taken himself off murmuring something about fishing. Kate had no belief in his fishing: she was convinced that Giles had gone to pursue his own private investigations at the quarry pool. Caroline had gone into Lancaster to look for curtain material, and now, at five minutes to one, Kate found herself alone with a B.B.C. voice which uttered platitudes about deep depressions. She counted Giles's stockings in the mending-basket. There were fifteen pairs in the basket, waiting for a rainy day. Well, it was raining now, and Kate decided to make a virtue of necessity. After all, perhaps the garden did need rain.

She was immersed in a synthesis of knitted stockings, a theory of her own about the pre-Roman occupation of Lunesdale, and gloomy forebodings about Giles and the quarry pool, when a knock sounded at the kitchen door.

Expecting the worst, she hurried to the door, and held it against her shoulder as the rain swept in. She did not at first recognise the tall man in a streaming Burberry and sodden hat.

"Good day, Mrs. Hoggett. I'm sorry to bring you to the door on such a day." The voice dispelled her uncertainty.

"Macdonald! Oh, I *am* so glad to see you. Come along in. Let me have that coat... Is Giles all right?"

"I sincerely hope so," said the chief inspector. "Why shouldn't he be?"

"He's gone detecting on his own. Come along to the fire," said Kate. "There's nobody I could be more pleased to see."

When Kate Hoggett liked anybody, she did it in no half-hearted fashion. Chief Inspector Macdonald, C.I.D., had stayed at Wenningby when the body of the unfortunate Gordon Ginner had been found in the River Lune, and both Kate and her husband had liked him very much indeed. They had not only admired his skill as a detective, they had enjoyed him as a guest, and found that, Londoner though he was, he fitted in with country ways and respected farming folk.

"What's all this about Hoggett going detecting on his own?" inquired Macdonald, when he had sat down with feet outstretched to the log fire.

"I thought you must have come up here to look for the corpse in the quarry pool," said Kate.

Macdonald shook his head. "Indeed I haven't. I've been up to Ulverston and Heysham, on a case concerned with Customs evasion, but I have heard nothing about a crime in Lunesdale."

"It's only a hypothetical crime," said Kate. "It was like this." With admirable brevity and clarity she told Macdonald about Broadgarth, about Caroline's ruin, the quarry pool and Francis Rolph's mishap. She concluded: "Giles made Rolph report the facts to the police, but I think the inspector thought it was all moonshine, and that Rolph tripped up. Caroline believes it was all an accident, and she knows Francis Rolph much better than we do."

"And what do you think yourself?" asked Macdonald.

Kate lighted another cigarette. "I'm not quite sure," she said. "I admit that Caroline has a point when she insists that Francis has the artist mentality, for all that he's so practical with his hands. She says that when he's been working at something which particularly interests him, he gets vague and absentminded and excitable. That's true, in a way. But I have found him to be an accurate observer, which very few people are. Then he's a practising architect. He's accustomed to scaffolding and heights and unfinished buildings, and I've never heard of him tumbling or getting vertigo while he's on a job."

"I think that is a very cogent point, Mrs. Hoggett," said Macdonald. "Balance is, to some extent, sub-conscious. Your husband has all the attributes of muscular balance, but he uses them unconsciously: his muscles are adapted to compensation, if you see what I mean. Now an architect must acquire the same faculty, so that his muscles answer in reflex fashion—that is, before he's had time to think about it. I shouldn't expect such a man to tumble about, even in a moonlit wood."

"Then Giles made quite a good point," went on Kate. "He says it's foolish to say that Francis Rolph could confuse being tackled rugby fashion with tripping over a bramble, even a bramble that's rooted at both ends. Rolph used to play rugger, and Giles says that being tackled isn't a bit like tripping backwards over a bramble."

Macdonald laughed. "That also is perfectly true," he agreed, "and nobody knows more about tackling and being tackled than Hoggett does. Now you've told me all about Miss Bourne's ruin and Rolph's trouble: may I now hear about Hoggett's hypothetical corpse?"

Kate laughed. She felt much more cheerful now that she could tell Macdonald the whole story.

"Well, you know what Giles is like," she said. "He's very quick at tumbling to some things. He did see the implications of the iron dogs and the salmon line and the chaff sack at Wenningby Barns, didn't he?"

"He did," said Macdonald promptly, "and I shall be the last to forget it. Also, he's got a nose for the unusual. If anything departs from the normal in his own environment, your Giles is on to it like knife."

"Don't tell him so," pleaded Kate. "I admit he was quite smart over that business at Wenningby Barns, but it's made him biased. He's got a departure from the normal in Rolph's accident, and his bias makes him determined that there is a profound mystery to be elucidated. Rolph said the men he heard were panting, as though they had been carrying something heavy. Inspector Bord believes that Rolph heard the queer noise that owls make when they are courting, and I know just what he means, because one of the few times I ever got frightened in the country, it turned out to be owls which made the noise that frightened me."

"Owls…" said Macdonald meditatively. "I think I have heard them when they're mating. They hiss, don't they?"

"Partly," she replied. "The noise is between a hiss and a groan. One night, years ago, when we were staying at Wenningby Barns, I heard the queerest sound. I thought it was like a very big animal breathing heavily. It went on and on, and Giles insisted on going out to the barn to see what it was. I was honestly frightened, because it *did* sound like a very big animal panting. I know I yelled to Giles to come in; and then two big brown owls flew out of the barn, almost touching us. I've never forgotten it."

She paused, and then added: "It's quite reasonable to assume that Francis heard the owls, and didn't know what it was. If he tripped and stunned himself, he'd have been concussed and wouldn't have remembered anything properly, and he might easily have imagined he heard footsteps."

"Perfectly true," agreed Macdonald, "but is the wish father to the thought, just a trifle?"

She laughed. "Oh, yes, I admit that. I don't want to believe that someone knocked Rolph down and left him for dead. It's a most unpleasant thought."

"It certainly is," agreed Macdonald.

"And I'm certain Giles believes there's a corpse about somewhere," she went on, "and I don't like him going poking round in the quarry pool on his own. He'll be getting himself knocked over the head next."

"I don't think he will," said Macdonald comfortingly. "I've a great respect for his ability to take care of himself. Also, though it may sound illogical, some people are far more prone to get knocked about than others, just as there are bad card-holders at bridge, against every law of probability. It's contrary to the mathematical laws of chance, but it happens."

"I know it does," she replied promptly, 'because I'm a bad cardholder and Giles is a good one."

Macdonald laughed. "There you are. I don't think you need worry about him. I still remember him on the rugger field. Now let me get the hang of his theory about a possible victim."

"It's *my* theory of Giles's theory," she admitted honestly. "He won't risk putting it into words to me, because he knows I should find all his loose ends. Alice Wynne had a row with her husband, who is a very unsatisfactory husband anyway, and David, Alice's husband, walked off after complaining that Alice had been encouraging Tom Field to get familiar. Tom Field is a friend of David's, or was supposed to be until they quarrelled. Both men have disappeared from the locality. In Field's case that means nothing. He's what they call an agricultural contractor and he's always moving around. He owns his own tractor and gear and does ploughing and ridging and sowing and tree-felling anywhere he can get a job, so he may be up north beyond Kendal, or down south near to Preston for all I know."

"And you think that Giles postulates that David Wynne killed Tom Field, and hid his body in the quarry pool?"

"Something of that kind," she agreed.

"But Rolph said that he thought he heard two men," went on Macdonald.

She nodded, adding: "He probably imagined it, though. You know how easy it is to imagine things in a wood by moonlight, especially if you're not used to the country at night."

Macdonald laughed. "Nobody knows that better than I do. When I was down in the dales by moonlight, I could have imagined anything. Well, thanks for the exposition. You have been most lucid. Now I'd better go and see what Giles is up to. How do I get to the quarry pool?"

"It's about four miles away and it's still streaming with rain," she said.

"I've got my car," he said.

Kate looked surprised. "Then why were you so wet when you arrived?" she asked.

Macdonald chuckled. "That's not fair, Mrs. Hoggett. You mustn't turn detective methods against a detective."

"Sorry. I withdraw the remark and it shall not be repeated," she said. "You drive up to the Chapelton-Lonsdale road, turn right when our road meets the main road, and drive on about a mile, until you see a very rough track on the right, at the far side of a beech coppice. Here's Giles's map—it's all marked on the Ordnance Survey. You see…?"

"I see," said Macdonald. "I'll go up there now. If he's not there I'll come straight back."

"Good—and stay the night if you can and I'll make a ham omelette for supper," she replied.

3

Macdonald had no difficulty in finding the track. He made his way to Caroline's cottage and inspected it thoughtfully. He agreed with Miss Caroline Bourne, it was a lovely site for a house, even seen in the teeming rain, with mist shutting out the fells. He stood on the little eminence outside the cottage and considered, his head slightly cocked as he listened to the trickle of rain, the sighing of the wind in the trees, and the distant plash of water. This place was marked on the Ordnance Survey Map. It was quite easy to find once you were aware of its existence, but you could drive along the main road, past the end of the woodland track a hundred times, without noticing it, without guessing at the existence of cottage or ruin or quarry pool. Even if you drove along the track to visit Broadgarth, you would never guess at the existence of the quarry pool. Such places had often been put to nefarious uses in times past, and nobody knew that better than Macdonald did.

Leaving the cottage, he walked slowly into the wood towards the pool, carefully avoiding the faintly marked path. He stopped to inspect at one point, where he found a shallow wooden box turned upside down on the path. Macdonald grinned, he couldn't help it. This was one of Kate Hoggett's precious seed-boxes.

"She'll be annoyed if he's borrowed several of them," thought Macdonald, "and, by Jove, he has! Good old Hoggett, sticking to his routine."

There were two more boxes farther along the path. Leaving them undisturbed, Macdonald walked on to the ruined shippon and went inside. In the farthest and driest corner lay a heap of clothes, carefully covered with a sack, and a pair of shoes. A rod, a creel, and a deplorable sodden hat completed the exhibits. Giles Hoggett, truthful as ever, having uttered the word "fish" had brought his gear with him:

no one else in the kingdom owned a hat that was the replica of that one, meditated Macdonald.

He left the ruin and walked on to the quarry pool, and was surprised, as Caroline had been, by its size. It looked ominous, dark and dangerous, with its enclosing ridge of rock, the dripping trees, the rain-pocked water. Macdonald noted the treacherous slippery rocks, the steep fall from the ridge, the brambles and briars, the creak and whisper of swaying boughs and shivering leaves. He stood again and listened, found himself startled as a heavy splash sounded in the water some twenty yards away. Macdonald's eyesight was good. He saw a head break surface as a diver came up in the inky water: he saw a well-remembered face marred with black mud-stains and clinging slime. Macdonald gave voice:

"Hoggett!" he roared. "Come out of it! Come out of it at once. What on earth will your wife say?"

FIVE

I

IF GILES HOGGETT WERE STARTLED BY THE QUITE UNEXPECTED apparition of a chief inspector from Scotland Yard roaring peremptory orders from the bank of the quarry pool, he gave no signs of perturbation. With long unhurried strokes he swam back to the side and began to scramble out, his long sinewy person in a black bathing slip looking unexpectedly boyish, his grey hair darkened by the water and bedizened with yet darker water-weeds. It was not easy to scramble up the rocky verge, and by the time Macdonald joined him, Giles was ruefully surveying his grazed knees, rather as a schoolboy might, after a tumble on a gravel path. Despite the fact that he was shivering, Giles achieved more dignity than might have been expected in the circumstances.

"You're the very man I was thinking of, Macdonald," he said. "I'm uncommonly glad to see you."

"Thanks very much. If you don't get sciatica to-night it'll be a miracle, Hoggett. Go and get some clothes on, do, and let the explanations wait."

"You've seen Kate?" asked Hoggett.

"Yes. I have. Go on, man, you'll have pneumonia in addition to sciatica if you're not careful."

Giles hobbled with such haste as he could over ground which was painful to bare feet, while Macdonald stood and surveyed the quarry pool. He guessed it was deep, its bottom and sides treacherous with uneven rock, its depths pocketed with mud and dangerous with snags and weed. "A good thing you're safely out of it, Hoggett," said the C.I.D. man to himself.

Macdonald strolled back to the ruined shippon. Hoggett was towelling himself vigorously.

"I see you've brought your rod and creel," said Macdonald.

"Yes. The fish should be rising well," said Giles. "You see I have put some boxes along the track?"

"Yes. I noticed that. Footprints?"

"Some very interesting ones, very deep," said Giles as he struggled into his shirt. "Has Kate told you about the circumstances?"

Macdonald nodded. "Yes. I called in at Wenningby to see you both. I've been up Furness way for a consultation, and I took some time off to pay you a visit."

"Furness way?" Hoggett looked surprised. "I thought you'd heard from Bord about Rolph's accident."

"No. He hadn't reported it to C.O.—not to my knowledge, at least," rejoined Macdonald. "Now, look here: the sooner you get back to a good fire the better, that pool must be perishing cold—but I'd better have a look at those cherished footprints you've taken so much trouble about."

Giles Hoggett pulled on his jacket and raincoat and put on his deplorable hat: the much-battered, dingy, rain-sodden felt suited him in some odd way: it added character to his long-limbed figure, inasmuch as it endowed him with potential ferocity. Macdonald, who knew Hoggett as the kindliest of men, knew that this appearance was quite misleading, but he liked the hat all the same.

"The trouble is that there's been too much trampling about," said Hoggett, as he led the way to the first inverted seed-box. "Of course the footprints I have covered may have been made by Bord and his man, but I think this one is authentic."

He raised the box carefully, and exhibited a very deep, rather shapeless footprint. "You can see this print is much more deeply impressed than that farther along," said Hoggett. "The farther one is mine, and both must have been made before it rained. Now I weigh 13 stone. The chap who made this one must have weighed a great deal more, unless he were carrying something very heavy."

"There's also the possibility that the man stood still for a considerable time," observed Macdonald.

Hoggett nodded. "Yes, there's that—but according to Rolph's evidence, the men whose footsteps he heard walked on until they came to the shippon. You can't see any useful traces there, because the ground's covered in leaves, overlying the old flagstones. Rolph thought that they halted there when they heard him dislodge a stone. If you look under the next box, you'll find a similar deep footprint, and a third closer to the cottage. If your theory's right, the man must have halted at least three times. They're not my footprints, nor Rolph's, nor my wife's, nor her cousin's. You can see specimens of all their tracks around the cottage."

Macdonald took a step backwards and studied his own footprint, where he had been standing on the track. Even though the ground was soft after the rain, the print was still not as deep as the one Hoggett had covered with the box.

"Say if I heave you up and study the resulting footprint," said Macdonald, stepping back on to the path. "Ready? Fireman's lift… Losh, I haven't done much weight-lifting lately. Now what about it…?" He drew back to the side of the path, and then said: "Well, it looks as though you might be right. Our combined weights seem to have made an impression, and Bord doesn't weigh twenty-six stone. I'll just measure these, then we'll go back and reassure your wife. You can show me Rolph's footprints as we pass the cottage."

2

As the two men regained the Broadgarth track and turned towards the main road, Macdonald said:

"Well, you seem to have established certain points, Hoggett. There are a few deeply marked footprints which weren't made by you or Rolph—or by a woman. It's a pity that the nature of the ground is so variable that we can't get enough footprints to denote length of stride, neither can we be certain that there were two men together, as Rolph believed. Hallo, who's this?"

A man's figure was seen approaching them along the track, advancing from the road. He had a sack round his shoulders, and a cap on his head. He wore the heavy clogs common to farm workers in dirty weather. He advanced steadily, a youngish man, Macdonald noted, with healthy red cheeks and heavy build.

"It's Tom Field," said Hoggett.

The newcomer showed no sign of nervousness. He walked straight up to the two men and said:

"Good day, Mr. Hoggett. Is Miss Bourne at Broadgarth now?"

"She owns Broadgarth, but she is not living there yet. What do you want?" asked Hoggett.

"Well, I was wondering if she'd want any timber felled, or hedges cut, or such-like, or maybe any ploughing. I've got my tractor and saw, and I might have some spare time later on."

"I don't think Miss Bourne wants anything of the kind at present," replied Hoggett. "If you'll give me your address, I'll pass it on to her."

"That's not so easy. I'm moving about like, never sure where I shall go next. Could you give me an idea when she's moving to Broadgarth?"

"No. I can't tell you," replied Hoggett. "Had you got an eye on any of the timber in this wood?"

"Can't say I had. I don't know it, but I'm always looking for business. Good day, Mr. Hoggett."

"Good day," rejoined Giles.

Field turned back the way he had come, and Macdonald made for his car, which he had left some twenty yards from the main road, Hoggett following.

"He's no local," observed Macdonald as he got into the driving seat.

"No. Indeed he's not," agreed Hoggett. "Our lads around here aren't so ready with questions and demands for jobs. That's what you might call a new phenomenon, Macdonald."

"How so?"

"Well, recently we have got accustomed to some of the farmers' sons buying their own tractors and setting up as agricultural contractors, but they generally work in their own neighbourhood, for farmers who know them, and they live with their own families. This young Field comes from away. His people live somewhere between Wigan and Preston, I'm told, so he's looking for work a long way from home."

"Is that to be counted against him?" asked Macdonald, who had guessed the answer to his question already.

Hoggett replied: "We are a settled community around here, Macdonald, as you yourself know. We tend to trust the familiar, the families who have had dealings with one another for years, sometimes for generations. There's been a lot of inter-marriage in the valley, of course. For instance, I'm related—distantly, perhaps—to several of the farming families around Wenningby. It boils down to this. If a young fellow leaves his own district and goes touting for work farther afield, we're inclined to ask ourselves the reason. There generally *is* a reason."

"I know you're suspicious of Field," rejoined Macdonald. "The thing I'm trying to find out is what grounds you've got for that suspicion, apart from native caution and ingrained conservatism."

Hoggett looked very serious. "I told you that Field had been associated with David Wynne, who left home some days ago. Wynne has a small farm, only twenty acres, between Wenningby and Chapelton Lonsdale. It's poorish land, only fit for grazing. He recently rented another eighteen acres from old Mr. Shaw, and he's been ploughing some of it. That's where Field came in. Wynne employed Field and his tractor to plough and cultivate and to clear some scrub and coppice. Field kept his tractor in Wynne's buildings, and also stayed with the Wynnes for a time. Now David Wynne is a young man of whom I've a poor opinion, and Field was the worst sort of influence for Wynne; encouraged him to go out drinking and betting, wasting his money and neglecting his work—neglecting his wife, too. Then Wynne and Field quarrelled, and it came to blows, I'm told. After that, Wynne accused his wife of encouraging Field's advances; and then Wynne disappeared. Of course I'm suspicious. I'm not less suspicious now that I've seen Field around the coppice—near the quarry pool, in short." Hoggett paused and then added: "Did you notice his clogs, Macdonald?"

The chief inspector chuckled. "I thought we should come to those clogs. I'll admit at once that Field's clogs were exactly the sort and size of footwear to have made those prints we examined. But tell me this, Hoggett. How many of your farming neighbours wear clogs in dirty weather?"

"All of them," said Hoggett. "A few of the younger ones like Gilbert Claughton have gumboots, but they only wear them if the land's properly flooded. We're a thrifty lot hereabouts."

Macdonald laughed. "You're a man after my own heart, Hoggett. You may invent a case to fit your theories, but you're prepared to blow all your theories sky-high by telling the exact truth when you're asked for it."

"I was also prepared to dive into that black hole," began Hoggett, and Macdonald laughed again.

"Prepared to? You *did* dive into it, I caught you in the act—and you're old enough to know better than to be so reckless. That's a damned dangerous water, Hoggett; don't let me catch you doing it again. Got that?"

"I can't say I enjoyed it," said Giles ruefully.

3

Kate Hoggett was immensely pleased when Giles and Macdonald returned to Wenningby together.

"Did you catch any fish?" she inquired of her husband, not quite kindly, but it was Macdonald who replied.

"No, Mrs. Hoggett, he caught no fish, though I'm not denying that there may be some queer fish in the stretch of water where I found him. However, if he's going to co-operate with me, I've warned him off that particular stretch. Further angling there will be regarded as poaching."

"Excellent," said Kate. "Hallo, here's Caroline. This is Chief Inspector Macdonald, Caroline. Miss Bourne."

"How do you do? Is it true you've been detecting in my ruin?" asked Caroline.

"I suppose it *is* true, to some extent," replied Macdonald. "May I add that I found what I expected to find there, but it had no direct connection with crime."

"I'm delighted to hear it," said Caroline. "Honestly, Chief Inspector, I think it's a bit hard that Giles and Francis Rolph are intent on staging a crime act on my land. It's the first land I've ever possessed, and I do think I might be allowed what the lawyers call peaceful possession without let or hindrance. Francis tripped over a briar and broke his crown. I assure you that's all that happened."

"Come and have tea and leave crime alone for a bit," said Kate.

"Amen to both," said Caroline as they drew up round the fire. "Giles," she went on, "do you know a place called Hauxhead Castle?"

"Of course. It was Sir Charles Brough's property. It has recently been sold and is now a hotel, I gather. It's a very fine house, in beautiful surroundings, near the head waters of the Lune."

"Is it an old house?"

Kate intervened here. "Very old; older than Levens, I believe. It was a religious house, originally, a Cistercian foundation, but it was mostly rebuilt in the great days of the Kendal wool trade. The old banqueting hall is still intact, and the outbuildings are magnificent. How did you hear of it?"

"I've just had a letter from the present owner. He offers me a commission to do some illustrations for what he calls a 'brochure'—revolting word—and also suggests that I should write a short history and description of the place."

"How did he come to know of your existence?" inquired Giles, and Caroline protested:

"Don't be so deflating! Quite a lot of people know of my existence. After all, I did exhibit at the Lunesdale Artists' show, and he said he had read my articles on the old pack-pony bridges—though I admit Kate gave me all the information in that one."

"Who is the owner of the castle now that it's been turned into a hotel?" queried Macdonald.

Caroline turned to him. "His name is Sholto Barren. Judging by his letter, he's quite a knowledgeable person. If I undertake the commission, he offers me hospitality at the castle. You can't say it isn't a handsome offer, especially as he is willing to let me name my own price for my drawings."

Giles snorted. "I should have nothing whatever to do with it, Caroline. It probably means that he'll get your drawings and you'll get nothing but your hotel expenses."

Caroline began a vigorous protest, but Kate cut in trenchantly: "Do you know anything about this man Barren, Giles, or not? If you don't, you've no business to make unjustifiable statements like that."

Macdonald began to laugh. "But I know just what Hoggett means. He's like me. He distrusts any man who begins by saying 'Name your own price.'"

"Of course," said Giles. "Macdonald's a man of sense. He knows that hotel keepers with Christian names like Sholto aren't likely to ask you to name your own price if they're on the straight."

"Well, with due respect to Mr. Macdonald, and to you, too, Giles, I think your northern forebears have made you unreasonably suspicious. This man Barren must be simply rolling. It costs the earth to equip a place like Hauxhead Castle as a first-class hotel, and it obviously *is* a first-class hotel."

"So it may be," said Giles, "but I don't like it. I hear that they've started one of these country clubs there, with a licence for members of the club, *and* their friends. It's not the sort of place we want in these parts. If I were you, Caroline, I should be very chary of having anything to do with it."

"Well, Giles, I think you're a bit high-hat," protested Caroline. "You know I always listen when you give me advice, especially about things up here, but this time I think you're being prejudiced. A job's a job, and this Hauxhead job sounds a jolly attractive one. It may be very useful to me professionally, because I want to get known up here, and I shall need to make some money if I'm going to farm Broadgarth. It's bound to cost me a lot to begin with."

"Good for you!" said Kate cheerfully. "Giles is getting too authoritarian altogether."

"Well, if you insist on doing it, see that you get your contract down in black and white," said Giles, and Caroline snorted:

"Contract indeed! I may not know anything about land tenures and farming, but when it comes to contracts, you're an infant in arms compared to me, Giles. I'm as hard as iron, as polite as Lucifer and as gullible as an Aberdonian—which is—not very... Kate, be like Galsworthy's Aunt Em and come and show me where the Portulaca was. I want to talk about Hauxhead."

Giles stretched his feet comfortably out to the fire when Kate and Caroline had gone outside to the greenhouse.

"I think it was worth while to warn her," he said magnanimously. "Caroline's rather hasty, but she's sensible enough in her own way. Now, getting back to this business about the quarry pool, Macdonald. What's your real opinion about it?"

"My first reaction is this," replied Macdonald. "It's not a safe place to dive into. You could strike a snag, or get caught by an overhanging rock under water. I know you're a strong swimmer, but so am I, and I know I wouldn't risk diving into that pool, so kindly avoid doing so in future, or your wife will blame me if you get into difficulties."

"Oh, no, she wouldn't, she'd blame me," said Giles quickly, "but I'll defer to your judgment in the matter. What I really want to know is this: Do you think the whole thing's a mare's nest?"

"No, I don't," replied Macdonald decidedly. "You've got something, to use the debased lingo of to-day, and you can follow it up, provided you leave the quarry pool alone. Your strong point is dealing with people, particularly the people of your own locality. It's like this, Hoggett. You've got a theory that the disappearance of David Wynne is connected with Rolph's mishap, and it's not for me to say that you're wrong. You've got a nose for the abnormal in your own environment, and I'd sooner trust your hunch than the scepticism of the local inspector. But since you've started this hare, I suggest you follow it up yourself. You've a much better chance of getting at the real facts of Wynne's disappearance than I have, because your neighbours trust you; so get on with it. I know you well enough to realise that you may be able to put us on to something, and you won't queer our pitch."

"Right," said Hoggett with alacrity. "I'll talk round the subject in the neighbouring shippons, according to custom. I'm a bit puzzled about Field's appearance at the coppice this afternoon, Macdonald. It looks as though I'm wrong about him. If he'd done anything desperate, he wouldn't have risked being seen there."

"I don't know," said Macdonald slowly. "I've been thinking about Rolph again; thinking of him, that is, from his assailant's point of view. I take it, from your wife's description of events, that nobody could have known that Rolph was staying at Broadgarth. Assuming that Field, or some other fellow whom we will call Field for the moment, came to the coppice in the small hours on some nefarious business, it must have been a staggering shock to realise that there was a witness in the coppice. Put yourself in Field's place for a minute, and think."

Giles rubbed his head. "Yes, I see your point," he replied. "I hadn't thought about it from Field's point of view. He wouldn't have had the least notion who Rolph was. He'd have realised there was somebody on the ridge whose presence there was a menace to him. He *dared* not let Rolph see anything."

"That's it. Also it's worth remembering that Field probably didn't know if he'd killed Rolph or not, but Field does know that Miss Bourne has bought Broadgarth, and that she might well wander through the coppice to the quarry pool. He wouldn't like the idea of her finding Rolph's body there. The fat would have been in the fire from Field's point of view if a police investigation developed round the quarry pool. All this is hypothetical, but it's worth considering."

Again Giles Hoggett pondered deeply. "You mean that Field may have come to the coppice to see if Rolph's body was still there—with the intention of tipping it in the pool to conceal it?"

"Maybe. I think Rolph may consider himself lucky that Field didn't try to do that very thing immediately. I take it that Rolph wasn't robbed? You didn't mention anything of the kind."

"No, he wasn't robbed. I'm sure of that because Inspector Bord asked him that question most particularly."

"Yes. Bord would have thought of that. The very fact that Rolph made no mention of any loss would speak volumes to a policeman. It was probably on that account that Bord was so sceptical. Violence with robbery is a commonplace to us cops. Violence to an unknown man without robbery is far less substantial."

"Yes. I see. You know a policeman's reactions and I don't," admitted Hoggett. "Another thing occurred to me: wasn't Field much too cool and collected when he spoke to us this afternoon to allow of any supposition that he felt in any danger?"

"Was he?" asked Macdonald. "I don't know Field, but I do know his type. He's got rogue written all over his face in my judgment. Didn't you say that Field had been interesting Wynne in the dog-racing track over at Strand? I know perfectly well that thousands of honest working men enjoy the dogs, but so do some very questionable gentry. No man is more glib and more brazen than some of the racecourse hangers-on. Field is just that type."

"Is he? It's a type I don't know, but I've always mistrusted Field—and Wynne, too, for that matter."

Macdonald was pondering again. "If Field had been up to any criminal business around the quarry pool, it was very necessary for him to have a good excuse for being there if anybody saw him," went on Macdonald after a while. "That inquiry about the possibility of working for Miss Bourne was very skilful. He had a justification for being in the coppice; examining timber with an eye to felling it. I noticed your astute inquiry as to whether he had an eye on any particular trees, but Field was too cunning to fall for that one." Macdonald was silent for a moment, then he went on: "You tried to dissuade Miss Bourne from going to Hauxhead, Hoggett. I think you're wrong there. You'd better go into reverse as cunningly as you know how."

"But why? I thought you agreed with me over the 'name-your-own-price' offer."

"So I do," chuckled Macdonald, "but Miss Bourne's emoluments are neither here nor there so far as I'm concerned. The point is, I don't want her haunting the coppice and the quarry pool. From her point of view it isn't safe. From my own, it's undesirable. I want the place left alone, severely alone. It would be an admirable idea for her to go and draw at Hauxhead. She says it's a first-class hotel."

Hoggett began to laugh. "I see. I gather you'd also prefer her to go on thinking that Rolph tripped over a bramble?"

"That's it. Don't think I underestimate her. She's no sort of fool. But the minute she becomes convinced that there's a mystery to be elucidated on her newly acquired land, it'll be the devil and all to keep her off it. She'd be much better at Hauxhead."

Hoggett laughed to himself. "All right. I quite see that. But there's my wife to consider as well. Kate does *not* believe that Rolph tripped over a bramble."

"I know she doesn't. That fact doesn't worry me at all. Your wife's a very unusual woman, Hoggett. She's got eyes that see and a tongue which keeps its own counsel. Your Kate won't go mooning round the quarry pool. She's got far too much sense. Have you realised that it's your wife who has put forward the best piece of objective evidence we've had in this case yet?"

"Has she? What was that?"

"You think it over," said Macdonald.

4

A moment later Kate and Caroline came back into the room.

"Giles, I *am* going to Hauxhead," declared Caroline, "and Kate's coming over there for a week-end while I'm there. She's agreed to work up the historical facts for me and share the proceeds."

"You must learn by experience, Caroline," said Giles. "If you don't get paid, it'll do you no harm. I hope you'll have an enjoyable time there; and if Kate goes to spend a week-end with you, I'll persuade Macdonald to come down to Wenningby Barns with me and we'll do some fishing."

"Perhaps you'll get a few more trout if he's there to help you," said Kate unfeelingly. She turned to Macdonald. "You're staying the night with us, aren't you?" she asked.

"I'm afraid not, Mrs. Hoggett. I've got to get on with my own job, but I hope to see you again before I go back to London."

"Thank goodness!" exclaimed Caroline, and to Kate's indignant expression she replied: "I only mean thank goodness he's not intent on investigating my quarry pool. If he won't even stay the night he can't be taking it very seriously, can he?"

"I take everything seriously," replied Macdonald, "but I can't be in two places at once. I hope you'll enjoy Hauxhead, Miss Bourne, and I hope to see your pictures of it some time. In spite of Hoggett's suspicions about 'naming your own price,' and mine, too, for that matter, I should think the place must be well worth drawing."

"I'm sure it is. Come over and see it, and I'll see if I can get Francis Rolph to come up, too. Then you'll see what he's really like, and why I say he probably fell over a bramble. But he'll be marvellous company at a place like Hauxhead. He's a genius at stone buildings."

"I should think he's had enough of the stone in this district," said Kate. "His head must be aching still."

"I know. It was rotten luck, wasn't it?" said Caroline contritely. "But he did me some marvellous drawings," she added happily.

SIX

I

WHEN MACDONALD LEFT THE HOGGETTS, HE DROVE OVER TO Carnton to see Inspector Bord. The inspector chuckled when he saw the C.I.D. man.

"Speak of angels," he exclaimed. "I was just talking about you. Has Mr. Giles Hoggett been writing to you about his latest problem?"

Despite Bord's chuckle, Macdonald sensed that the Carnton man was more than a little vexed: it is not customary for the C.I.D. to appear in country areas without having been invited to participate in a case. Macdonald hastened to explain himself.

"No, Hoggett didn't write to me, and I haven't come up here on his account at all, though I have been to see him and his wife. I came up here to help the Excise men. They've got evidence at last against a man they have suspected for a long time—one William Maredeth. I expected to be able to collect him at Heysham as he came off the Irish boat, but he must have got wind of our intentions. He wasn't on the boat. Have you ever heard of him?"

Bord rubbed his head. "Maredeth? Why, he was one of the men who put up the money for the new greyhound racing-track at Strand. I gather there's been trouble there once or twice, but that was due to some toughs—proper welshers, I believe. I've never heard any complaints against the promoters. What's Maredeth been doing?"

"What hasn't he been doing," responded Macdonald. "He's suspected of currency offences, smuggling, black market in petrol, and a variety of other felonies. He gets about the country a lot, always popping up in different places. He's got several small businesses which do legitimate trading with the Continent and Eire, so he has been able to get abroad more or less as he wishes."

"And he's given you the slip?"

"Yes, for the time being. I shall get him sometime. It happens that I know his face. He gave evidence for the defence in a case I was working on. He lied, and I knew that he lied—and he knew that I knew that he lied, but I couldn't prove it—so it would have given me a lot of pleasure to take him into custody."

"A pleasure deferred," chuckled Bord. "Anything I can do to help you?"

"Any information gratefully received," said Macdonald. "You'll be getting the usual chit from C.O. about him. We didn't anticipate any trouble in collecting him, but there must have been a leakage somewhere. He's got a house up Ulverston way, and probably several other residences as well. The Excise men have proved—to their own satisfaction at any rate—that Maredeth is the consignee for various crates containing contraband in addition to legitimate goods, all from Ireland. It's probable I shall be in your area for a bit, as well as in Westmorland and Yorkshire."

"The hunt's up, eh? Well, I don't fancy his chances with you on his tail," said Bord. "While you're here, I wish you'd tell me what you make of Mr. Hoggett's latest. He's told you about Rolph?"

"Yes. He told me. I want to know what *you* make of it, Bord, if you care to tell me. It's your pigeon, not mine."

Bord scratched his head. "It's hard to say, Chief, and that's a fact. I didn't make much of this architect chap, he's a flippant sort of cuss. He's told Hoggett this story about being knocked over the head in

Broadgarth Coppice, and Hoggett believed it. By the time Rolph had thought it over, I think he wasn't that anxious to report to us, but Hoggett insisted, and brought him here. To my mind, it's far more likely that Rolph tripped and knocked himself silly on those rocks than that he was assaulted from behind. It's a damned dangerous place, and a wood can be pretty spooky at night, especially when you're not accustomed to the country. Rolph's a Londoner, and he's a nervy customer. I believe the noises he heard were owls and such-like." He paused, and then added: "There wasn't much I *could* do, was there? No description of assailant, no motive, no robbery—all pretty thin. I went and had a look at the pool. Plenty of footprints, of course, but as the whole party from Wenningby had been playing around there, that didn't help much. I asked the patrolmen if they'd seen any suspicious characters about, or any strangers. I went and saw Thwaites at Bromsgrove Farm nearby—all quite negative."

Macdonald nodded, and Bord went on again: "Look here, Chief. You know Hoggett; I don't know so much about him. It occurred to me that after that business in the dales, when I believe you found him a very useful chap, he might have got detection on the brain a bit—if you won't take it amiss."

"Of course not," said Macdonald cheerfully. "There's a lot in what you say, but I do think that Hoggett's got a nose for the unusual. I'm not sure what it is: he's observant: he spots a lot of things you might not expect him to: he knows the valley folk very well indeed, and he's got two sets of qualities. He's a countryman by extraction, with generations of country forebears, but the fact that he's got a trained mind, in the academic sense, and has lived in a university town, makes him different from the usual farmer. In addition to all this, he's got an awareness—which he doesn't put into words—about conditions in his own valley. He *knew* Rolph's story was thin. He didn't expect you to believe it, but he believes himself that there's something amiss."

Bord swallowed down something like a snort. "What matters to me is this, Chief. Do *you* believe it?"

"I believe that something odd has been going on around that quarry pool," said Macdonald. "Whether it's anything criminal I've no means of judging, but there *is* evidence that folk have been using the track between the cottage and the pool."

"Likely enough," said Bord. "There'd be fish in that pool: free angling and no one to interfere. The Bromsgrove folk never go up there, and the last owner of Broadgarth was bedridden for months."

"Good enough," rejoined Macdonald. "Who do you reckon the anglers are?"

Bord scratched his head. "I've no evidence," he said defensively. "Might be anybody."

"Very well," agreed Macdonald, "but let's think it out a bit further. Do you think the fishing in that pool is good enough to attract anglers from Lancaster, or Chapelton Lonsdale, or Carnton here?"

"Well, no," said Bord. "It's too far away, and there aren't any bus services. More likely some local lads."

"Agreed," said Macdonald, "but remember this. Hoggett knows his own district. He can tell you the owners or tenants of every farm within a radius of five miles of the quarry pool. He knows exactly which farmers have hired men, and he knows just how hard they work. All the farms thereabouts have too little labour and there's precious little time for amusement and no transport. When Hoggett says there's nobody in his own locality who'd be likely to go angling in the quarry pool, I'm disposed to believe him."

"Well, who does *he* suggest the trespassers are?" asked Bord.

"He's got a few ideas. I've told him it's up to him to prove or disprove them," rejoined Macdonald equably. "I went to the coppice myself this afternoon, because I wanted to find Hoggett. He was there all right. As we came away, a young fellow came along the track:

his name was Tom Field, and Hoggett tells me he's an agricultural contractor from farther south in the county. These chaps get about a bit with their tractors and gear, I gather."

Bord nodded. "True enough. I've noticed it myself. Some of them are disposed to fell timber for firewood without being too particular as to getting the owner's permission.".

"Firewood," murmured Macdonald. "There's been quite a racket in that line, hasn't there, with the coal shortage and one thing and another?"

"Admitted," agreed Bord. "Has there been any timber felled in that coppice?"

"No—but did you go into the cottage?" inquired Macdonald.

Bord nodded. "Yes. That's been stripped all right. I supposed it was the military; no end to the damage they did."

"Certainly, but how long ago is it since there's been a military camp or searchlight station within three miles of the quarry pool?"

"Well, it'd be a matter of years," agreed Bord. "Four years anyway. Too long to trace anything."

"Four years," said Macdonald. "I found this in the cottage, thrown into a corner under some splinters and fragments of floorboard."

He produced a cigarette carton which had once contained twenty cigarettes. It was still fairly crisp, and the lettering on it was as legible as when it was printed. "Erindale," he read out. "This brand has only been sold in England for about twelve months. In any case this carton has obviously not been lying in that cottage for a matter of years. Months, possibly, but not years. Getting back to firewood, Bord, it's not beyond the bounds of possibility that the timber looted from the cottage was cut up and sold for firewood. It would have been well worthwhile, granted the immunity from interference which could be counted on in that isolated spot. I'd say the timber in the cottage was worth more than the fish in the quarry pool."

"That's an idea," admitted Bord. "This chap Field, for instance… but it'd be hard to prove anything."

"If no one has seen him at it, it'd be impossible to prove anything," agreed Macdonald, and Bord said quickly:

"You think Field might have gone for Rolph, then—on the principle of no witnesses wanted?"

"I don't think Field would have attacked Rolph on account of firewood," said Macdonald. "That would have been risking too much for too little. In any case, the timber had already been looted, hadn't it. But I think the timber might have attracted Field's attention in the first place. It's all surmise, I know, but I think it might be worth your while to try to find out a bit about Field, as quietly as possible. To-day is Friday, April the 2nd. Rolph was at Broadgarth on Wednesday, the 31st. It'd be interesting to know what Field was doing on that night."

"I'll see to it," said Bord. "What was he doing in the coppice to-day—or didn't you speak to him?"

"I didn't speak to Field myself, but he spoke to Hoggett. He wanted to know if Miss Bourne were at Broadgarth, as he thought he might get a job on her land."

Bord looked a bit startled. "She isn't living in the house by herself, is she?"

"No, and not likely to be. Hoggett will see to that."

"It's a lonely place, Broadgarth. Not safe for a woman to live by herself there," growled Bord.

"Why not?" countered Macdonald. "Have you ever known a crime of violence in these parts, such as an attack against a woman living alone in a house?"

"No, never," said Bord, and Macdonald went on:

"Then why say it's not safe? You can't have it both ways, Bord. If you think it isn't safe, you must mean that you think there's a possibility of violence."

Bord scratched his head. "We're living in rum days, Chief. There's more crime being committed in this country than ever before. When I was first in the force, there was virtually no crime in this area. Occasional drunks, occasional tramps, some petty larceny—but nothing that couldn't be dealt with summarily. To-day, with black market and deserters and maniacs and perverts—well, by gum, anything might happen anywhere."

Macdonald nodded. "I quite agree. Even a peaceful rural community like this one may get its share of the violence which permeates the world. That's why I'm doubtful if we can take it for granted that Rolph tripped over a bramble."

Bord snorted. "I wish you'd seen Rolph yourself, Chief. Perhaps you could have made out if he were really serious."

"I shall probably look him up, unofficially, when I'm back in town," said Macdonald. "I'll let you know what I think of him. He's a fine architect, you know; I've seen some of his exhibition drawings—plans for rebuilding the blitzed areas."

"All the same, he's not used to the country at night, not this country, anyway," said Bord. "Look here, Chief. What d'you want me to do about the quarry pool? Put a man on to watch it?"

"No. You haven't the men to spare," rejoined Macdonald. "If you want my advice, it's this: get what information you can about Field and his associates, but don't let him know you connect him with the quarry pool. It's like this. If he's been up to any games there, he's quite in the dark as to anybody connecting him with that spot. Hoggett hadn't advertised Rolph's story. If you interview Field, do it in connection with something like timber-felling without permission, and keep your ears open for any local gossip."

Bord scratched his head. He looked very thoughtful, and Macdonald left him to his thoughts.

2

When Macdonald left Carnton, it was growing dusk. The rain had ceased and the sky was clearing, but the moan of the west wind promised more rain to come. Macdonald drove slowly, pondering over the story he had heard from Hoggett and wondering if by sheer chance it had any connection with his own errand.

As he drove, he tried to visualise the map of the country he was working in, and, much more difficult, to memorise the county boundaries. Very few people could state accurately the borders of the northern end of Lancashire. The county, so Macdonald pondered, seemed to be almost pushed into the sea by the West Riding of Yorkshire and the south-western tip of Westmorland. At Lancaster, the county of Lancashire is only thirteen miles wide: it then thrusts into Westmorland near Kirkby Lonsdale, but is in turn pushed to the sea coast at Arnside. Northwards and westwards from Arnside, Lancashire occupies the peninsula of Furness and runs up beyond Coniston water to the Langdale Pikes. From consideration of the complexities of the county border (which he felt he ought to be familiar with and wasn't), Macdonald considered the coast round Morecambe Bay, with its treacherous sands; Heysham (the port for Belfast), Morecambe, Hest Bank, the River Keer, Warton, Arnside, the River Kent, Grange, Cartmel and Ulverston. He believed (without being very certain) that the sands of Morecambe Bay at low tide had, in past centuries, been used as the roadway from Hest Bank to Cartmel. He wondered if the route over the sands were known to-day. "I must ask Mrs. Hoggett. It's just the sort of thing she'd know," he said to himself. Broadgarth and the quarry pool were only about five miles from the sands—a point worth remembering. Morecambe sands, Furness, Coniston, Duddon Vale—grand country for playing hide-and-seek in, he meditated, thinking of his defaulting trader, Maredeth.

This brought him back to the various reports he had heard to-day. It seemed that he had one definite link, albeit a slender one, between Hoggett's suspicions concerning Rolph's assailant, and the case which had brought him (Macdonald) to Lancashire. Hoggett had said that Tom Field and David Wynne had frequented the dog-racing track at Strand. Bord had said that Maredeth had been one of the financiers who put up the money for the track. Macdonald admitted to himself that the connection between his own legitimate business and the (not proven) attack on Rolph was so slight that he had not even mentioned it to Bord. Macdonald knew well enough that Bord did not believe Rolph's story, and Bord's statement that he had no facts to go on in instituting an inquiry into it was justified. Nevertheless, Macdonald chuckled to himself a little. He had suggested two independent inquiries: one to Hoggett, one to Bord, and he knew that they would be pursued independently. Bord would make guarded official inquiries concerning Tom Field and his whereabouts on Wednesday night. Hoggett would pursue quite unofficial inquiries, though very competent ones, concerning the disappearance of David Wynne. Hoggett believed that a crime had been committed, and that Rolph's mishap was ancillary to that crime. Macdonald's attitude was that Hoggett had raised the hare, and Hoggett could put his suspicions to the test, since Bord did not believe that that particular hare existed.

Meantime, Macdonald's cogitations had brought him to the road below Bromsgrove Farm, the nearest house to Broadgarth. Finding a recess where he could leave his car off the road, Macdonald got out, locked the car, and made his way in the dusk along the track leading to Bromsgrove.

3

The daylight had faded and the moon had not yet risen, and it took the C.I.D. man some time to get his eyes accustomed to the gloom. He was walking on a rutted track, between dry-stone walls, with occasional thorn trees. Always alert to learn the characteristics of the country he worked in, Macdonald had been interested when Kate Hoggett had told him about the old bridle-tracks which had been used by the pack-pony trains in the days of the wool trade. Kate had shown him one particular track last time he had been in Lunesdale: it connected up with a bridge over the Lune some ten miles from Lancaster, and ran north to Kendal. The tiny hump-backed bridges over intervening becks still survived along that cross-country track: bridges without a parapet, just wide enough for a pony to cross when the becks were in spate. Macdonald hazarded a guess that the track he was on now, with its old walls and yet older thorn trees, might well be the route of one of these ancient bridle-paths. In which case, he argued, the track might well continue beyond Bromsgrove to Broadgarth, and run north past the quarry pool to join up with the Kendal track, and, quite possibly, with a track which ran to Hest Bank and thence over the sands to Furness. If a man wanted to play hide-and-seek in this little known area of England, meditated Macdonald, he might do worse than learn about the old wool-pack routes which avoided the main roads.

The chief inspector walked about a quarter of a mile before his eyes picked out the black void which he knew must be the Bromsgrove steading, but it was feeling more than sight which kept his feet on the track when it divided at the Bromsgrove gate and led to a field gate a little to the east of the house. From here he could see the light in the mullioned kitchen window of Bromsgrove, and he stood still a moment, expecting a dog to bark. He heard no dog, but a very young lamb bleated unhappily somewhere near at hand, and a calf raised its lusty young voice somewhere in the shippon.

Satisfied that it was possible to pass Bromsgrove after dark unnoticed, Macdonald climbed a gate and set his course for the higher ground of Broadgarth. He could see the ridge of woodland to his north, and he saw the Great Bear shining in a ragged patch of clear sky above the woodlands, and he walked steadily on up the rising pasture. He had not yet been to Broadgarth, but he knew that it stood on an eminence, surrounded by its small pastures and meadows. At one point he found his way blocked by a fence which contained no gate and guessed that he must be at the point where Bromsgrove land ended and Broadgarth began. This "fence," a hedgerow, reinforced with wire and staples, was certainly not Broadgarth property. Negotiating the fence in the dark was a painful business, but he was soon through, and able to see the sturdy block of Broadgarth farmhouse. He stood still for a moment to consider. Rolph said that he had worked at his drawings by lamplight until nearly two o'clock, and Macdonald had a sudden thought concerning the conditions in this place two nights ago. The man inside the house, working in the lamplight, with a good wood fire to warm him, must have felt so secure and remote, cut off from the outside world. But there were no curtains at the windows: the light would have streamed out, indicating that the house was occupied, and any one could have looked in at the windows. From where Macdonald stood now, when the kitchen door was opened any one could have seen Rolph come outside and turn past the lighted window, facing uphill towards the coppice. If there had been a watcher, how surprised he must have been, pondered Macdonald. It was not usual to sit up till the small hours in these parts, nor usual to go for a stroll to meditate in the moonlight long after midnight.

With the west wind whistling past his ears, Macdonald left the farm-house on his left and climbed up towards the woods. Rolph had left the light burning in the kitchen when he went out—Hoggett had supplied that item of evidence—and it seemed to Macdonald quite probable that the light would have been visible from the coppice. He went on until he topped the bank and entered the wood close to the quarry-pool ridge.

It was beginning to rain again now, and it was very dark. Macdonald stood still and listened: he heard the wind soughing in the trees; he heard a car change gear on the road, a long way away to the west, and then he heard another very strange sound. If he had not talked to Kate Hoggett that afternoon Macdonald himself might have said he heard "deep breathing, as a man breathes when he carries a heavy weight." It was a pair of owls, courting in the ruined shippon to the east of the quarry pool. Macdonald stood still, fascinated by the queer sound, and then he was startled by a different sound. A blackbird suddenly called its alarm note, and flew past Macdonald, giving an imitation of a decrepit alarm-clock, surprisingly loud and challenging. "Now, did I put you up, or is there somebody else there?" asked Macdonald of himself. A second later he got his answer, for the owls stopped their courting duet in the shippon and flew out calling that familiar "To-whit, tu-whoo," loud and complaining. Something had disturbed the owls, too. Then came a knocking sound, and an unhappy voice spoke in the darkness:

"Is there anybody there? Please, is there anybody there? Oh dear, oh dear, what *shall* I do?"

SEVEN

I

IN REPLY TO THAT PLAINTIVE QUESTION, MACDONALD STOOD perfectly still and waited to learn what would happen next. The voice he had heard sounded like an old man's voice, and certainly its owner did not belong to the north of England. A few seconds later there was the sound of a tumble, followed by a series of groans, and Macdonald made his way cautiously towards the shippon. He moved quietly, but he must have been heard, because the voice spoke again.

"Help! Help! If anybody is there, please come and help me. I have lost my way..."

Macdonald felt suspicious to his fingertips. Was this a ruse to make him show a light, or a genuine call for help? Because he was a cautious man, Macdonald crouched low before he gave an answer; he had no intention of being flung headlong on to the rocks as Rolph said he had been thrown.

"Who's there?" he called, sharp and clear.

"I'm here... a stranger. My car has broken down and I am looking for help. I thought there was a farm nearby and I have lost my way. Oh dear, oh dear, I am in sad trouble."

It was such a tremulous old voice that Macdonald was almost ashamed of his own suspicions.

"If you could help me back to the road," went on the gentle plaint.

As he moved forward, Macdonald switched on his torch, and he saw a very respectable old gentleman sitting on the ground by the old shippon: his white hair shone in the torchlight and he was bending forward, holding his ankle.

"I lost my way in the wood after I dropped my torch," went on the gentle troubled voice. "If you could lead me back to my car I should be most grateful. I am indeed in trouble."

Macdonald came close up to the other and said, "Can you get up?" as he held out a hand. It was taken with alacrity.

"I thank you... I am too old to do such foolish things. Ah... thank you. If you could assist me back to the road I should be infinitely obliged. My name is Warrender. I am driving to join some friends at a hotel in Chapelton Lonsdale. My car is on the road, by the track. I thought there was a farm nearby, but I am sadly out in my reckoning."

"You are, indeed," said Macdonald. "The track is back in this direction. What farm were you seeking?"

Holding the tremulous old gentleman firmly by the arm, he led him back along the rough path, flashing his torchlight around at intervals, while the rain beat steadily down.

"I am afraid I do not remember the name of the farm. It sounds very foolish. I knew this district so well at one time. I used to shoot here when Sir John Greyland was alive many years ago. I was convinced there was a small farmstead a little way along this track. May I ask your name, sir? I am indeed indebted to you."

"I am a chance visitor to this locality. I took a shortcut up from Bromsgrove Farm," replied Macdonald, "but I can hardly believe that Bromsgrove was the farm you had in mind. It is away over the fields. Now this track will take you back to the main road."

"I am most fortunate that you chanced on me," said Mr. Warrender. "May I trespass on your kindness to the extent of asking for your assistance as far as the road? I did not realise what a blind old fool I had become."

"It's a dark night," said Macdonald. "I will see you safely back to your car."

"I am more than grateful," went on the other. "I wish I could offer you a lift, but my car seems quite obdurate. I waited for a long time hoping that help might arrive. It was the more tiresome because the lights have failed also."

"I'll see if I can do anything about it," said Macdonald.

He did not add that he was anxious to see the car and to take its number, provided the car really existed.

When they reached the road, Mr. Warrender said: "I left the car a few hundred yards back; this way. I was driving from Lancaster. This is a very lonely road. I expected that a lorry might pass me, for I know there are but few private cars on the road just now, but though I waited for a long time, nothing came past... Ah! I think I see my car. Thank heaven for that! At least it will provide cover from the rain."

By this time Macdonald was quite uncertain what to make of the old gentleman who held his own arm so tightly. For Mr. Warrender *was* an old man, and at the moment a very shaken, tottery old man. Moreover he was a man of education: even while stumbling over the rough track at Macdonald's side his spasmodic utterances had the unmistakable hall-mark of the courtesy and certainty which only a man of some standing achieves.

Macdonald fairly pushed him into the car—it was a Stanhall, and its coachwork proclaimed it to be not far from new: the more surprising then that it should have broken down so completely.

"If you will give me your ignition key, I will see if I can spot the trouble," said Macdonald. "If you wish me to do so, that is."

"My dear sir, I should be profoundly grateful," said the other.

"I should put that rug round you; you're very wet," said Macdonald.

It took the C.I.D. man a very short time to find the fault in the car: in fact he went straight for it; a lead had worked loose from the battery. The nut might have been faultily turned, or it might have worked loose. Macdonald did nothing to remedy it. After tinkering for a bit in the light of his torch, he put his head in at the window and said: "The best thing I can do for you is to phone from the call-box some way back. I'll send out a garage man, but in the meantime, if any passing car offers you a lift, I should take it and get to the nearest hotel."

"I can't tell you how much indebted I am to you," said Mr. Warrender. "You are indeed a friend to one in distress. If I might know your name?"

"My name is immaterial, but I promise to send you help quite shortly," said Macdonald, and turned away into the rain.

2

Macdonald made great speed over the half-mile to the call-box. Once there, the call he put through was not to a garage but to Giles Hoggett.

"Can you do a job for me, Hoggett? I found an old gentleman in the quarry wood. He said he had lost his way. He is now sitting in his own broken-down car a few hundred yards west of the Broadgarth turning on the Chapelton Lonsdale Road. Can you drive out there and ask if he's in trouble and offer him a lift to his hotel in Chapelton Lonsdale?"

"Certainly I can," rejoined Hoggett with alacrity.

"Good. You know nothing about him, remember. When you get to the hotel, he will certainly ask you in for refreshment. See what you make of him. He may be genuine. He may not. I'll ring you later this evening."

"What about his car?"

"I'll get Bord to have it towed in. You might phone Bord and report the car is abandoned, telling the owner you are doing so."

"Right! What if he's driven on?"

"He can't," replied Macdonald laconically. "Got the idea?"

"Certainly," said Hoggett.

Macdonald hung up the receiver, feeling that Giles Hoggett was the very man he wanted on this occasion.

3

It was not more than twenty minutes after Macdonald had left him that Mr. Warrender became aware of the headlights of a car on the road behind him. He immediately stepped out of his own car into the rain and waved an exceedingly capacious white handkerchief. The oncoming car pulled up and Giles Hoggett's kindly voice asked:

"Are you in trouble? Could I give you a lift? I was driving into Chapelton Lonsdale."

"I should be *most* grateful, most grateful," exclaimed Mr. Warrender. "My car has failed completely, and I shall have to abandon it and leave it here. I am afraid I am deplorably wet..."

"Jump in. There's a rug there," said Giles cheerfully. "I'd better push your car off the road as the lights have failed. There's plenty of room on the verge."

He jumped out, put his hand in at the window of the other car, loosed the hand-brake and put his broad shoulder against the window and guided the car on to the verge.

"What about locking it?" he inquired.

"No, I think not. A man who helped me when I had lost my way in the wood promised to phone a garage for me and I hope they will tow it in. Dear me, what a deplorably wet night! I had better take my suitcase—yes, and the rug—and perhaps the maps... and those books... Thank you very much... it is indeed a downpour."

"We can do with it. Now the sowing is finished, we are glad of rain for the grass," said Hoggett, as he packed Mr. Warrender and his possessions into his roomy old Austin. "Did I hear you say that you got lost in the coppice?" he inquired.

"Indeed I did: a most regrettable and discomforting experience," sighed Mr. Warrender. "My engine stopped about half a mile back. As it was on a down gradient, I let the car run on hoping that it would pick up again, but it was so very dark I thought it wiser to pull up. I had a torch, and I got out to prospect. Having known this district well in years past, I thought I could find my way to a farm which lies along the track beyond the old bailiff's cottage. Unfortunately I dropped my torch, and in the darkness I missed the track and got confused in the wood. Very fortunately for me, a Scotsman found me—a kindly gentleman, though reticent. Indeed, I fear he may have suspected my bona-fides, or perhaps thought that I had escaped from a mental home. In any case, I could not blame him."

"A Scot?" inquired Hoggett. "Did he tell you his name?"

"He did not. He only told me that he was taking a shortcut up from Bromsgrove Farm," was the reply.

"Oh, I think I know who he is—a very reliable fellow," said Hoggett serenely. "If he promised to phone a garage for you, he will certainly do so... Hallo, this seems to be a police car... We had better stop and report your car. The police are inclined to be fussy."

He flicked his headlights on and off as a signal, and drew up carefully by the hedge. As the police car stopped, Giles leant out of his window.

"Inspector Bord? Hoggett of Wenningby here. Can I have a word with you?"

Giles Hoggett was enjoying himself enormously. His brief statement of identity had something of a patent of nobility about it, and his demand for "a word" was spoken with an easy authority which he could express very definitely when he wished. Still leaning out of the window he continued:

"This gentleman with me has had to abandon his car as the engine and lights have failed. It is parked on the verge close to the track leading to Broadgarth. Perhaps you could make arrangements about having it towed to Chapelton Lonsdale, Inspector."

"May I see this gentleman's driving licence and identity card, please?" inquired Bord.

"Of course. My name is Warrender—Judge Warrender," replied Giles's passenger. "Here are the relevant documents, Inspector—driving licence, insurance certificate, identity card. A *very* wet night. I was fortunate in receiving succour so soon."

"You will make arrangements about Judge Warrender's car, Inspector?" inquired Hoggett urbanely. He knew quite well that Macdonald had already given instructions on that account, and Hoggett was quite human enough to enjoy being slightly cavalier to Inspector Bord. After all, Bord had condescended to Hoggett in a somewhat patronising way over Rolph's report. Bord returned the "relevant documents."

"I will make arrangements about the matter," rejoined the inspector. "Will you tell me where you will be staying, sir?"

"The King's Head Hotel in Chapelton Lonsdale," rejoined Warrender. "I am much indebted to you, Inspector, as I am to Mr. Hoggett here."

Giles Hoggett called good night and sketched a salute with a wave of his hand as he let the clutch in. He had enjoyed that little meeting. Meantime Mr. Warrender was saying:

"Hoggett? Not Mr. *Giles* Hoggett, surely?"

"Yes. I am Giles Hoggett."

"God bless my soul! My dear sir, I am doubly fortunate to-night. I have often wished to meet you. I went to Camford shortly after my return to England and called in at your most excellent bookshop there. You have been of great service to me in times past, finding and dispatching me some old law books when I was in India. Nathaniel Warrender—do you not remember my name?"

"Of course I do," said Hoggett. "I ought to have remembered it at once, but since I turned farmer I have almost forgotten I was ever a book man."

"A book man... a felicitous description," burbled Judge Warrender. "Yours was the best bookshop in England, Mr. Hoggett. I hope your farm is as excellent."

"I'm afraid it isn't," admitted Giles, "but I am very happy farming. So happy that I can't imagine why I ever did anything else. Of course, my forebears farmed here for generations. I was interested to learn that you knew this district in years past."

"Oh, I knew it very well indeed," was the reply. "It would be nearly forty years ago that I shot with Sir John Greyland over all this woodland. I remember the coppice along this road. The bailiff—Matthew Crabbe—was in charge of the planting, and he had a cottage by the quarry above the farm-house... Woodgarth, was it?"

"Broadgarth," said Hoggett. "James Braithwaite farmed it until 1915, and Brawne, the old keeper, had a cottage on Broadgarth land—a lean-to against one of the shippons."

"Excellent! Excellent!" exclaimed Warrender. "I remember Broadgarth, and Mrs. Braithwaite often gave us tea in her kitchen. Is the bailiff's cottage still inhabited?"

"No. It's not been lived in since Crabbe died in 1918. In fact it's quite derelict," replied Hoggett, "without windows or doors or flooring.

The quarry is now a sizable lake. A spring must have found its way through a fissure in the rocks."

"Ah, I think I heard of that," said Warrender. "Curiously enough, this locality became a topic of conversation on my last homeward voyage from India. Another passenger mentioned Deepdale, Greyland's house, and we got talking about this district. I spoke of the quarry, which I had heard was flooded and had become quite a lake. Do you know who owns the land now, Mr. Hoggett? I know Greyland's estate was broken up after his death."

"Part of his land belongs to his granddaughter, though she never visits it," said Hoggett. "The strip of woodland with the old cottage and the quarry pool has been bought recently by the new owner of Broadgarth."

"Indeed! I am sorry to hear that," said the other. "I long cherished a fancy to buy some of Greyland's property, particularly the woodland, and to build myself a house up here. I have many happy memories of Crabbe's cottage; a very beautiful site, I remember."

"I heard that there was someone from away bidding at the Broadgarth auction," observed Hoggett. "Perhaps it was your agent, Judge Warrender."

"Oh, dear me, no!" rejoined the other. "I should not embark on farming at my age—but I should like a small property in 'Lonsdale south of the sands,' as I think it was named in olden times." He chuckled. "Perhaps it was my wish to identify myself with happy memories of long ago which led me into such trouble to-night," he went on. "I had not seen these woods since 1918, but I was so sure that I remembered my way about them. Alas! I learn that Crabbe's cottage is a windowless ruin, and the stone quarry has become a lake. Perhaps that explains why a churlish young man denied the existence of the quarry and the cottage."

"Who was the young man?" inquired Hoggett, his curiosity very alert again. He was driving slowly, anxious to protract this interesting conversation.

"It was at a garage between Preston and Lancaster," replied Warrender. "I stopped to have my brakes adjusted, and while I was strolling outside the garage I saw a young tractor driver and asked him if he knew the country north-west of Lancaster. He said that he knew it well, and I asked him which road to Chapelton Lonsdale took me nearest to Deepdale. He said that I should do well to keep south of the river at Lancaster and drive via Hornby. I was sure that was not the route I wanted, and I asked him if he knew Crabbe's cottage and the quarry, and he said that no such place existed anywhere north of the river."

"Of course the quarry pool is right away from the road, and though it is familiar enough to those who live in the locality, it is quite unknown to those who only use the main road," said Hoggett. "I wonder if you can describe the tractor driver, Judge? It is possible that I may be able to place him."

"He was a powerfully built fellow, dark, but of a ruddy countenance," replied the old gentleman. "I sensed that there was something aggressive about him, a type more common to the towns than to the countryside."

"It is curious you should have mentioned him," said Hoggett. "There has been some complaint about poaching or similar offences, I believe, and I wondered if your tractor driver could be identical with a fellow suspected of such pursuits. Ah, we are just approaching Chapelton. The old bridge is on the right there—you will remember it, I expect?"

"I do indeed. One of the finest bridges in the country, and the most beautiful river-reach I have seen the world over," said Warrender. "I cannot tell you how greatly I am indebted to you for your kindness, Mr. Hoggett. I hope that you will spare a few minutes to partake of a glass of sherry with me, or a whisky and soda or such-like. I should like to drink to our further acquaintance after this happy chance from which I have so greatly profited."

"Thank you very much," replied Giles cheerfully.

4

It was shortly after ten o'clock that Giles Hoggett returned, to find his wife looking somewhat disconsolate.

"If you are going in for detection as a full-time job, you'll have to get a hired man to look after the cows," she said indignantly. "Kitty tried to strangle herself in her neckband and Bluebelle has been roaring the whole evening. You know cows always hate disturbances. They like to feel quiet and confident, and they always know when you're neglecting them."

"Kitty ought to have more sense. It's only because she tries to snaffle Bluebelle's hay," replied Giles. "I've had a most interesting evening, Kate. The old chap who got lost in the coppice turned out to be an old customer of mine. He said he hoped my farm was as good as my bookshop. I told him it wasn't," Giles added hastily.

Kate yawned. She had not enjoyed her solitary evening, having been worrying about her husband.

"What was he doing in the coppice, anyway?" she inquired.

Giles scratched his head. "I'm not sure. Even now I'm not sure," he said, "although I liked him very much. But I think he'd seen Tom Field, and I don't know what to make of it. It's quite a story—"

At that moment the telephone rang and Giles said, "That'll be Macdonald."

"All right. I shall go to bed," said Kate, "and remember to go and see that Kitty's all right before you come up. And tell Macdonald that the cows are all upset," she added as a Parthian shot.

Giles came up to bed a few minutes later.

"I still can't make up my mind. There *are* suspicious circumstances," he averred; but Kate declined to answer.

Giles tried again: "You see, I can't understand—"

"Go to bed," said Kate, "and if you don't buy some new braces soon, you'll be reduced to safety-pins and string."

Giles knew this to be true, so he refrained from further conversation.

EIGHT

I

MUCH AS HE THOUGHT ABOUT THE MATTER, GILES HOGGETT could come to no satisfactory conclusion about old Mr. Warrender. On the face of it, it seemed quite ridiculous to connect that distinguished and courteous old legal luminary with questionable doings at the quarry pool. Giles's native common sense bade him dismiss the whole incident as one of those odd coincidences which occur in most people's lives, but his observation also told him that Macdonald had been exceedingly interested in his, Giles's, detailed report of his own conversation with the old gentleman.

"I can't make head or tail of it," said Giles to himself, and decided to dismiss the matter from his mind while he concentrated on his own private "hare," what he believed to be the focus of the disturbances which had resulted in Rolph's broken crown. In short, Giles decided to go to see Alice Wynne, and try to discover for himself what had led up to David Wynne's disappearance.

In an urban area, it is not so very rare for an ill-tempered husband to "walk out" on his wife and leave her stranded. Abandoned wives are quite numerous, and Giles knew it, but for a farmer in Lunesdale—or anywhere else for that matter—to leave his land and his cattle was absolutely unheard of. Everybody in the neighbourhood agreed on that point. David Wynne had gone away and left his milking cows, his heifers and calves, his sheep, his pigs, his spring sowing—everything that makes up that complicated organism called a farm. The only explanation that the majority offered was that David Wynne had gone mad: it was the action of a lunatic, neither more nor less.

Giles had known Alice Wynne nearly all her life. She was the daughter of a farmer who had once been one of Giles's own tenants—in his bookselling days—and she was the niece of old Richard Blackthorn. Giles had seen her christened, in 1924. He had seen her married, in 1944, and regretted that she had taken a husband "from away," and a Welshman to boot. Giles knew that William Aughton, Alice's father, had set Alice and David up on their little farm, and undoubtedly Mr. Aughton would come to the rescue in the crisis occasioned by David's absence. Alice was a good farmer herself, better than her husband, in Giles's opinion, but a young woman could not be left unaided to deal with the work of a farm.

Pondering over his best manner of approach, worrying in his kindly way over Alice's troubles, Giles went and found some sections of heather honey left over from last year's crop. Honey was valued by farming folk, for sugar and sweet things were about the only foods in short supply in a dairy farming district. Packing his sections carefully, Giles set out and drove the two miles to Ashdale, where the Wynnes had their small "family farm." He left his car on the high road, and walked along the track which led to the little old stone house, a much poorer house than Caroline's Broadgarth.

It was ten o'clock in the morning. The milking and "mucking out" would be finished, the midday meal in the course of preparation. Crisis or none, a farm worker must eat, and eat well, for farming is heavy work.

As he approached the fold yard, he saw Alice at the pump, and to his relief she greeted him with a smile.

"Good morning, Mr. Hoggett. A good rain we had."

"Good morning, Alice. We wanted that rain, didn't we? It'll make all the difference to the hay crop. I have brought you some heather honey. My wife wants me to get last year's honey out of the way, so that she can clear up the dairy."

"Thank you, Mr. Hoggett! I always like that heather honey."

She looked full at him, with shrewd yet candid grey eyes. She was a fine girl, thought Giles, strong and straight, with rosy cheeks and curly hair.

"You'll have heard about David, Mr. Hoggett?"

"Indeed I have. I'm very sorry you're in such trouble," he replied.

"Will you come in a minute? I should be glad to talk to you, Mr. Hoggett. I've known you a long time, haven't I?"

"Of course I'll come in. I was only thinking as I drove here, Alice: I saw you christened. We're old friends."

She led the way into the kitchen. "I'm in a bit of a mess like, there's a lot to do, but Bill—my youngest brother—he's come along to help, so it's not so hard now. It fitted nicely, him wanting to work away from home."

She paused, and then added: "It's not so bad as folks think, Mr. Hoggett. I know David. He just got mad, in one of his moods. He's like that. He'll come back when he's thought it over. He did it once before, only nobody knew. Maybe it was my fault. I was driving him. He wasn't reared to farming, like me, and he let things slide, and I was always on at him. Some things in farming, if you leave them, you never catch up again. You know, Mr. Hoggett. Your folks farmed, didn't they?"

"I know," replied Giles. "There are some things you can't leave."

"It was I who made him rent that land up t' hill," she went on. "That's not bad land if it's cultivated. Tom Field ploughed it for us on contract. You remember Tom?"

Giles nodded, and she went on: "I don't think much of Tom Field. He's what my Dad calls 'a nowt,' but he's got t' gear and he can do the job. I made David have him here for t' ploughing and sowing, and David took it wrong, silly thing."

Giles understood all right: Alice, who was reared to farming, was ambitious to make a success of their holding. She persuaded her husband to rent the extra land, knowing that Tom Field had the gear to plough and cultivate. "We'll want Tom again, we must get that land ploughed and harrowed this month," she would have insisted, and David "took it wrong," pretending that Alice wanted Field to stay in the house because she was fond of him.

"What a pity," said Giles simply. "He should have known you better than that, Alice."

"Eh, but he's daft when he gets these moods on him," she said, "but he'll get over it, and be sorry later. I've heard from him, Mr. Hoggett. He sent me some money; I reckon he'll be back soon."

That was a facer for Giles, but because he was innately kindly, his first thought was for Alice.

"I'm very glad to know you heard from him and that he's all right," he responded warmly. "Did he say where he is now?"

She shook her head and took a crumpled sheet from her apron pocket. "No, he didn't say, but he's a terrible poor hand at writing. Never wrote a line if he could help it. Look, 'tis like any kid's writing."

That was just what David's writing *was* like, thought Giles, as he put on his glasses and studied the crude scrawl; any child might have written the ill-formed letters. "Sending you this to go on with. David." That was all.

"You're sure it *is* David's writing?" he asked.

"Why, of course it is. No one else would send me five pounds, would they now?" she retorted. "The only thing that worried me was where he got the money, for he hadn't any when he left here. That I do know. Maybe he won it dog-racing; I can't abide that business."

"You didn't notice the postmark on the envelope?" asked Giles, but she shook her head.

"I never thought to look. I'm afraid I threw the envelope on the fire." She hesitated a moment and then went on:

"I was wondering if you'd help me, Mr. Hoggett. You're good at figures and such-like, and I know you won't talk about us. It's like this. David did all the money part, payings and such-like. I don't like figures myself and I hate bills. I like to pay cash and know where I am, instead of having a lot of old bills coming in. I just don't know where we are, and that's a fact."

She paused, her face frowning in concentration and Giles waited, much too understanding to rush in with offers of help before he understood what she wanted.

"David sold two stirks to Mr. Ash over at Barcombe," she went on, "and I know he bought a heifer from you, Mr. Hoggett—she's a beauty, too, just calved and she's got a real good bag. Well, I don't know if Mr. Ash paid David or if David paid you."

She opened the drawer of the dresser and produced a small notebook. "David kept his accounts in this, but I can't make head or tail of it. Dad had a look, but he's worse nor me at figures. David has put things down in a way, but it looks an awful old muddle to me."

She handed the book to Giles, who began to study it. It certainly was an "awful old muddle."

"I wondered if you'd look at it and see if you could make sense of it, Mr. Hoggett," she said. "I'm ashamed to bother you, but I'd rather ask you than any one I know. After all, you knew Dad, and you know me—"

"Of course I'll see if I can help you; I'm very glad you've asked me, Alice," he replied, and she went on:

"It's like this. I'm not one to interfere, and I wouldn't have touched David's book, but he did go away and leave me to make do, didn't he? And I thought maybe if I could get things straight while he was away—well, he might be glad, and we'll start straight again when he comes back."

"A very good idea, and I think you're being very sensible," commended Giles. "I'll do my best to get you an idea of the position, if I can make out these notes; but hasn't your husband got a banking account?"

"No, not a proper one. He's got a savings bank book, but I can't find it. I did tell him he'd have to have a banking account now we're sending milk away. The milk's paid for by cheque, isn't it?" She went back to the kitchen drawer and produced another sheet of paper. "I've written down the names of people we deal with," she told Giles. "There's the corn millers and the vet and the tradespeople, and some of the farmers David's bought stock from, or sold to. I thought the names might help you."

Giles nodded. "Yes, Alice, that'll be very helpful," he said. "Now I wonder if you'd tell me just how it was that David went away? I don't want to seem inquisitive, but there are a lot of stories going round, and perhaps I could stop some of it if I knew the facts."

She flushed. "I'm ashamed when I think of it, Mr. Hoggett, and that's a fact. You see, I lost my temper. Tom Field had been ploughing the high intak and David came in to milk in a rare bad temper and said how he wasn't going to have Field doing any more jobs. I said we'd got to get the job finished or the ploughing'd be wasted, and if it was the money he was worrying about I'd pay for it myself—I've got a bit put by—and then David said he was fed up with me and Tom carrying on, and I was that surprised I got mad and told him off proper. Then, when we were in the fold yard, Tom came in and said something silly about David bullying me, and before I knew what they were up to David went for him with his fists. It was awful, because Tom's much stronger and heavier, and he knocked Dave over and told him he was a dirty Welshman, and then he just cleared off."

Alice was nearly crying by now, but she went on with her story. "I tried to help David, but he was so angry he wouldn't listen, and he just shouted out he was fed up and he was going away, and he'd kill Tom next time he saw him. He just walked off, and I went in and had a real cry. I thought he'd come back when he'd got over his temper, but he didn't, and next morning I had all the milking and that to do, and when David didn't come back by evening I phoned a message to Dad, and he came over and stayed a bit."

Alice wiped her eyes, while Giles said what a pity the whole thing was, and she nodded, recovering her poise again.

"I know, Mr. Hoggett. I told you I was ashamed. I know I've got a temper, but generally I'm careful not to get angry with David. I know he's moody and that—he can't help it, he's made that way, and you know I'm very fond of him. It was what he said about Tom and me made me fly out at him. That wasn't right."

"Certainly it wasn't right. I know you've been a very good wife to David," replied Hoggett. "Where do you think he will have gone, Alice?"

"Oh, back to North Wales, to his married sister, I expect," she replied. "He's always saying he wants us to go there and try to get a hill farm, but he did promise he'd settle down here if I married him, and I don't want to go and live in Wales. It'd be like living amongst foreigners."

"What time was it when he left home?"

"Oh, just coming dusk. Dave was late for milking, and I'd done most of it. Reckon he had a long way to walk; there's nowhere hereabouts he'd have gone for the night. I felt awful about it when he didn't come back that night, and then I remembered how he'd gone off before, and I was sure he'd come back. I've been working so hard since he went that I've had no time to cry."

"You haven't seen Tom Field again?"

"Goodness, no! He'd have a rolling-pin at his head if he showed his face here. I reckon it was his fault, David behaving like that. Tom must have said something silly and Dave was always jealous."

Giles Hoggett put the notebook in his pocket. He would have liked to ask some more questions, but he didn't feel that he could do so at present. He held out his hand, saying: "You know I will help you in any way I can, Alice, and I hope you'll hear from David again, and that he will soon come home."

"I'm certain he will," she replied, "and thank you for coming, Mr. Hoggett. I wouldn't have talked about it like that to any one else, but it does help to talk, and you've always been kind to me, ever since I used to get into rows at school."

"Remember me to your father," said Giles, and she nodded.

"I will. He said you might help with that notebook if I asked you. Thinks the world of you, Dad does. Good-bye, Mr. Hoggett, and thank you."

2

Giles walked back to his car and drove a short distance. Then he got out and walked to a gate whence he could see across the wide valley of the Lune. With his arms resting comfortably on the gate, the spring sun shining on his bare head, he was aware of the familiar beauty of Lunesdale in April: the foaming white of blackthorn and damson blossom, the intense green of the holmland across the river, the whole backed by the misty lilac of the fells from Claughton to Clougha. But, while the accepted loveliness of sky and fell and blossom breathed serenity and deep content, Giles's mind was troubled. Standing looking over the gate, as so many of his forebears must have stood before him, watching lambs which leapt in sheer exuberance of spirit, Giles analysed his own forebodings. In his pocket was the untidy little notebook in which David Wynne had "put things down." Tucked away in the notebook, unnoticed by Alice, was the letter which she said was from David, two untidy lines of childish writing. Giles took the book from his pocket and studied the letter, comparing it with the entries in the book. He was certain the book and the letter were not written by the same hand, and if he was right, his worst suspicions were justified.

He went over the story Alice had told him. David had come in late to milking and had quarrelled with her about Tom Field. Tom had then come into the fold yard, and his interference had resulted in a fight between the two men. David had been knocked down, and Tom had gone off. A short while later David had followed him, having threatened to kill him. Giles, who knew all the routine of farming, knew that Tom Field had been ploughing. It was probable that he had gone back to get his tractor and gear from the field where he had been working—more than probable, it was certain, argued Giles. Before the two men had come to blows, it was understood that Tom was to "finish the job." That would have meant that his tractor would stay at Ashdale until he was through with the work there. Tom had not been to Ashdale again, so it was obvious he had taken his gear away with him. As Giles saw it, David and Tom might well have left the farm about the same time, David on foot, Tom on his tractor. Had they met, and had the fight been resumed, with disastrous consequences for David? Tom Field was a very powerful fellow: had he hit harder than he had realised?

Giles, standing very still as he leant on the gate in the sunshine, had a grim vision of the two men: it was "coming dusk" as Alice put it, and Tom saw David lying in the road and realised what he had done. Would Tom have left David's body lying there, knowing that Alice would bear witness of their quarrel? Would he not have heaved the body on to his trailer, covered it with a sack, and got away from the farm as fast as he could? Giles was certain that Tom's first thought would have been to hide the dead man—in a ditch, in a wood, in a cleft in one of the steep rocky gills. Later, perhaps, Tom had thought of the quarry pool—as safe a hiding-place as could be devised for a weighted body. That would explain the attack on Rolph. It would also explain the letter to Alice. If Alice could be made to believe that David had written to her, there would be no search for David.

Unconsciously gripping the gate, Giles began to fit together the pieces of the puzzle. He had first heard of Alice Wynne's trouble on the day of the Broadgarth auction—that was Tuesday, March 30th. David had left home the previous evening, March 29th. It was on March 31st that Rolph had rung up saying that he was in Manchester, and he had come on to Lancaster, and spent that night at Broadgarth. It seemed probable to Giles Hoggett that on the supposition that Tom Field had killed David Wynne, and hidden his body hastily in some hiding-place not far removed from Ashdale, then Tom would probably have gone away somewhere, and waited to see if the papers or the radio reported the finding of David's body. Then, as nothing was reported, he began to wish he had hidden the body more securely, and two nights later had come back to carry out his plan. Tom would thus have known nothing about the selling of Broadgarth until after his return. When he saw Rolph standing by the quarry pool, he must have panicked, and attacked the unknown man with the one thought of ridding himself of a witness who could bring him to the hangman. It all fitted in, thought Giles dismally, and then, as he watched the lambs, he took himself to task for indulging his imagination in a manner so morbid.

"It's pure assumption," he said to himself. "Just because Rolph said he was attacked and because David Wynne has gone off in one of his moods."

Then he remembered about the notebook in his pocket, and the letter which was in a different handwriting. It was no use pretending that there wasn't something suspicious about that.

Giles scratched his head unhappily. "I must talk it over with Kate," he said to himself. He knew that Kate could always see the errors in his sometimes hasty assumptions. Giles had read Logic and Philosophy at Cambridge, Kate had read Science at London; but, illogically it seemed to Giles, the scientific training had developed a more logical mind than the one trained in the humanities.

NINE

I

ON THAT SAME FINE SUNNY MORNING WHEN GILES HOGGETT went to see Alice Wynne, Kate had got through her household chores as quickly as her meticulous habit of mind would allow. The sun was shining, the sap rising after the rain: in short it was gardening weather, and the garden called. Kate was a gardener to her capable fingertips, and never happier than when tending her seedlings and the flowers and vegetables she raised with so much skill and understanding of their various needs. Giles had taken himself off, neglecting his own share of the digging, but Kate went into her garden rejoicing and busied herself with the final pricking out of seedlings for her summer bedding. She was aware of the birds all around her, the blackbirds who had built so foolishly on a stack of wood against the potting-shed, the thrushes who were rearing a family in an elderberry tree close to Giles's chopping-block, the greenfinches who nested in the big conifer, the chaffinches in the pear trees; she knew them all, and they were so used to her that they almost followed her round the garden in the hope of food.

She had just finished her last box of antirrhinums and was brooding over some *Lilium regale* seedlings which she had raised from her own seed when a man's voice spoke to her from the door of the greenhouse.

"I do apologise for interrupting you, but what a lovely garden! Your primulas make me green with envy. That Kashmeriana is a triumph."

Kate was muddy: she was also very busy; but few gardeners can resist intelligent appreciation of their flowers. She turned and studied a tallish fellow—good build, good country tweeds, not too new, good knitted stockings, and a lean sunburnt face. He waved a hand towards Kate's beloved herb garden, where lilies and irises raised healthy spears between the thyme, sage and marjoram.

"'Lilies of all kinds, flower de luce being one,'" he quoted. "Surely that was the guiding thought."

She laughed. "Yes. It was really, but there's not much to see yet."

"There will be," he said. "May I introduce myself? John Wilson. I think you must be Mrs. Hoggett. Is your husband at home?"

"No. I'm afraid he isn't. Can I give him a message?"

"Well, perhaps you could advise me. I am told that Mr. Hoggett is a beekeeper. I wondered if I could give an order for honey later in the year."

"I don't think so," she replied. "He doesn't really sell his honey. We like to keep it, and he gives a lot away. It's nice to have something to give to one's neighbours—they're all very generous to us."

He laughed. "How sensible! You're very lucky people in this valley."

"Lucky?" Kate disapproved of the word. "We work hard. Things don't grow by themselves, and collecting swarms of bees in the middle of haytime isn't always pure delight."

"Don't take me wrong," he protested. "I know enough about gardening and farming to realise the amount of work it entails, especially these days. When I said you were lucky, I was envying you the fact that you have the land to work: you own this lovely place, and the work you put into it is infinitely worthwhile. I'm in the poor position of trying to buy a property up here for myself, and being frustrated at every turn. You don't know of a nice house for sale, do you, with garden and a bit of land, just like this?"

It was Kate's turn to laugh. "No, I'm afraid I don't. There are occasionally farms or small holdings sold by auction, but most of the landowners round here don't want to sell. I know my husband wouldn't sell an acre of his own free will." She paused, and then added: "I don't mean that he's really the exclusively possessive type, but his forebears owned some of this land since Elizabethan days, and he loves every field of it."

"I understand that, and respect him for it," replied Mr. Wilson, "but I still say you're lucky, even though you *do* work hard." He chuckled a little. "I did have a shot at buying a small holding not far from here—Broadgarth. I expect you know it—but I was lucky really because I didn't get it."

"Why lucky?" inquired Kate, very alert at the mere mention of Broadgarth.

"Well, there's bound to be trouble there sooner or later," he replied. "It's a matter of water. Water can be the devil."

"Lack of it can," she replied, "but there's plenty of water at Broadgarth."

He laughed. "I should say there is. It's not lack of water but excess of it that will be the trouble there."

"But why?" she demanded. "It's not a damp house. It stands on an eminence—at least on a terrace, so there's natural drainage."

"Quite, quite; but do you know the quarry pool?"

"Of course. It's rather beautiful, and it doesn't interfere with Broadgarth."

"Not now, but it will in course of time," he replied. "However, I mustn't interrupt you any longer—"

"You can tell me what you mean about the quarry pool and Broadgarth," she insisted. "It's not fair to say things like that without evidence."

"Oh, I'm not saying it without evidence," he replied. "Don't imagine it's sour grapes. How long have you known the quarry pool?"

"Not very long, but my husband has known it for years."

"Then he would know that the quarry has been slowly filling up, and the pool getting larger for years," went on Mr. Wilson. "You know the pipe track from Lake Greenthwaite which supplies the town of Warrigan? The track passes just across the end of the woodland above Broadgarth, doesn't it?"

Kate nodded. This was correct, and she knew it.

"That pipe was laid twenty years ago," went on Wilson. "Forgive me if I'm being long-winded over this, but you did ask me to justify my statement."

"Go on. I'm interested," said Kate.

"Well, I'm an engineer, and I know a bit about some of the difficulties the pipe track engineers met," he went on. "Water was one of them; this is a very well-watered district." He paused, and then said: "I think you're probably a very well-informed person, Mrs. Hoggett," he said. "Do you know anything about the geology of this locality, and the manner in which the springs arise?"

"I'm no geologist, but I know we are on the Millstone Grit here. So is Broadgarth," she replied promptly. "The stream which gives us our water supply here rises at a point just below a thick cap of morainal detritus overlying the solid rock; the rain water probably seeps through the detritus, enters clefts in the Grit, and rises as a spring through some fault in the rock."

He smiled. "Excellent. Couldn't have been better expressed. As you say, the same conditions hold good at Broadgarth—same rock, same morainal detritus on the slopes above. Well, when the pipe track was laid, the engineers had to deflect certain springs. I think I'm right in saying that the quarry filled with water—after having been a dry quarry for centuries—after the engineers laid the pipe track."

Kate considered. "That seems reasonable," she admitted.

"Very well. Now it's in the highest degree improbable that the quarry floor has no cracks or fissures in it," he went on. "The spring isn't only filling the quarry, there would have been a much more considerable outflow if that were so. It's sinking through a fissure until it finds impermeable rock. What will happen then?"

"You mean it's bound to rise again when it finds a passage?" said Kate.

"Just that—some other fault, some fissure in the rock which will give it a passage," he replied. "Finally, have you inspected the Broadgarth well lately?"

Kate remembered Caroline saying: "I hope that well never overflows. It's almost full."

Kate knew that every farm and small holding in the district had a well, but it was very unusual to have a well in which the water was not several feet below ground level.

"I see what you mean," she admitted. "You think the water sinks through the quarry floor until it reaches impermeable strata, after which it's got to find an outlet."

"That's it," he said cheerfully, "and if I know my stuff, the outlet is going to be below Broadgarth farm-house, and I'm not exactly keen on seeing my kitchen flagstones washed up. I apologise for inflicting you with all this, but you did challenge me to produce evidence, didn't you?"

"I did," she admitted, and he went on:

"Well, I'm sorry I can't do a deal over the honey, but I think Mr. Hoggett's very wise to hold on to it. Once again, congratulations on your garden."

2

Kate went back to her gardening in a very troubled frame of mind. Who Mr. Wilson might be, or where he came from, she had no idea at all, but she realised that he had talked sense. Kate was angry with herself for not having thought out the implications of the quarry pool for herself. The quarry *had* filled with water within the last twenty years, after having served as a workable quarry for centuries. Kate knew quite well when stone farm-houses had first been built in Lunesdale, between 1650 and 1680. The Broadgarth quarry had been worked to supply stone for the farm-house, the small holding and Caroline's derelict cottage, and the quarry had become a pool after the pipe track was laid. This and Mr. Wilson's other arguments were sound enough, and it seemed to Kate that Caroline's newly bought farm-house, which Giles had advised her to buy, might become valueless and uninhabitable in the near future. Kate was a very conscientious woman, and this thought troubled her a great deal.

3

When Giles came back from Alice Wynne's, he was intent on telling Kate all the evidence he had collected, but Kate refused to listen until she had poured out her story of Mr. Wilson's visit and his opinions about the course of the water in the quarry pool. Giles's first reaction was indignation.

"Who is this fellow," he demanded, "and what business is it of his?"

"It doesn't matter who he is, or if it's his business," she said. "What he said was perfectly feasible. He had looked at Broadgarth with a view to buying it, and he believes it's a wash-out. Caroline bought it on your advice, Giles, remember that, and if a spring is coming up below the house, it'd cost a lot of money to drain it off."

Giles looked troubled at that. "But there's no proof," he insisted. "It's only an idea."

"There's the well," said Kate. "Did you look at it?"

"No. I didn't. I knew there was plenty of water there."

"Then you ought to have looked at it," insisted Kate, "before you advised Caroline to buy the house."

Giles scratched his head and looked unhappy. He also was a very conscientious person.

Kate went on: "I can't make out what's at the back of all the things that have happened at Broadgarth. I wish you'd never taken Caroline to see it."

"At the back of it? I'm afraid Tom Field's at the back of it," said Giles gloomily, "but I couldn't have foretold that."

"No. It isn't only Tom Field," said Kate. "I've been thinking. When you rang up about the coppice, when Caroline wanted to buy it, you were told that someone else had inquired about it. That was very odd, you know. No one has wanted to buy it all these years."

"Well, can't you explain that by remembering that Broadgarth was on the market," said Giles, "and any potential buyer might have thought, as Caroline did, that it would be wise to buy the coppice through which runs the approach to the farm. Apart from any ideas about the ruined cottage, it was good business to buy the woodland which divides Broadgarth from the road, if only to prevent any one else buying it."

Kate pondered. "Look here, Giles. Can't you find out who else was after Broadgarth, apart from Mr. Harrow and the people we know?"

"I don't see the point," he argued, but Kate insisted.

"I want to know. You're good at finding things out. Ask the auctioneer, and the agent who arranged the sale of the coppice."

"I know what I will do," said Giles. "I'll go and see Emma Brough. She was in charge of the house when it was on view. I'm certain she'll have noticed everybody who came to view it. She's a very shrewd body is Emma Brough; and now, Kate, you can hear my part of the story."

Giles retold Alice Wynne's story almost verbatim. He was very good at recapitulating interviews such as this one, and he fell naturally into the local accent and idiom. It was not until the conclusion of his narrative that he produced David Wynne's notebook and the letter, for Giles had a feeling for drama. Laying down the two documents he said:

"Well, there it is. That is my evidence," rather as a counsel might have concluded a speech to the jury.

Kate studied the ill-written documents with a frowning face.

"Neither you nor I am competent to make a judgment over similarities in handwriting," she said. "It's an expert business. You'll have to show these to Macdonald, and he will get an expert opinion on them—at least, I suppose he will."

"Certainly," agreed Giles, "but can't you see for yourself that the handwriting in the book is dissimilar from that in the letter?"

"No, I can't," she replied. "The handwriting in both is childish. You can't expect anybody who writes as badly as that to show any consistency in the forming of their letters."

"But notice the capital D's, and the small g's," urged Giles, but Kate refused to be impressed.

"I agree they're different," she said, "but if you look at the different pages of writing in the notebook, you'll find the same letters formed in different ways on different pages. Of course you may be right, I'm not saying you're not right, it's just that I won't give an opinion. Now, look here, Giles. I think you'd better go and look at that well at Broadgarth, and when you see Mrs. Brough, ask her about the well. Now the place is sold, and off their hands, you'll probably find she's quite willing to tell you if the water in the well has risen of recent years."

Giles scratched his head. "I doubt if she'll do that, she'll be afraid I shall get Caroline to back out—throw it up, as they say when a cow is returned after a sale."

"You've got to find out," said Kate firmly. "You might even get on to the pipe track authorities, and ask if a stream was deflected near the quarry pool."

Giles looked worried. He had no belief at all in this theory about the behaviour of underground springs. His classical education had omitted any rudiments of geology and he was hopelessly unscientific. He had never heard of any farm-house rendered untenantable by the rising of a spring. Broadgarth had stood for nearly three hundred years, he knew that, and he believed it would stand for another three hundred. Because Kate had dealt rather severely with his own theories, he decided to be a little superior himself.

"This man Wilson," he began. "Where does he live, Kate, or where is he staying?"

"I've no idea, I didn't ask him," she replied.

Giles looked very solemn. "I am rather surprised at that," he said portentously. "We ought to know who he is. He has no business to be going round saying that Broadgarth is a worthless property. I'm not sure that such statements aren't actionable—I must inquire about that. You see, if Caroline changed her mind and wanted to sell, rumours about possible inundations might prejudice the sale."

"Not nearly so much as the appearance of a spring under the kitchen floor would," retorted Kate.

Giles scratched his head. "You're taking this wild idea very seriously, Kate. Do you really think this chap knew what he was talking about?"

"What he said made sense," she replied. "He knew enough elementary geology to know how springs are formed, and how they behave in the sort of rock formation we've got here. If *you* started talking to anybody about rock faults and morainal detritus, you'd make a much worse mess of it than he did, although you got an honours degree and are what is called an educated man."

"I shouldn't start talking about morainal detritus," said Giles serenely, "but lots of chaps can pick up jargon of that kind and use it effectively. Still, if you passed him as sound, he must know a bit about it."

"He does," said Kate. "He knew about the pipe track and its passage. Now *we* know all about the pipe track and where it runs, but it's not what you'd call general knowledge. He knew the pool was a quarry pool, and he knew the quarry had been worked for centuries. That's a bit odd, Giles. He *must* have been studying the locality for reasons of his own. I wonder why."

"Because he thought of buying Broadgarth," said Giles, but she replied impatiently:

"So did Mr. Harrow think of buying Broadgarth, but he didn't bother about geology."

"He didn't need to. He knows Broadgarth land is good fertile land, as I know it," replied Giles. "Still, I agree that his interest in the place is a bit odd, and I wish you'd asked him his address."

Kate grinned, quite suddenly, and her square, sunburnt face looked suddenly youthful again.

"All right, you old misery. I'll let you score that one, but you can easily find out about this Wilson man. He must have gone to view the house, and he's the sort of person your Emma Brough would remember."

"Perhaps he was the chap who put up the little townee at the auction who bid against Caroline," suggested Giles, but Kate shook her head.

"No, I don't think so. If this man had wanted an agent to bid for him, he'd have sent his lawyer, or some person of good position. He's the type they call gentry in the south; a little aware of his own importance, although he was quick enough not to try the *de haut en bas* manner to me."

"Did he say why he came here?"

"Oh, yes. He wanted to give an order for your honey crop. I told him you didn't sell."

"So he knows a bit about us," mused Giles, and she replied:

"Oh, yes. He was quite sure who I was, so he must have got to know something about us."

"If he's been talking about us in this district, he'd surely have heard about Caroline buying Broadgarth," said Giles. "I wonder if it was good nature which made him try to give an indirect warning about Broadgarth, although I'm quite certain he's talking nonsense."

"I'm not," said Kate. "What he said was elementary good sense. I ought to have thought it out for myself. Also I don't believe good nature is one of his characteristics, although he's got good manners. He hasn't a good-natured face."

She paused, and then added: "There must be *some* reason why so many people are suddenly interested in Broadgarth and the quarry pool. There's your Mr. Warrender. I expect he's an old fraud. He imposed on you because he talked charmingly, and because he said you'd been a very good bookseller. You'd believe in anybody who said that."

Giles grinned. "It showed sound judgment on Judge Warrender's part," he claimed cheerfully, and Kate snorted:

"Who said you weren't complacent, with that grin on your face, too. You leave your private detecting alone and go and see Emma Brough. You've got to find out about that well."

"It's very good water," said Giles. "I never fancied water out of a tap myself."

"I don't fancy it under the kitchen flagstones," retorted Kate.

TEN

I

WHEN CAROLINE BOURNE ARRIVED AT HAUXHEAD CASTLE, she was more than ever glad that she had ignored Giles Hoggett's suspicions and had accepted the commission offered to her. Not only was the position of the hotel a glorious one, set high above the river, encircled by fells, but the castle was the most beautiful house Caroline had ever stayed in. Its ancient stonework satisfied her critical eye as soon as she caught sight of it. Here was nothing bogus, nothing "restored," it was an ancient place furnished and run by experts, with a garden which was kept up as very few gardens can be kept these days.

When she was taken up to her bedroom, Caroline was amazed. She had obviously been given the "State Bedroom": a vast, panelled apartment with great oriel windows facing south. There was a four-poster bed hung with genuine embroidered curtains of Queen Anne's day, and the oak chests, tables and presses were Jacobean. The windows were wide open and the sun streamed in over crystal bowls filled with fragrant narcissus.

Caroline went to the window and looked out at the sunlit fells. She had a sudden feeling of discomfort. Why had she been given a room like this? Then came a knock at the door, and a pleasant-faced woman, clad in a charming flowered smock, came in.

"Miss Bourne? I am the floor manager. Mr. Barren told me you were coming, and told me to show you anything you wish to see."

"That's very kind," said Caroline, "but do you think he really meant me to have this room? I feel it's too generous altogether."

"Mr. Barren said you were to have it, madam. You are going to paint, aren't you?—and Mr. Barren hopes you will sketch this room."

"I certainly shall," replied Caroline. "It's about the loveliest room I have ever seen."

"It is beautiful, isn't it?" replied the other. "It's very comfortable, too. Your bath is through here. This little room between was a 'powder closet.' You see there are hanging cupboards for your frocks. It's not possible to get period furniture that makes suitable modern wardrobes, and Mr. Barren didn't want to spoil the bedroom by furniture of the wrong period. The bathroom opens out of this one."

Caroline looked at the lovely modern bath, with its showers and mirrors and crystal fittings. "But all this must have cost a fortune!" she exclaimed.

"I expect it did," the other replied, in her pleasant tranquil voice. "Mr. Barren was very anxious that everything should be well done. You see there are so many people waiting to complain that a great house is ruined and cheapened by being used as a hotel. He was determined that there should be no complaint over this one. Actually, he has improved the place a lot by removing Victorian and Edwardian horrors."

Caroline studied the quiet-voiced woman. She was certainly an educated woman, and Caroline went on:

"I can see you're interested in the house, in the same way that I am, and you probably know all about hotels. But do tell me, can a place like this ever really pay? I mean, give a return on the capital expended?"

The other smiled. "Oh, yes, indeed it can, if it's properly run. A first-class hotel *does* pay. Of course this place is calculated to appeal to wealthy tourists, particularly those from the States and South America. They pay, too, you know, a surprising sum, but the place has got to be just right." She smiled at Caroline and led the way back to the bedroom. "I do hope you will enjoy being here, and I shall look forward to seeing your pictures. Please ask me for anything you want, anything at all. Luncheon is served at one o'clock. I hope you can find your way about all right. The staircases are confusing at first, but you will find directions everywhere."

Caroline murmured her thanks, and a few moments later made her way down to the panelled entrance hall and thence to the "Banqueting Hall." It deserved its name, she meditated—and how well it was arranged, with the tables widely spaced, flowers everywhere, silver and glass gleaming. About a dozen tables were already occupied, and a white-coated waiter led Caroline to a table reserved for her by a window. She was studying the menu when she looked up to see another waiter beside her, with the wine list in his hand. He was quite an impressive-looking man, in a handsome uniform. Caroline looked up at the wide face with its multiple chins, and the shining bald head. "He looks like a bishop," she thought. He bent towards her, smiling and obsequious, yet somehow benevolent.

"Mr. Barren asks if you like Claret, madame. There is a Chateau Lafitte, a good vintage year, well matured or would madame prefer a 'Collins'?"

Caroline stared back. A 'Collins,' how often had she enjoyed that drink. Suddenly she exclaimed:

"But I've seen you somewhere before. I know your face."

"Yes. I know madame's face. In London. At the Café Napoleon perhaps, at the corner table."

"Why, yes… but you weren't our waiter. He was an Italian, a little dark man."

"Yes, madame. Giuseppi d'Alerno. I did not have the honour of waiting upon madame, but I remember that she enjoyed a 'Collins.' May I suggest the Claret to-day? It is to be recommended."

"No. I'll have a Collins. How do you like Hauxhead?"

"Very much, madame. It has quality—like the Chateau Lafitte."

He beamed at her and moved on, pontifical and assured. It was not until later that Caroline found that her drinks also were included in her "contract." There was nothing to pay. Just as she got up to leave the dining-room, the large wine waiter came up to her.

"Mr. Stern would like a word with madame, if it is convenient. He deputises for Mr. Barren when he is away. Mr. Stern is in his office. Charles will show you the office if that is agreeable."

"Certainly," agreed Caroline.

Stern got up from his table when Caroline entered. "May I introduce myself, Miss Bourne? John Stern. Barren so much regrets that he had to be away. I am his second in command. I hope you approve of Hauxhead."

"I should be hard to please if I didn't," she replied. "I can't get over that glorious bedroom you have given me. I'm quite overpowered."

He laughed. "Shall we say that we combine business with pleasure? We are very lucky to have got you. Barren knows that you will produce just what he wants. It's very important to us to have this thing done properly. The average hotel brochure is abysmal. We want to give you a good impression, you know."

"Yes, I understand that, but I feel you're doing me much too well. Business is business, after all, and I do expect to pay for my own drinks."

"Forget it," he laughed. "Barren asked you here as his guest. He is a great admirer of your work, you know."

It was then that Caroline became aware of a sense of discomfort. She was always honest with herself, and though she knew she had something of a reputation both as a writer and a painter, she felt that Stern was "laying it on with a trowel." She studied him for a second or so before she replied. He was tall, well-groomed, his accent was pleasant, but there was something about him which made Caroline sceptical of his good faith. Smiling sweetly, as though she enjoyed his flattering attitude, she asked:

"Which part of my work?"

"Oh—er—both your writing and painting. An unusual combination of talents. I believe you have already written about the antiquities of Lunesdale, and illustrated your own work."

"I wrote about the pack-horse bridges and I drew the one at Merchants Corner," she replied, "but it was quite a slight piece of work. As a matter of curiosity, how did Mr. Barren get my address?"

He laughed. "Well, I don't know exactly, but you're something of a celebrity, aren't you? I expect the bookish folk in Lancaster knew all about your whereabouts. Then I believe Mr. Hoggett of Wenningby is pretty well known in the valley. You're staying with him, aren't you? Now I wonder if you'd mind talking business for a moment?"

"Not at all. I should welcome it."

"Splendid. Now Barren told me that he had asked you to fix your own terms."

"Yes, but I can't do that until I know what you want. What length is the text to be? How many illustrations do you want? Are they to be line drawings, half-tone, or do you want any colour prints?"

Mr. Stern looked rather taken aback. "Well—er—what would you suggest?" he asked.

"He doesn't know a thing about it," thought Caroline to herself. Aloud she said: "It depends on how much you want to spend and how many copies you expect to print. Blocks for colour prints cost a lot. Do you intend to sell this handbook, for instance?"

"Oh, no. It's for publicity. Barren intends to send copies to his agent in the States, and elsewhere. The tourist trade is very important, you know."

"Yes," agreed Caroline, thinking rapidly. She began to wonder more and more why *she* had been asked to undertake this commission; why not some big man, if publicity in the States was the target? "Well, I think the best suggestion is this," she went on. "To-day and to-morrow I will look around and do some quick sketches: then I will do a lay-out—a sort of scheme to give you some idea of what I'm aiming at, and Mr. Barren can consider it when he comes back. As to terms, since it's a bigger job than I anticipated, I think you'd better deal with my agent. I warn you he'll probably object to my parting with my copyrights for a fixed sum. If you intend to print in thousands, I think a royalty basis should be arrived at."

He laughed. "You're very businesslike, aren't you? I don't think you need worry, Miss Bourne. Barren is very generous."

"I'm not worrying," she retorted, "neither am I questioning his generosity. But when I sell my work, I prefer to have advice over contracts." She paused, and then added: "I think it'd be much better if I paid my own expenses here, you know. After all, a job is a job."

He laughed. "We needn't go into that. You're Barren's guest—the guest of Hauxhead, if you prefer to put it that way. I'm so glad you like this place. It's very beautiful country, too—but I believe you know Lunesdale well."

"Is this where he gets down to brass tacks?" she asked herself. "The business talk was all eye-wash. He doesn't know what a half-tone block is." She smiled again, and accepted the cigarette he offered. "Yes. I know it pretty well, as far as a body 'from away' can know it," she replied. "Actually I've just bought a small property of my own, not far from Wenningby."

He smiled, and suddenly there flashed a suspicion into Caroline's mind. Stern was interested—and pleased—at her last remark. Why on earth should he be?

"Have you really?" he said. "How enterprising of you! You're not going into the hotel business in opposition to us, by any chance?"

"Goodness, no! I'm not a capitalist. It's just a little old farm-house, very old and humble, but it has its points. There's some woodland, and a very beautiful water, a quarry pool, really. There is a ruined cottage near the pool, and I'm going to rebuild it."

"It sounds quite exciting," he said. "I hope you had the place properly surveyed before you bought it; but you're so businesslike, I'm sure you saw to all that."

"No, I'm afraid I didn't, but I knew the land was valuable, and the woodland is so beautiful I fell in love with it at sight."

"Well I do hope you won't find you've been too rash," he said. "The trouble with some of these old farm-houses is that the fabric is often in a bad way—beams rotten, flagged roofs leaking like riddles and dry rot everywhere. You ought to get a surveyor on to it. Barren would send our man over for you."

She laughed. "Thanks, but I'm not having it surveyed. I take it on trust."

"I hope you'll be justified. What's the name of the place?"

"Broadgarth."

"Why, that's funny," he said, and hesitated.

"What's funny?" she inquired.

"Why, somebody was telling me of some queer story about a stranger being attacked in a wood. I hope that wasn't on your property."

She laughed ruefully. "News does travel, doesn't it? Actually there *was* an accident by the quarry pool. A man I know tripped over a bramble and knocked himself silly on the rocks, and somebody's exaggerated it into a case of assault, complete with police investigation, I suppose. It's incredible the way people exaggerate things."

"Isn't it?" he agreed. "What a shame to have your property maligned and credited with dark deeds of assault. And so it was nothing but an accident? Well, well!"

Caroline laughed. "Rumour's always like that," she said. "Now I think I'd better get on with my job. Is it true you've got a maze in the garden?"

"Quite true; clipped yew, and quite bewildering. I'll give you a key to it; it's really rather involved. And do be sure to have a look at our Elizabethan 'Knot' garden."

"I'm going to have a lovely time," she declared. "Thank you so much for giving me that wonderful room. I'll make a really good drawing of it."

2

"Now what on earth was he getting at?" asked Caroline of herself, "and why is he interested in Broadgarth? It's all quite mad. That *was* the *Lunesdale Observer* he had on his desk, and he'd been reading it, too."

She went across the beautiful hall, and found the office, discreetly placed in an alcove.

"Do you have newspapers here? Oh, yes, I see you do. Can I have the two local ones now, and order a *Times* for the morning. Thank you so much."

She went up to her room, the papers folded under her arm, and when she was behind her own closed door, she opened the *Lunesdale Observer* and found the column she had already read at Wenningby that morning. Under "Auctions" she read a brief notice. "Broadgarth Farm. Sold at Carnton, March 30th. Auctioneer, Robert Sharp. Buyer, Miss Caroline Bourne of Wenningby. Price, £2000."

"So he knew all the time," she said to herself. "He had got the paper open at that page. What on earth does it all mean? Why have they got me here and given me this room? They could have commissioned anybody. They must be simply rolling…"

She sat and pondered, and at last got to her feet, saying: "I might as well enjoy it now that I *am* here, but somehow I think I shall be recalled… by urgent business. There's something phoney about this commission."

ELEVEN

I

INSPECTOR BORD WAS CONSCIOUS OF A SENSE OF IRRITATION. HE had acceded immediately to Chief Inspector Macdonald's courteous request that he, Bord, should go out the previous evening to collect Mr. Warrender's car and to check up on its ownership with a view to ascertaining where the owner intended to stay during the next few days. What had upset Bord was Mr. Hoggett's association in the matter. "Not that I dislike Hoggett," Bord argued to himself. "He's a very polite, kindly fellow. A good landlord, I'm told, and much esteemed in his own locality."

But Bord was aware that Mr. Giles Hoggett had already assisted in one police case in Lunesdale, and that he had also been "much esteemed" by the C.I.D. Detective Inspector Peter Reeves had been outspokenly enthusiastic concerning Hoggett's acumen in detective work; but Bord didn't like amateurs. When Giles Hoggett had brought Francis Rolph to report on the alleged assault at the quarry pool, Bord had rather enjoyed pointing out the nebulous nature of the evidence, and discouraging Mr. Hoggett from feeling that it was of any importance.

With the advent of Macdonald, and his attitude of inquiry towards the Rolph episode, Bord had wondered if he himself had made a mistake in tactics, from the point of view of his own professional status, that was. Then came his meeting with Giles Hoggett and Mr.

Warrender yesterday evening, when Hoggett had certainly had the laugh on his side. Hoggett had been asked by Macdonald to ascertain Mr. Warrender's bona fides without police questioning, and Bord, while acknowledging that there was good sense in Macdonald's employment of Hoggett for this purpose, could not help feeling slightly irate about it. In the first case, Bord had condescended successfully to Hoggett. Now the position was reversed. Being a very efficient police officer, despite his tendency to distrust amateurs, Bord felt that the best way to put Giles Hoggett in his own place was to pursue the matter mentioned by Macdonald; to find Tom Field and "put him through it" concerning his recent activities. Bord knew that his constables generally knew all about the farming business in their various villages and he anticipated no difficulty in learning where Field was employed at the moment. To his surprise his inquiries brought only negative results, for no report of Field's presence in the neighbourhood came in. Bord had a vague suspicion, which he ought to have translated into a solid conviction years ago, that the farming community tended to hold its peace in the presence of a police inspector. Edward Troutbeck and Richard Blackthorn would both gossip happily by the hour to Giles Hoggett and other fellow farmers, but when a policeman passed the time of day he was answered by a polite agreement about the weather and nothing else.

Thinking the matter out, Bord thought his best chance of getting the information he sought was to go to the cattle market, which was held that day in Carnton. Here he knew he would find a cross section of the local farming community, whose aggregate of information would cover a wide area.

Bord strolled into the market: it was the day when milking cows were auctioned, and the air was full of loud complaints from unmilked dairy cattle, who had every cause to resent this break in their usually placid routine of home comforts and kindly attentions. Bord soon spotted a group of farmers occupied in profound contemplation of a fine young Friesian cow. She was a good beast—Bord could tell that, for she had a big bag, and was in excellent condition. What Bord did not know was that the cow had been bred on Mr. Hoggett's farm, sold by him as an in-calf heifer, and that now, after her second calving, she was expected to make a good price. Bord noticed at once that when he joined the group, silence became general.

"That's a fine beast," he observed genially.

"Aye, she's not too bad," was the guarded rejoinder.

Bord turned to Mr. Clough of Tressingham. "Can you tell me if Tom Field is working hereabouts just now?" he inquired.

Clough pushed his hat back and scratched his head. "I can't say. I haven't seen him," he replied, and returned to his contemplation of the Friesian. "Aye, I've seen worse," he said judicially.

Bord was puzzled. Without being very acute by nature, his training had made him observant of those he interrogated, and he knew that somehow these farmers were "holding out on him." He tried again. "I want a word with Field sometime. Hasn't he been working near Wenningby recently?"

"Maybe he has," agreed Mr. Clough vaguely. "I don't hire a tractor man myself. My Bob's got a tractor and he does all t' ploughing and sowing, faster than his dad ever did it. Aye, if you want a nice Friesian, Inspector, you might do worse than this one. Ah, there's Mr. Turner now—" and with that Mr. Clough made off.

Bord had no means of telling that a prolonged discussion had been in progress around the mild-eyed milking cow whom Kate Hoggett had once called Black-eyed Susan. With the long memory of farmers, all these men had known that the Friesian had been Giles Hoggett's beast, and with Mr. Clough's gambit, "I mind that was Mr. Hoggett's heifer," the group had started on a vigorous, if guarded, discussion concerning the Wynnes and Tom Field, with a later admission that

"Mr. Hoggett was seeing into it." They were quite satisfied that Giles was capable of probing any mystery—if mystery there were—about David Wynne and Tom Field, and none of them had any wish for a police inquiry into the matter at the moment. After Mr. Clough had taken himself off, Joe Thorne put a word in. Joe was hired man at Bromsgrove.

"Reckon Field may have gone south for the potato ridging," he hazarded. "Ploughing's about done our way."

Bord turned to Joe. "Where does Field live?"

"Couldn't say for sure. Reckon it's Preston way," said Joe.

"Who did he work for last in this district?" asked Bord.

Joe scratched his head. Every one knew that Field had worked at the Wynne's place until he had quarrelled with David.

"Last?" he countered vaguely. "I couldn't say. Did some felling and sawing for Overfield some time, and some ploughing for t' Wynnes, but which was last I couldn't say. Gets about, Field does. Be over t' fells to Slaidburn one day and up Silverdale another."

Bord nodded and turned away, determined to waste no more time with men who, for one reason or another, were evidently determined to avoid giving a plain answer. Field's address could be got from the county offices where his tractor was registered, and further inquiries could be pursued at the Wynne's farm, wherever that was, and at Overfield.

Because Ashdale proved to be the nearer, Bord drove out there as soon as he had found the address and direction.

2

From her kitchen window, Alice Wynne could see the track which led to the farm, and the gate on to the high road. She saw Bord's car pull up, and the inspector get out and open the gate. She had about two minutes for thought, and she thought hard. Her heart was thumping, for the sight of a police inspector filled her with foreboding. Without knowing much about her husband's activities when he took himself off for occasional days of unspecified "business," she was apprehensive concerning the nature of that business. She knew he sometimes went "to the dogs," and she not only disapproved of every sort of gambling as "plain silly," she also feared it. For a long time now she had been afraid that David was getting into bad company, and the sight of a police inspector coming up the track filled her mind with consternation. "He'll get nowt from me," she decided, as she seized a broom and barrow and decided to get busy cleaning out the poultry houses.

Bord met her just as she was well underway with the barrow. It was a gusty day, and he had to shout to make himself heard.

"Mrs. Wynne?"

"Yes. What is it? Don't tell me it's Foot and Mouth, or Swine Fever."

"No. Nothing of that kind. Can I see your husband?"

"He's away to-day. Can you leave a message?"

Bord was a bit put about. He knew that the farmers had very clear ideas about the undesirability of strange men—police or otherwise—calling on their wives in their absence, and he was anxious to give no cause for complaint.

"I really wanted to see Tom Field," said Bord. "He's been working here, hasn't he?"

"Field? He did t' ploughing up t' hill, that new land we've got—but that's finished days ago. Haven't seen him since. My young brother's come to work here now, seeing 'twas a bit too much now we've got the arable."

"Can you tell me where Field is working now?"

"I don't know—how should I? These tractor men don't know from day to day where they'll be. He finished here, that's all I know."

"Would your husband know where Field's to be found?"

"Why should he? It's what I told you, they move on from one place to t' next."

Alice seized her broom to indicate that she wanted to get on with her work, hoping that the inspector would go, but he went on: "Just a minute. Sorry to keep you, Mrs. Wynne. I can see you're busy, but can you tell me how your husband gets in touch with Field when he wants him. Does he write to him?"

"That he doesn't. Never writes a letter if he can help it," rejoined Alice. "He sees him at t' market, maybe, or working somewhere else, or sends a word when he hears he's in the district. We're not much of letter-writers here…"

"Then your husband doesn't know Tom Field's address?"

"Not that I know of. Field doesn't live hereabouts; somewhere near Preston, I think he said, but I don't remember exactly. Anyway, it doesn't matter to us, not now we've got my brother here working."

"How long was Field working here?" asked Bord.

Alice considered. "Not so long," she said, in the usual idiom of the district. "Two full days that might've been, and some odd hours, maybe. I didn't rightly notice."

Again Bord had the feeling that Mrs. Wynne, also, was avoiding giving him any information at all, and he sensed that, in spite of her expressed indifference, his questions worried her, and that she was anxious to be rid of him. "There's something wrong somewhere," thought Bord to himself. He altered the angle of his inquiry.

"Did Field fell any trees on your land, or in this neighbourhood?" he asked.

Alice was plainly surprised at the question, but she answered tersely enough: "He felled no trees here. We're tenants, and the timber isn't ours. As for what he did anywhere else, I can't say. We've enough to do with our own business, without watching other folk's."

She asked no questions, Bord observed. Knowing the natural curiosity which is generally felt over a police visit, the inspector thought this was unnatural. "She knows something, and she's keeping it to herself," he thought. He went on:

"Did Field ever mention the coppice above Broadgarth or the quarry pool?"

She stared back at him, her eyes very alert. "Not that I know of," she replied. "He was ploughing, and you don't talk all that when you're driving a tractor."

"But he stayed in the house with you while he was working?"

"Yes, he did, but he went out in the evenings. I go to bed early, 'tis hard work on a farm at this time of year." She paused, and then added: "If it's Broadgarth you want to know about, you'd better go and see Mr. Hoggett. His cousin has bought Broadgarth, and he'd know all about it. Drat the beasts! They've broken out again!"

A trio of inquisitive bullocks had appeared at the fold-yard gate, and Alice, broom in hand, set about them, intent on chasing them back whither they had come. Bord stood still in the chill breeze. He had learnt nothing from his visit, but he was more than ever convinced that something was being concealed from him. He felt the more irate. He had not come here to be advised to go to see Mr. Hoggett, but he didn't see what else he could do at the moment. Dignity would not allow him to pursue Alice Wynne and the bullocks. Regulations—and natural common sense—debarred him from going into the house. He turned away, pondering deeply, and went back to his car.

3

Bord sat in his car and thought hard. He remembered that he had heard somewhere that David Wynne and Tom Field had been seen together at the dog-racing track at Strand, and enlightenment dawned on him, as he thought. "They're in it together, whatever it is, Wynne *and* Field," he said to himself. While it was satisfactory to have arrived at an idea, however rudimentary, Bord found his satisfaction short-lived. If Wynne and Field were involved in illicit dealings together, then it seemed all Lombard Street to a china orange that Mr. Giles Hoggett had been right in his hypothesis that the affair at the quarry pool required police investigation, and Bord had to admit that he himself had been too slow in making a start. Field seemed to be off the map, and Wynne... "Damn all!" said Bord bitterly. "They've beaten it together and left me standing. That's why she wanted to be rid of me."

He sat with shoulders hunched, still thinking. The odd part of it was that Alice Wynne had suggested that he, Bord, should "go and see Mr. Hoggett." "That's queer, that is," thought Bord. Not by any stretch of his imagination could Bord believe that Mr. Hoggett was "in" this too. Bord knew a law-abiding citizen when he met one, and though he might disapprove of Mr. Hoggett's ventures into detection, he knew that any supposition that involved Mr. Hoggett as an abettor of illegal transactions of any kind involved argument so fallacious that it fell to pieces of itself. Bord then reconsidered the matter of Broadgarth itself. Certainly Miss Bourne had bought the property: certainly, also, she was not living there at the moment. The pastures were already being used by Bromsgrove, and the owner of Bromsgrove was liming the meadows, but the house was empty. "I'll go and have a look at it," said Bord to himself, and turned the ignition on. Any sort of action was preferable to none.

4

After the middle-day meal, Giles Hoggett set off to find Mrs. Brough. Kate, again left to her own devices, found the matter of the Broadgarth well came between her and her seedlings, and suddenly she decided to go and have a look at it. Giles had said that Mr. Wilson's theories concerning the well were just so much nonsense, but Kate wanted to see for herself. So she set off, not keeping to the road, but going cross-country, which was much more interesting. She climbed the gill behind the farm-house, and considered once again the spring which filled the Wenningby reservoir: above it was another spring which Kate called the "Holy Well." It was just below the gaunt little stone church, and the clear trickle provided the water for the font when Wenningby infants were baptised. She crossed the road by the church and took an almost disused path, still rising, and running direct north across the fields to Bromsgrove and Broadgarth and eventually, Kate knew, to the shores of the bay. It was an ages-old route, disused now, save by Bromsgrove children on their way to and from school. Thus she arrived at Broadgarth by the fields, as Macdonald had done the evening before. It was a fine sunny day, and the sturdy stone block of Broadgarth farm-house and barn had something of the quality of a fortress about its massive reticence. Kate had enjoyed her walk, and no misgivings had entered her head. The familiar fields, the peaceful solid bulk of the plain stone house, seemed friendly and sensible, so that Kate did not give a thought to Giles's wild theories about the quarry pool. She was intent on her own business; that of examining the well to decide for herself if it seemed abnormal. She walked round the house, for the well was close to the back door; it had the usual wooden cover, but there was no pump. "Caroline had better get one of those rotary pumps fixed," she thought, as she bent to lift the stones which had been placed on the cover to keep it in place lest some inquisitive ewe or bullock tried to shift the cover.

It was just as she bent down that she became aware of a movement on the far side of the garden hedge. As she lifted the first big stone, she suddenly realised that the moving object she had seen could not have been a sheep or a cow, it had been something tall and narrow and dark. Kate straightened herself and looked again, but there was nothing there. It was then that misgiving entered her head. There had been a man moving behind that hedge, and now he was hidden. Kate remembered Rolph's tumble, and Giles's forebodings, and she was suddenly angry. Her anger was directed against herself. She had come here alone, telling nobody of her intention, and she was too far away from any other habitation to be heard if she called out. On impulse, the age-old impulse to get your back to a wall if in danger of attack, she drew back into the angle made by the porch and the wall of the house, and found she was still holding the big stone she had lifted from the cover of the well. Kate was sturdy and muscular, and she kept hold of the stone. It wasn't too heavy to throw, but it was heavy enough to do a lot of damage if thrown properly.

5

Inspector Bord drove on to the Broadgarth turning after leaving Ashdale. He left his car by the roadside and strolled into the coppice. It was very peaceful and beautiful there, but Bord was as indifferent as Peter Bell to primroses, and as for Mrs. Hoggett's wood muscatel, it was only "another weed" to him. He looked into the cottage and metaphorically kicked himself because he hadn't thought of Tom Field in connection with the looted timber. Doors were worth a lot these days, and Bord knew it. He followed the track to the ruined shippon and looked inside. There were footprints and two cigarette ends—one a Players and one a Woodbine. They had been dropped by Macdonald and Giles Hoggett, but Bord did not know that. He collected them conscientiously and went on to the pool. Bord would have agreed with Hoggett in describing it as "a black hole." For the first time it struck him that it looked ominous. He knew nothing about "Millstone Grit" and had never considered the fact that this obdurate stone always tended to look dark when wet; the darkness of the water was due to the dark rock which surrounded and cradled it, but Bord thought it looked "unnatural." How deep was it? he wondered, and fretfully threw a stone into it, an action which taught him nothing. "I suppose we'd better drag it," he thought, and then set off to reach Broadgarth. He approached it from the rear, and as he reached the hedge surrounding the garden he heard footsteps. On the alert at once, he halted and peered through an unobliging elder tree. He could see very little: a neutral coloured raincoat and dark beret. What was the chap doing there, by the back door?

Bord crouched down and considered. He, like Kate Hoggett, was alone: he was also unarmed. If there *were* anything in this elusive case, it was possible that violence might occur. For the first time, Bord found himself taking Rolph's injury seriously. He determined to outflank the intruder by the back door, and on his way round the barn he picked up a serviceable piece of wood, stronger than a walking-stick but handy enough to grip. Not a very correct looking weapon, perhaps, but better than nothing.

6

Kate Hoggett heard the footsteps approaching round the house and she stood still and waited, wondering if the stone she held was too heavy to throw. When she saw Bord's face appear round the angle of the house, she was so exasperated she nearly threw the stone at him. She had worked herself up into an idiotic fit of nerves over a policeman. When she saw Bord hastily throw away his wooden post, Kate felt better. She grinned derisively. "A stone's worth more than a stick on some occasions," she said to herself, and then snapped out:

"What are you doing here?" unconsciously emulating Giles's "landowning voice."

Bord grinned, too, rather shamefacedly.

"I'm sorry if I startled you, Mrs. Hoggett. I was just looking round to see that everything was in order. I admit I mistook you for an interloper." He paused, and then added: "Judging by that stone, you weren't feeling any too easy in your own mind about this place. You asked me what I was doing here. I hope you won't take it amiss if I ask you the same question."

"I came to look at the well," rejoined Kate. "Do you know anything about wells?"

Bord looked nonplussed; wells were the last subject he was interested in.

"I'm afraid I don't," he said. "What's the matter with it?"

Kate pushed away the remaining stone from the cover of the well with the toe of her solid shoe, and then lifted the cover. The water was only a few inches below ground level.

"Have you ever seen a well as full as this one?" she demanded. "It looks as though it might overflow any time."

"Good heavens!" ejaculated Bord. "You mean you think something is concealed in it, and the water has risen accordingly?"

Kate groaned. "No! I don't mean anything of the kind," she snapped back. "I'm not looking for corpses. I'm trying to find out if the house is liable to flooding." She studied Bord with open amusement. "We both seem to be making fair-sized fools of ourselves," she said. "You go crouching behind hedges in a manner which suggested no good, and I stand patiently with a stone ready to throw it at you. Now you hopefully suggest there's a corpse in the well. There isn't. Mrs. Brough would have known if the well water had risen suddenly."

Bord scratched his head. Despite the trenchancy of her speech, he liked Mrs. Hoggett. She was sensible and practical, and she gave a plain answer when asked for it.

"Look here, Mrs. Hoggett. I admit I'm stumped over this business. Your husband brought Mr. Rolph to report about his accident, quite rightly, but there wasn't enough concrete evidence to make a case of it. There was nothing I could do. Now I'm beginning to wonder if there isn't further evidence to be got if I could get hold of someone who was willing to be frank."

Kate Hoggett saw the humour of this approach, but she also saw that Bord was not feeling in the least humorous about it. Taking a key out of her pocket, she said: "Shall we go inside? It's cold here, and I want to have a look at the kitchen. Miss Bourne is away, and she left the key with me."

"By all means," agreed Bord.

The still air of the house felt warm after the keen air outside, and Kate walked across the kitchen and sat on the table, swinging her sturdy legs. She felt enormously amused, and thought how much tickled Giles would be when she told him about Bord's change of front. Bord removed his hat politely when he entered the house, and continued the conversation by saying:

"I have just been to Ashdale. So far as I can gather, both Tom Field and David Wynne have gone away."

"Have they?" inquired Kate, unhelpfully.

Bord flushed. "That's the sort of answer I've been getting all day, Mrs. Hoggett."

Kate continued to swing her legs. "Look here, Inspector. I don't know anything about this business. It's my husband who is interested, and you can't expect me to repeat anything he's told me in confidence. If you want any information from him, you'd better ask him for it."

"Of course," agreed Bord, but something about his worried face made Kate respond more directly than she had intended.

"You know, you made a mistake in thinking that Giles was talking through his hat about the Rolph business," she said.

"But I didn't," began Bord.

"Oh, yes, you did," she replied. "You thought he'd got swollen headed over that case at Wenningby Barns. You said you wanted somebody to be frank, so I'm taking you at your word. I don't think Giles has many of the qualities of a detective, but I do know that he's uncannily quick at noticing anything amiss, as we say round here. He's got a sort of instinct for sensing the unusual. If you'd ever played three-handed bridge with him you'd know, as I know, that he can smell a good hand in Dummy." She paused, and then added: "I suppose you think I'm talking nonsense?"

"Oh, no, I don't," protested Bord.

Kate went on: "If Giles had come into this kitchen with us, he'd have noticed at once something that you might not notice at all, because you're not used to stone farm-house kitchens."

Bord looked wildly round the bare gaunt room, and Kate went on: "It's nothing you can see. It's the temperature. This room's warmer than it's any business to be. If you put your hand in the oven, I believe you'll find it's warm, and nobody is supposed to have been here for over three days."

Bord went to the fireplace and put his hand against the firebricks. "You're quite right," he said resignedly. "Someone's had a fire here not many hours ago."

TWELVE

I

IT WAS NEARLY TEA-TIME WHEN KATE RETURNED TO WENNINGBY, walking home by the same route she had taken to go to Broadgarth. Bord had offered to drive her home, but she had refused the offer. She did, however, accept a cigarette from him, when, rather diffidently, he held out a well-filled cigarette case. Kate had not had a cigarette since breakfast-time and this was corn in Egypt.

"I can't offer you one back," she said honestly. "Giles ought to have gone into Lancaster to-day to get our quota, but he can't even remember to get the cigarettes these days."

"Bad luck. I've got a new packet—do take it," said Bord.

"No, I won't take it, but it's a very generous offer," said Kate warmly, "especially as I haven't been particularly polite."

"You nearly threw a stone at me," said Bord. "I shall always remember that."

"What about you, with half a gatepost to protect you?" she retorted.

They had parted on quite friendly terms and Kate was still chuckling over her afternoon when she got home, and perceived that yet another visitor was inspecting her primulas. It was Macdonald, and she went to greet him.

"Come and have tea. I thought you were in London," she said.

"I was in London for precisely two hours. I should like some tea very much, thank you," he replied. "Where's your husband?"

"Talking to Emma Brough. They'll talk for hours. She was the body who showed Broadgarth to viewers," said Kate, as she led him indoors. "Sit down and I'll get tea. I've just been up to Broadgarth. Inspector Bord thought I was 'loitering with intent,' and came after me with half a gatepost, while I nearly chucked a large stone at him, because—well, because the prevailing dementia is catching."

"It sounds quite a lively afternoon," said Macdonald, and she replied:

"Bord was really very decent about it. He gave me a cigarette."

"Excellent. That reminds me, I've brought you a hundred Players. Giles was talking about smoking colt's-foot leaves yesterday."

"A hundred Players! Glory! I'm right out. I'll open the last pot of strawberry jam for you, and there's some cream and farm butter."

"Thank you very much," he replied warmly. "How's things?"

"Utterly crazy," she replied. "I'll tell you all about it in a minute. What about you?"

"Well, in confidence, I'm not doing too well at the moment. My man has gone to earth."

"And I suppose you feel exasperated," said Kate as she got busy with the teapot. Macdonald came across to carry the tea-tray. He grinned at her.

"Well, since it seems probable that he's gone to earth somewhere in this locality I'm not complaining. Now tell me all about the prevalent dementia you mentioned just now."

"I suppose I ought to leave Giles's part for him to tell you," she said. "Hearsay isn't evidence, is it?"

"Not in a court of law," agreed Macdonald, "but from my point of view I profit if I get individual accounts both from you and your husband. You tend to stress different points—so carry on."

Over the tea and the strawberry jam Kate gave a factual account of Giles's visit to Alice Wynne, and of the discrepancy he had noticed in the writing of David Wynne's letter and that in the notebook.

"Giles believes that if the two *are* different, it's a proof that something's badly wrong," she said.

"It isn't a proof, but it's an indication," said Macdonald. "But you say his wife was quite satisfied?"

"Oh, yes. She's certain David wrote the letter; and I know that Inspector Bord went to see Alice to-day, and she just told him David was out for the day."

Macdonald pondered. "You're pretty certain in your own mind that Alice Wynne is straight?" he asked. "You don't think her husband had any real cause for complaint?"

"About Tom Fields? Goodness, no! Alice is perfectly straight, we've known her all her life. Besides, David may be a bad farmer and a moody Welshman, but he's got something attractive about him and she's in love with him. Tom Field is just a lout—and a grubby lout at that. Alice'd never look at him." Kate drank her tea appreciatively: she was thirsty after her walk. "So Giles is now absolutely convinced that Tom Field killed David Wynne, and put his body in the quarry pool. Inspector Bord, having failed to discover either Field or Wynne when he wanted them, has at last decided that a crime *has* been committed, but he rather favours the Broadgarth well as a depository for corpse and/or loot."

"The Broadgarth well?" queried Macdonald, and Kate said:

"Yes. This is my part of the story... Help yourself..." She pushed the strawberry jam towards Macdonald and told him the details of Mr. Wilson's visit. Macdonald was so much interested that he forgot the jam, and sat with his chin on his fists, listening hard.

"I only did geology up to matric," he said, "so mine's pretty hoary, but the ideas seem to hang together all right so far as I can judge. What's your opinion?"

"Oh, he didn't make any floaters: the idea's sound enough. I had another good look at the position of Broadgarth. Although it's on high land, it's a fact that the house is in a bit of a dip—the ground slopes towards it on three sides, and it's a lot below the level of the pool and the coppice. In fact the more I thought about it, the less I liked it, until I remembered that Mrs. Brough showed Caroline the well without being asked to. Mrs. Brough's pretty shrewd. She'd never have shown prospective buyers the well unless she thought it was an inducement to buy. In other words, Emma Brough sees nothing wrong with the well."

"Yes. That's a point," agreed Macdonald. "But if Mr. Wilson was treating you to an intelligently composed fiction, he could only have been doing it for one reason: to make an inducement for Miss Bourne to sell Broadgarth when she gets a suitable offer for it."

"Yes, but *why*?" insisted Kate. "If this had happened a century ago, the explanation would turn out that Broadgarth was on a valuable coalfield, or there were iron deposits, or something. Now, even if they strike oil, private owners can't exploit it, can they?"

"I believe not, though I'm not well up in the new Act," said Macdonald, "but I don't think it's that. Is Miss Bourne at Hauxhead?"

"Yes, having a wonderful time. She wants me to go over. They've given her a state bedroom and her own bath, and she says the castle is lovely. They've got a spinning gallery, like the one at Borwick, and a panelled banqueting hall—early Jacobean. Incidentally, old Mr. Warrender's going on there. Giles told Caroline to talk to him. She talks quite well, you know, and elderly intellectuals dote on her."

Macdonald began to laugh.

"It's a wonderful story, the whole thing," he said. "It all hangs together so nicely. Is your Mr. Wilson also staying at Hauxhead?"

Kate looked chagrined. "I don't know," she said. "I didn't think of asking him. Giles was awfully snooty about it. He said I ought to have found out who Wilson was and where he came from. I know I ought to have asked him, but I'm not in the habit of asking people questions, and habit's very strong."

"Yes," agreed Macdonald. "I've noticed your habit of not asking questions. It's a very rare and very admirable habit. It's because I'm aware of that peculiarity of yours that I can come and eat your strawberry jam and talk to you without being too careful of what I'm saying."

"Well, you're not eating much jam now," said Kate. "Do have some more. Oh, and I haven't told you my *real* discovery. Bord will tell you, but I got there first. He just didn't notice. I took him into the house to talk—I'd got the key. The fireplace in the kitchen was still warm. Someone's been there, making a fire. It must have been last night. I bet it was Mr. Wilson."

"Do you? What was he like, by the way?"

Kate considered: "Fiftyish, or rather less: about five feet ten or eleven, lean, well built, sunburnt and healthy looking," she replied. "His hair was greyish and he'd got light-coloured eyes, grey-blue, a thin mouth that shut tight and a definite chin. Well-kept hands—he's not been doing any manual work lately—and his clothes and shoes were good without being ostentatious. What you'd call a country gent. I can't see him mucking out a shippon. He knows a bit about gardening. Not the man you're looking for by any chance?"

Macdonald shook his head. "Totally unlike. My bloke's stout and rubicund with a sizable underwaist and several chins. This Wilson doesn't sound the type to camp out in an empty farm-house."

"No. I suppose he doesn't," she agreed. "Perhaps Tom Field's a likelier guess."

"Much likelier; but how did he get in? Any windows left open?"

"No. All secure. The visitor must have had a key."

"You say you've got the door key. There isn't generally a second key to the front door of a farm-house, is there?"

"No. Very seldom. But the one I've got is the back door key. I suppose Caroline has the other. The front door wasn't bolted. I suppose no mechanic would have any difficulty in turning the lock without the proper key. It's a large keyhole, you could almost get your fingers in it."

Macdonald nodded. "Yes. Those ancient locks aren't difficult to open. Tom Field, for instance, would be able to manage that job all right."

"Yes—but—" Kate broke off and Macdonald said:

"Well? What's the idea?"

"Only this. If Field *has* committed a crime, and the quarry pool is involved in it, wouldn't he have got as far away as possible, as quickly as possible? Surely he'd never stop at that spot."

"I don't know," said Macdonald. "It would be quite an astute place to hide in for a limited period. No one would expect him to be there. Obviously Bord didn't think about it. Then there are all the farm buildings to play hide-and-seek in. Your dark barns and shippons must offer many a place of concealment to a man accustomed to such buildings."

Kate agreed, and Macdonald went on: "I think your husband has good grounds for suspecting Field, you know. He may have been concerned in various questionable enterprises, and I shouldn't be at all surprised if it was he who had looted the timber from the cottage. It would have been so easy, for he's known to deal in timber, and his tractor-trailer outfit gives him the safest and easiest of transport. Once a man has started on the slippery road of illicit enterprise, he is in the position of one who has given hostages to fortune. In other words he's vulnerable, and he may find himself committing a bigger crime to conceal a smaller one."

Kate sat with her chin on her fists and pondered, and Macdonald smiled across at her.

"You think it out, Mrs. Hoggett. You've got most of the data; nearly as much as I have. And now, after thanking you for a noble tea, I'm going to cadge local information."

He held out his cigarette case, saying: "I want you to tell me about Morecambe sands, and the old path over the sands from Hest Bank to Cartmel."

2

Kate started off with a characteristic disclaimer. "I don't know enough about it to be reliable," she protested. "You'd do much better to ask some of the fishermen who live on the shores of the bay."

"I'm asking you for two reasons, Mrs. Hoggett. When you have given me information, it's always been accurate, and you don't run about telling other people what questions I've asked."

"Well, I'll do my best, but all I know about the sands is what I've read, and I'm talking from memory, so I don't guarantee anything," she said. "The sands were used at low tide to get from Hest Bank to Cartmel right through medieval times. The monks of Cartmel Priory provided guides and kept the posts and signals in order. It is a very hazardous crossing, and I believe there is only just time to make it in between the tides, but I know the stage coaches went across the sands in the eighteenth century."

"Well, that indicates that the going must be good at certain stages of the tides," said Macdonald. "The sea comes in with a rush, doesn't it, when the tide turns?"

"Yes, but the crossing is complicated by the two rivers, the Kent and the Keer," she said. "The rivers cut channels through the sands and you've got to know where to cross them. There's an old saying about many a good mare lost 'twixt Kent and Keer. The story goes that one man got off his horse because his pack was slipping and he stopped to make it fast; and the delay resulted in his being caught by the tide, and he and his horse were drowned. You can't afford to stop for anything. Once the tide comes in, the sands become quicksands and swallow you up."

"How much distance is saved by crossing the sands instead of going round the bay by road?"

"Oh, I should think about thirty miles—quite a lot when you're riding," she replied. "Of course the sands are used to a limited extent now; the cockle gatherers and the shrimpers go out, and take their carts, too, but they all know the sands well. You ought to drive up to Grange and go on to Furness Abbey; the sands are a beautiful sight at low tide—miles and miles of them."

"I've been thinking over all the various things you've told me about this district," he said. "You know much more about it than most of the men in the police force, for instance. You told me about the old pack-horse tracks, and the pack-horse bridges, which very few people know about. Don't you think it's just possible that a man like Tom Field, who knows the farm-land well, might know these tracks, too, and even the road over the sands? You see, if we look out for a fugitive, we watch roads and railways and buses and cars and lorries. But from what you've told me, there are other ways which we don't know anything about, whereby a man could get north to Barrow or Maryport, and thus out of the country."

"I suppose it's possible," she said, "but I doubt very much if Field would know the sands, or risk crossing them, unless he has friends to guide him. He comes from farther south—Preston way—so I shouldn't expect him to know the sands." She paused, and then added: "If you want to know about the sands, you should ask some of the older fishermen. I can only generalise, and you want specific information."

"Admittedly; but I don't want it to be known that I'm asking questions about the sands—old fishermen are generally great talkers. Hallo, here's your husband come back."

Giles welcomed Macdonald warmly, and the C.I.D. man asked: "Well, was Emma Brough interesting?"

"Yes, very interesting. We had a fine 'crack,'" said Giles. "Kate will have told you about Wilson and the well at Broadgarth?" He turned to his wife. "I told you the chap was talking through his hat," he said serenely. "Mrs. Brough swears the well is all right. She says it's always full up every spring, and has been for years: it drops several inches by midsummer and the water is lowest in September. It never overflows and it's never been known to go dry. So that's that."

"But why did that Wilson man come here and spin all that yarn?" demanded Kate indignantly.

"Because he wants Broadgarth for himself," said Giles. "He came to view it on the same day that Caroline and I went there, and he wanted to buy it direct. He did his best to persuade Emma Brough to let him deal direct with the owners, and not to have it put up for auction. He said they could name their own price."

"Why didn't they?" asked Kate.

"Because Emma Brough and old Polly Makin thought they'd do better out of an auction, with folks bidding against one another. They were afraid, if they mentioned a price, they might hit on too low a figure. The odd part was that Wilson didn't even turn up at the auction."

"He can't have wanted it very badly, then," argued Kate. "Did you find out where he lived?"

"He told Emma that his address was Hauxhead Castle," replied Giles, "so perhaps he will be trying his stories direct on Caroline. I must have a word with her over the phone and tell her not to take him seriously. Incidentally, Caroline made quite an impression on Emma Brough. Emma liked the way she bid up, bold and clear."

"Of course she did," agreed Kate. "It was Caroline's determination that ran the bidding up. It'd have gone for £1200 if she hadn't been there."

"Yes, but it wasn't only that," said Giles. "You see, there was a new auctioneer, a chap named Sharp, who has recently gone into partnership with old Gus Stebbing; Stebbing was known all round the district, but he was ill, and this chap Sharp took the Broadgarth auction unexpectedly. Emma Brough said he would have ignored Caroline's bid altogether if he could have, but she spoke up so loud and clear that he couldn't ignore her."

"But why on earth should he have wanted to ignore her?" demanded Kate. "The auctioneer wants to get a good price, doesn't he?"

"Yes, of course, if he's on the straight, but occasions have been known when an auctioneer's been got at, and he uses his skill to knock a property down to the chap who's bribed him. I'm not suggesting that such a thing *did* happen in this case, but Emma Brough is pretty shrewd. She suspected that auctioneer: she thought he was trying to let the small townee have the final bid, but Caroline settled that little game by her clear bidding."

"Did she know who the townee was?"

"No, but she had a very interesting idea. She said Tom Field went to view Broadgarth, and Emma believes that Field is one of a syndicate, or else that he's got some other chaps in with him, and that they had managed to get the deposit for about £1800, thinking that was enough to outbid any one else."

"But why on earth should a man like Field want to pay an inflated price for a small holding of twenty acres?" demanded Kate. "Two thousand pounds is an enormous sum of money for Field to put up. He's quite a youngster."

"Well, I've got one idea and Emma's got another," said Giles. "I believe that Field knew that Wilson was out to buy the property. Field hoped to buy it and then to sell it again at a profit. Emma believes that Field was trying to get the place for some of his dog-racing friends: the owners and trainers sometimes like a nice quiet place for their kennels, where the bookies don't know what they've got up their sleeves. The Broadgarth buildings would make good kennels, and a big dog-breeder might think the place worth paying a stiff price for on account of its remoteness."

Kate looked shocked. "But they'd never be allowed to use that land for breeding dogs alone: the county agricultural committees wouldn't let them."

"Quite true," said Giles, "but that's where Tom Field was in a good position. He could do the necessary haymaking and ploughing, so that the land was cultivated and everything looked normal, while his dog-owning friends could keep their kennels on the quiet. You must admit that it was a very shrewd idea of Emma Brough's."

Kate nodded. "Yes. It's smart enough, but I don't believe it. Anyway, she's sure the well is all right, that's one comfort."

Macdonald put a word in here. "Did you ever find out who tried to buy the coppice and quarry pool, Hoggett, just after Miss Bourne asked to buy it?"

"I rang up Waine, the agent," said Giles. "He couldn't tell me anything about the actual person. He said the inquiry was made by a man who gave his name as Barton Smith. This chap said he'd noticed the woodland from the road and thought it was a good site for a house. Waine told him it was already sold to a lady who was buying property in the district, and there was nothing doing. Very decent of Waine, because at the time Caroline hadn't signed anything, and she might have changed her mind." Giles put on his most judicial expression and finally summed up: "I'm disposed to believe that Emma Brough used her imagination a bit in assuming there was anything phoney about the actual auction. It's plain that several people were anxious to buy

Broadgarth, but there's always intensive competition nowadays to get any small holding. The real problem remains—Field and David Wynne." He put his hand in his pocket and drew out Wynne's notebook.

"Kate will have told you about my visit to Alice Wynne?" he said to Macdonald. The latter nodded.

"Yes. Are these the specimens of handwriting? Thanks."

Macdonald studied the letter and notebook, while Giles watched him eagerly.

"Well, in my judgment you're right, Hoggett, but it's a job for the experts. Handwriting of this kind is difficult to assess, but fingerprints may tell us something. I'll go over it and tell you if I get anything definite, but I am disposed to agree with you that the two documents were written by different persons."

"Then there's only one reading of that," said Giles. "Somebody wrote that letter and sent the money in order to make Alice Wynne believe that her husband was still alive, so that she shouldn't start a hue and cry after him."

"It's the most obvious supposition, but you can't put it down as fact," said Macdonald. "Now I think I'd better phone to Bord. He ought to be back at his office by now, assuming he's writing his report. You haven't heard the evidence Mrs. Hoggett has collected; she's always the one who produces actual facts."

3

Giles's feelings when Kate told him of the still warm fireplace at Broadgarth were mixed. First he was excited, then horrified by the thought that Kate had gone to Broadgarth alone.

"Anything might have happened," he said portentously.

"Don't be silly," she replied. "The only thing you know for certain that set you off on this crazy notion about a crime at Broadgarth is that Francis Rolph fell down and broke his crown. The rest of the business is pure supposition on your part." She did not tell Giles that she herself had been within an ace of hurling a knobbly portion of millstone grit at a police inspector. Instead she went on: "I didn't go into the house alone. Inspector Bord was there, as he wanted to see the house, so we went in together, but it was *I* who noticed the hearth was warm."

"Did Bord ask you why you were there?" he asked.

"Of course. I'd a perfect right to be there. I'm looking after the place for Caroline," she replied. "I told him I was looking at the well." Suddenly Kate laughed, her laughter bubbling up, fresh and spontaneous. "He's not being superior any longer, Giles. He's really convinced you're on to something, and he's a bit fed up with himself that he didn't co-operate with you to start with."

"Why, has he found out anything else?" demanded Giles.

"He's found out that David Wynne and Tom Field have both disappeared from the district, and I'll bet any money that when I left him he started poking about in that well. You believe there's a corpse in the quarry pool—with very little evidence to go on. Now Bord believes there's a corpse in the well—with still less evidence."

"The *well!*" exclaimed Giles, but before he could say anything else, Macdonald came back.

"Bord isn't back," he said. "They say they had a phone message from him saying he was going to Preston. I'm a bit surprised, because we'd more or less made an appointment to meet at seven o'clock this evening."

"Preston? He's gone after Field," said Giles, and Kate put in:

"He can't have found a body in the well, then, or he'd have been too busy to go to Preston."

"Yes, I think you're right there," agreed Macdonald, and turned to Giles. "I'm going up to Broadgarth. Will you come with me?

You know much more about farm-houses than any of the police force."

"Of course I'll come," said Giles with alacrity.

"Right. If you could think out the best way for two men to approach the place unobserved it might be useful. It's just coming dusk. Bord seems to have gone after Field in Preston. For myself, I shan't be surprised if Field is still in Lunesdale."

Kate Hoggett sighed. "When you *do* come in, you'll find hot soup on the stove and cold pies in the dairy," she said resignedly. "I suppose Dick's done the milking. I take no responsibility for the cows, Giles."

"They'll be all right," he said callously.

Mr. Giles Hoggett had forgotten he was a farmer. As Kate said, detection was demoralising.

THIRTEEN

I

THE DAYLIGHT HAD QUITE FADED WHEN MACDONALD AND GILES Hoggett set out, though a luminousness in the southern sky showed the dark line of the fells across the river: early moonrise, thought Giles, as he opened the field gate across the road from the farmstead. It was Macdonald who had said they had better set out up the gill rather than by the road, and Giles had been a bit surprised, because he hadn't realised that Macdonald was quite so familiar with the locality as his suggestion implied. They climbed in silence: Giles knew the route well, and led without hesitation, for he had eyes which equalled a cat's in that queer colourless half-light which most people call darkness. He was sure-footed and he moved silently, keeping the deep cleft of the rocky gill on his right, aware of every tree and bush as a something blacker than the shadows about him. He could hear the water cascading over the rocks, for the beck was in spate, and he listened for the trickle of the higher spring, the "holy well" Kate called it, before halting for a breather, for it was a steep climb. The road was just above them now, and they would have to cross it: then they would skirt Edmund Troutbeck's newly sown oats and cross the meadow which had been limed earlier in the month.

Macdonald stood beside Giles close to the little reservoir of the "holy well," and somehow Giles was aware that the C.I.D. man was listening. They waited until a car travelling eastwards rushed up the switchback hill by the church, lost its impetus before the summit and had its gears changed with a clatter and protest, and then Macdonald touched Hoggett's elbow to indicate they should move on. They crossed the road and climbed a gate and set out northwards, climbing the steeply sloping field.

As he walked, Giles Hoggett could not help a faint feeling of satisfaction. Bord *had* been very offhand at first, and now the inspector was so hot on the trail that he had forgotten his appointment with a chief inspector of the Criminal Investigation Department: and *he*, Giles Hoggett, was in action with the C.I.D. The least conceited of men, Giles knew that he was there in the capacity of guide only. It was his local knowledge, his ability to see in the dark and to move without making a noise, that made him useful: still, however humble his role, it was very satisfactory to be made use of.

They walked on steadily, rising all the time, across empty pastures. It was too early in the year for the milking cows to be left out at nights, and the ewes with their lambs were all in pastures near the farmsteads. Giles had never known a more silent walk as he swung over the rough grass while the moon cleared the fell-top way back across the Lune.

They approached Broadgarth from the south, and by previous arrangement they parted before nearing the house: Macdonald, who had the back door key in his pocket, went to the rear, Hoggett to the front door. Hoggett stood in the shadows for some minutes before he heard a sound: then, for all Macdonald's care, the bolts on the front door groaned and the old door creaked as he opened it. By common consent the two men stood still and listened again, but no sound came. They both went inside, leaving the door unfastened. Giles realised, as Kate had done, that the house was unexpectedly warm; he stood very still while his senses assessed the "feel" of the house. There was nothing to hear: the solid old building was utterly still. The smell was that of all stone farm-houses: crumbling mortar, a faint mildew, old wood smoke, the smell of the chimney, and pervading it all the smell of hay and straw and shippon. Giles, analysing the smell as it were, with his experienced nose, was aware of stale tobacco smoke, too, very faint, but perceptible. As for light, his eyes soon accustomed themselves to conditions inside the house, for the moonlight drifted through the little mullioned windows and reflected back from stone flags and whitewashed walls.

According to plan, it was Giles who did the searching, because he knew the arrangement of the building. Macdonald stood motionless, in the darkest shadows behind the front door, which stood a crack open, inviting a fugitive to bolt for the open. As Macdonald had said, if a man were hiding anywhere in the house, he must inevitably know that some other person had entered it, for the old locks and doors could not be silenced. What the fugitive might not realise was that there were now two newcomers in the house: one to search, one to guard the two doors.

Having got his bearings, Giles Hoggett prowled round the kitchen. He could see the square table, and the camp-bed which Caroline had brought for Rolph to sleep on, and the folding garden chair which Kate had lent her. Giles thought how cosy a man could be, with a good log fire for company, and one of those blankets hung over the small window to hide the tell-tale glow of the fire. In his rubber-soled shoes, he walked across to the dairy, which opened out of the kitchen. There was enough light coming through the tiny window to show its emptiness. Even in that faint light Giles realised how well Emma Brough had set the place to rights before she left—every wall and shelf and slab freshly whitewashed, and all junk removed. "Clean as a whistle," he meditated. From the dairy and kitchen he prowled silently into the tiny parlour; bare as Mother Hubbard's cupboard. He felt round the darkest shadows, where eyesight could not help him, by the back door, and then before he went up the ancient stone stairway, he paused to consider, scratching his grey head thoughtfully. Mr. Hoggett's next proceeding puzzled Macdonald considerably: ignoring the C.I.D. man completely, Giles went outside very quietly and returned with something in his hand which Macdonald could just see was a very ancient bucket. Being positive that all Mr. Hoggett's actions had a rational purpose behind them, Macdonald's own vigil was enlivened by deducing the reason for carrying an empty bucket upstairs. As a weapon it was not handy. And then Macdonald tumbled to it. The house was gabled, like the barn, and there would be a loft above the bedroom ceilings. These rooms would be low, and the bucket would be just high enough to give the long-limbed Hoggett the necessary "leg-up" to reach the manhole in the ceiling which would give access to the loft above. Macdonald's reasoning was perfectly sound: Giles Hoggett went into each of the little moonlit bedrooms—white and bare—and then turned his bucket upside down and performed the not negligible feat of standing on it long enough to push back the trapdoor above his head. This performance could not be carried out in silence. Having shoved the trapdoor back, Mr. Hoggett (as he later told Kate) had an uncomfortable feeling of extreme vulnerability. Though his fingers could grip the edge of the manhole, his balance was precarious, and what he really expected was a wallop over the head from above, the man below being at an obvious disadvantage in this act. Nothing happened: holding on with his left hand and hoping the bucket would not crumple beneath his weight, Giles got a torch from his pocket in his right hand, managed to get his head through the manhole, and shone his torch around the loft, at the same time heartening himself by growling audibly and fiercely, "Come out of that," thereby inducing Macdonald to believe that the search was rewarded. But there was nothing there, and Giles got down from his bucket with mixed feelings of relief and disappointment. He went downstairs and whispered to Macdonald:

"It's impossible that any one is hidden here. I'm going to search the buildings, the barn first."

2

Caroline Bourne had admired the barn when she saw it in daylight. It was a noble structure, with its great beams and wide gable end, more impressive and more beautifully proportioned than many a church. When Giles saw it in the moonlight, its interior seemed vast. There was a gap high up in the stonework of the gable to admit light, but in addition to this the moonlight barred the floor from the space above the great double doors: it shone in puzzling lines between some of the flags of the ancient roof and even through gaps in the masonry of the walls. Giles knew all about barns, but he had to admit that Broadgarth barn in the moonlight was a creepy sight. He made for the hayloft above the shippon: the ladder was just like his own, comfortingly familiar, with a great rope hanging beside it to steady him, a rope worn smooth by many a gnarled hand. There was some hay left in one corner of the loft, and Giles booted it about, feeling oddly reminded of one of his own cows who tossed her hay petulantly to demonstrate that what she really wanted was a nice succulent mangold. He then went down to the floor of the barn again and swung himself over the "boostings," the wooden partition dividing the shippon from the threshing-floor. There was yet another door here, the door through which the cows entered their stalls, and he set this wide to admit as much light as possible. The cow-stalls were all lime-washed (Emma Brough again), the concrete floors swept and clean. Giles glanced round: there was a heap of sacks in the farthest corner. Sacks... well, there were always sacks about a farm: chaff sacks, grain sacks, fertiliser sacks. Conscientiously, yet with a queer sinking in the pit of his stomach, Giles grabbed the sacks and pulled them back. Quite unexpectedly, he had to put out a hand to the boostings to support himself. For the first time he realised to the full that crime detection was not always exhilarating.

3

Giles Hoggett stood there for several seconds. He remembered a lot in that short period of time. He remembered that when he had co-operated with Macdonald over the murder of Gordon Ginner in the dales, he, Giles, had never seen the corpse of the dead man. Macdonald had found it, tied up in a sack anchored to the roots of a willow tree in the river. Macdonald had said: "You can get out. I've found your sack." That was all. Giles had not even seen the stretcher men arrive, nor the stretcher carried over the green dales to the ambulance on the south side of the river. He realised now the whole thing had been like one of those problems in the detective novels he enjoyed so much. Now, with a man's body prone at his feet in the moonlight, and a mess of blood on the ground, black in the ghostly light, it wasn't anything like a detective novel. It was just grim and tragic and appalling. He could see very little of the body at his feet: the face was mercifully hidden, but he could see the dark head with its ruffled black hair, and he thought of Alice Wynne saying, "It's not so bad as people think… David's like that…" And David was here at his feet, a huddled, ungainly lump on the shippon floor. And Giles Hoggett, who had regarded detection as a stimulating mental exercise, just stood still and stared mournfully, because he was quite incapable of doing anything else. He had read about corpses, he had theorised about corpses, but he had never been brought up against the dreadful reality of the dead body of a murdered man. There was something paralysing about it, something which shook him to the very core of his being.

4

Somehow Giles made his way out of the door where sedate cows had been wont to amble to their stalls: he rounded the angle of the barn and eventually found Macdonald by the fold-yard gate. Giles could find no coherent words. He said miserably, "It's in there."

Macdonald did not ask him what "it" was, as most men would have done. Even in the moonlight he could see enough of Hoggett's face to guess what he had found. The C.I.D. man made for the door of the shippon, swift and quiet and resolute, and Giles followed him, thankful that he was not left alone to deal with this horror. As though instinctively, Macdonald turned in at the shippon door and in a second was bending over the huddled form. Gruffly, in a voice which he could not control, Hoggett said, "It's David Wynne. He's dead."

Macdonald, bending over the body, had switched on his torch, and the sudden light, reflected back from the lime-washed walls, made Giles blink. Then he heard Macdonald's businesslike voice:

"It's not David Wynne, you fool, and he's not dead. It's Bord. Hold my torch..."

If the roof had fallen on him, Giles Hoggett could not have been more surprised. Had an angel from heaven appeared in the beam of Macdonald's torch it could not have been more welcome than that prosaic voice informing Giles Hoggett he'd been a fool.

"Are you quite sure?" he asked.

"Quite sure. Hold that torch steady. You're too kind-hearted for this sort of thing: your Kate would have had the gump to find out if a wound was still bleeding. Cripes, he's had a swipe for his pains... that'll larn him. I've got a first-aid dressing somewhere... If you don't hold that torch steady I'll brain you."

Slowly, Giles Hoggett recovered his normal resilience. Obediently he held Macdonald's powerful torch at an angle which gave most assistance to the work of first-aid and least light on the tiny window which allowed a modicum of daylight to the cows. Giles was still suffering from the shock of surprise, surprise that the discovery of what he had taken for a corpse had so shattered all his usual initiative and powers of observation. Macdonald, his deft fingers busy with wads and strapping from his first-aid packet, put in a word here:

"A real corpse with a bloody head is a bit different from an imaginary or theoretical one, isn't it? You won't forget that in a hurry. Also it's worth while remembering that a preconceived notion plays the devil with the mind. You'd got a theoretical corpse in your head, labelled David Wynne, so you identified this chap with your own preconceived notion."

"Yes," agreed Giles humbly, "but you said Bord had gone to Preston."

"No, I didn't. I said someone had rung through *saying* that Bord had gone to Preston. I didn't even say I believed it myself. Well, that's the best I can do with this outfit."

"Shall I go for a doctor?" asked Giles.

"No, certainly not. You can find a door or a gate or a hurdle, something we can lift him on to and carry him into the house with a minimum of shaking. You can use your torch now."

"You mean it doesn't matter if I'm seen?"

"I mean that the chap who batted a police inspector over the head isn't likely to stay on the premises in order for me to arrest him. Attacking a policeman is one of those crimes which it's better to avoid... Get a hurdle if you can, it's lighter than a door and Bord's pretty solid."

Giles set off with alacrity. He remembered having seen a hurdle in one of the fences when he had taken Caroline round the farm. He didn't need his torch, for the moon was bright, and he carried back the hurdle and negotiated it through the shippon door handily and swiftly. It wasn't David Wynne and it wasn't a corpse, that was all that mattered for the moment.

"Good! Let it down here," said Macdonald, "just beside him. My coat over it, so. Now yours... right. You did ambulance work once, didn't you? Remember, this chap isn't dead, but a jolt's not going to make him more alive. You take his legs—gently does it."

Slowly, with infinite care, Macdonald lifted the heavy shoulders and they got the unconscious man flat on the improvised stretcher and negotiated it through the shippon door and over the cobbles of the fold yard and so into the house, where they laid it, hurdle and all, on the camp-bed.

"He won't notice that a hurdle's not comfortable, and the less we move him the better," said Macdonald. "Take one of those blankets and get it over the window. You can see that window from a distance."

Hoggett obeyed, and shut out the moonlight, so that dense blackness encompassed them.

Macdonald switched his torch on. "There are some candles up there—right. Well, now it's your job to light a fire. The only thing we can do for Bord at the moment is to keep him warm and quiet."

Tucking a blanket round the inanimate form, Macdonald went on: "A couple of warm bricks would help warm him up. Apart from that, there's nothing you can do but stay with him."

"If he recovers consciousness—?"

"He won't, or I'm a Chinaman. He'll lie like a log for hours. You can put a kettle on and boil some water. Doctors dote on boiling water; but there won't be a doctor here before daylight probably."

Macdonald straightened himself and then added: "You stay here. I've got other fish to fry. When I've gone, bolt the door behind me and don't open it unless you recognise my voice, or Reeves' voice. He's around somewhere. And remember this: the chap who laid Bord out took an almighty risk and knew what he was doing.

It's your business to stay here with Bord and see there's no more trouble. Got that?"

"Aye," said Mr. Hoggett, very soberly.

Macdonald added a word from the door. "Don't look so glum. After all, you found him pretty quickly, and you were very competent with that hurdle. You can tell Kate I said so."

Suddenly Giles Hoggett grinned. "It's all right. I know I'm a mug."

"If that's so, I could do with a few more mugs," rejoined Macdonald.

In a moment he was gone, and Giles obediently bolted both back and front doors and went back into the kitchen and found kindling and logs, while Inspector Bord snored on his hurdle.

Giles looked down at the rather ghastly face almost tenderly. "Bord must have been a bit of a mug, too," he thought to himself. "I wonder…" and his thoughts joined the wood-smoke and spread out far beyond the silence of the stone farm-house.

FOURTEEN

I

AS MACDONALD MADE HIS WAY ROUND THE BROADGARTH buildings, he was conscious of feeling more than a little exasperated, and being a very fair man he took himself to task first to decide if it was his own error which had precipitated things to this point, for he was quite sure that the attack on Bord meant that a climax was near at hand, and in that climax a number of persons must surely be involved. So far as Macdonald himself was concerned, the business which had brought him north was exactly what he had stated to Bord: he had come, on information received, to arrest a man named Maredeth, whom the Irish police believed to be travelling on the Heysham boat. When it became clear that the wanted man was not on the boat, Macdonald had gone to Ulverston, in the Furness district, because he knew that Maredeth owned a house there. Again drawing a blank, he had travelled south along the coast via Grange and Arnside, and it was during this journey that it had occurred to him that the old road over the sands might be put to modern use by the evaders of Customs and Excise. It had been a very wet day, but he had got out of his car several times to study the coast and the sands. He had gone to see the Hoggetts because Wenningby was very conveniently situated for his present inquiry, and on arriving there he had been told the story of Rolph's adventure at Broadgarth.

Macdonald was not prone to jump to rash conclusions, but in his own experience he had often found that any abnormal circumstances in an area subject to police investigation were worth investigating, because there was more than a fifty per cent chance they might be connected with the matter under investigation. Now Inspector Bord was an experienced police officer: he knew why Macdonald was in his district, and he had an equal chance with Macdonald to assess the possibilities implicit in Rolph's mishap. Bord had not believed in Rolph and he had started by being inimical to Hoggett, but Macdonald was too well aware of the tenuousness of his own half-formed theories to thrust them on Bord.

During the few hours he had spent in London early that same morning, Macdonald had set on foot a number of inquiries: some of these concerned Judge Warrender and the list of passengers on the journey from India he had mentioned to Hoggett. Some of them concerned the syndicate which had bought Hauxhead Castle and other similar properties in the north. Reports on these inquiries had not yet come in; there had been no time for them to come in. Macdonald had also tried to get into contact with Francis Rolph, only to find that he was out of town. A night's pondering over all the evidence he had collected up north, plus Giles Hoggett's medley of facts and theories, had developed a hunch in Macdonald's mind that the queer business at the quarry pool was serious, and that it might involve the murder which Giles Hoggett had postulated plus other dealings connected with the missing Maredeth. On reaching this conclusion, Macdonald had phoned to Bord, arranging to see him at seven o'clock that evening, and had included a guarded statement that things might be expected to be lively at Bord's end and circumspection was advisable. The total result of all the care which Macdonald had taken was that Bord had got himself knocked out, a thing which an experienced police officer should have avoided doing, and Giles

Hoggett, who might have been useful at a crisis, was occupied in looking after Bord.

Macdonald was convinced that there would be further alarums and excursions that night. He did not believe that it was Tom Field who had, unaided, both knocked out Bord and then sent a telephone message to ensure that no search for him should be set on hand immediately. That message was sent in order to gain time, the respite of one night. It could not have been supposed that Bord's absence would be disregarded for more than one night, and during the hours of darkness events must happen which would put both Macdonald's and Hoggett's theories to the test.

As he made his cautious way up the sloping fields towards the coppice and the quarry pool, Macdonald pondered over the chances of getting to a telephone, and knew that he couldn't risk it. If Hoggett had been available, it would have made a lot of difference, but Macdonald would not leave the helpless Bord alone in the farmhouse. Hoggett had to be counted out. There remained Macdonald himself, Detective Inspector Peter Reeves and a keen young C.I.D. recruit named Walsh, who had been in the Commandos and was a lad after Macdonald's own heart. These two men would be at the quarry pool. In addition to this party, another group of C.I.D. men were on duty between Hest Bank and Silverdale, on the shores of the bay, 'twixt Kent and Keer. Kate Hoggett's old jingle came into Macdonald's mind, "Many a good mare lost 'twixt Kent and Keer," and he wondered if his own reputation for forethought was going to be lost, too, buried in the quicksands of that treacherous bay. "There's only just time to cross between the tides," Kate had said. Time—that was the trouble. There wasn't even enough time to get to a telephone.

Macdonald had given Reeves a point at which to meet him. He had racked his brains over this: he wanted to leave the old cottage and the ruined shippon severely alone, also the track where Kate had noticed the trampled bluebells. He had thought of the oak trees, which Giles wanted to buy from Caroline—there were only three oaks in that coppice—but he wasn't at all sure that Reeves, with all his varied information, was able to distinguish an oak from a sycamore or an ash, so Macdonald had fallen back on the two-inch Ordnance Survey and stipulated the highest point of the ridge at the western end of the quarry pool.

As he crept through the undergrowth of the coppice, where the moonlight shivered on every bud and twig, Macdonald comforted himself with the thought of Reeves. Reeves would be at his point, he always was. Once or twice during his progress, Macdonald had stopped to listen when he heard a car on the Chapelton Lonsdale road: once he had heard the unmistakable grumble of a tractor. Was this Tom Field, he wondered, coolly risking everything to get to the quarry pool? Knowing that Bord was immobilised, Field might have thought he was safe for a few hours, safe to dispose of any evidence which might involve him with the relentless processes of the law. But the tractor rumbled on eastwards—some hard-working ploughman wending his weary homeward way in a manner undreamed of by the famous elegist. Macdonald skirted the pool and climbed the ridge on all-fours, remembering Rolph's experience when he stood up against the sky. Calculating that he had reached the point stipulated, Macdonald breathed "Reeves," and was startled by the closeness of the whispered response:

"Here, Chief! You're almost touching my boots."

Macdonald crept closer, until his face was a few inches from Reeves. Good campaigners both, the two C.I.D. men were snug on a ground-sheet, a camouflage net above them, invisible in the moonlight, so cunningly was it intertwined with twigs and dead leaves. Lying prone beside his two scouts, Macdonald whispered:

"We're in for a lively night. Bord's got himself knocked out, head cut right open. Hoggett found him in the shippon down there. That means if anybody's going to make a move, it'll be to-night."

Reeves grunted: a faint sound of acquiescence, not dissatisfied. "Do the others know?" he whispered back. "The others" were the party on the shores of the bay.

"No," replied Macdonald. "I only knew myself half an hour ago. We ought to warn them. The point is how. Their field telephone isn't laid yet."

"Send Walsh," breathed Reeves. "He's been learning his map by heart all day. He knows their point. Tell him, chum," admonished Reeves. Walsh took up the whispered tale.

"We got the Admiralty charts, as you said, sir. Bateson's posted in sight of the mussel-bed off Red Bank: Long and Grey are on Warton sands. I've got my bike just off the road. I can easily find them. Turn left at Broadgarth gate, first right, and it's a plain road to the coast through Western le Sands, four miles, all downhill. I'll cross the sands after that and contact Bateson."

Macdonald found time to remember that only that morning Walsh had never even heard of Morecambe sands. He was a Sussex lad. Now, having studied Ordnance Survey maps and Admiralty charts for a few hours he had got the district photographed on his brain apparently: roads, contours, railways and canals, all taped. Modern military training did that.

"Those sands," said Macdonald. "They're dangerous."

"Not inshore, sir. The quicksands are beyond the Keer channel. Nothing doing there. That's why Bateson chose the mussel-bed. We soon saw about having to cross the railway and the Lancaster-Kendal canal. Reckon we've spotted the only routes."

That whispered spasmodic conversation made Macdonald realise the amount of intelligent map-reading young Walsh had done.

"I do like chaps who know how to work quickly," he murmured. "All right, Walsh. Go and warn Bateson to look alive, and come back here as fast as you can. What about phoning for some more men—"

"Not for here, sir," put in Reeves in an urgent whisper. "It's too late. A couple of local chaps floundering in here at zero hour would just put the lid on it. Walsh and I took an hour to crawl in here. Tell 'em to mark the roads, but for the love of Mike keep 'em away from here. Walsh can come back. He's all right. Knows his stuff."

"O.K., sir?" murmured Walsh.

"O.K., laddie," replied Macdonald.

The chief inspector lay very still. He heard a tiny rustle of leaves, no more, but he knew that young Walsh was no longer in the shelter.

"Snakes also ran. Never knew such a kid," murmured Reeves.

2

Lying prone in the shadow of the net, Macdonald uncovered the luminous dial of his watch. Only half-past nine; it seemed hours since he and Hoggett had left Wenningby, and it might be many more hours before they got back there. He had time to admire the situation Reeves and Walsh had chosen. Below them, the quarry pool lay black for the most part. The rising moon only caught the narrow arm of water which ran southwards at its farther end. Between the bare meshed branches of ash and beech the stars glimmered and the sky was light. A willow bush on the farther bank, covered with fluffy, pollen-laden catkins, shone white under the moon, like white lilac. The gable and chimneys of the old cottage were black against the sky.

Macdonald valued Reeves' silent companionship: in such vigils as these he never fidgeted, he never fussed: he seemed almost to go into a coma, so utterly still was his body, so silent his breathing. Yet Macdonald knew that no bushman could be more alert than this nimble Cockney detective at his side; when action was called for, Reeves was like a released spring.

On that peaceful moonlight night sounds carried astonishingly. Distant cars and yet more distant trains made themselves audible; when cars passed on the road their headlights blazed spectacularly in the woodland; even cycle lamps threw up trunks and branches into black relief, but the first relevant sound they heard was not heralded by the lights of any vehicle. Even as his own quick ears picked up a distant sound Macdonald felt Reeves stir at his side. It was footsteps they heard: at first the rhythmic sound of a quiet walker on a hard surface: perhaps "felt" described it better than "heard" thought Macdonald: it was a sort of vibration, a regular beat. It ceased for a few seconds, and then became perceptible again nearer at hand. The walker had left the road and turned into the track at "Broadgarth gate," the junction of track and road. Then the footsteps left the track and took to the woodland: the rustle of undergrowth and an occasional cracking stick told their own story. Macdonald analysed the newcomer's progress by locating the sound. He had turned towards the old cottage and was prowling about in it. He walked right through the cottage apparently, for he emerged on the side nearer to the watchers, by what had once been the back door, only there was no door left. Very slowly the footsteps came along the track, pausing outside the ruined shippon and then continued to the verge of the quarry pool. There they ceased.

Macdonald had raised himself a little: if he had judged the sound correctly he thought he should be able to see the cautious walker, but he could see nothing, hear nothing. He half expected to hear the ripple of water made by a swimmer, and strained his eyes in the darkness to discover any movement on the surface of the pool. Again, nothing.

Reeves whispered against Macdonald's ear: "Reckon he's lying on the ridge, like us, watching out…"

Watching out—but what for? queried Macdonald to himself. Was he suspicious of the very silence, waiting for a sign, waiting for a signal? There was nothing to be done but to wait also: there was no point in breaking cover to investigate an eccentric who was doing precisely nothing.

Once again the two detectives settled into immobility. "Five minutes each, turn and turn about," breathed Macdonald. Reeves understood. One was to concentrate on the spot where the newcomer must be, one was to watch and listen over the whole area they could see. Both knew the intense difficulty of watching any given spot intently for an indefinite time, especially in that difficult half-light of the moon filtering through the branches. Macdonald took the first five minutes: the odd part of it was that when he concentrated on the one spot he became largely oblivious to the spaces beyond. He told Reeves later that he believed someone could have come up behind him without his realising it, so intent were his senses on trying to perceive any movement on the ridge across the pool. At the end of five minutes they changed over, and so it went on. Four times they had alternated watches: it was at the close of Reeves' second spell that Macdonald whispered: "A car has pulled up and backed off the road away to the west: that's the turning Walsh would have taken."

"O.K. Our chap's moving. Watch out."

Watch? Well, there was nothing to see, very little to hear. Just a faint scraping of cloth against rock, the least shuffle of leaves moved by an incautious foot. The unseen was crawling on all-fours—but where? Gradually Macdonald realised that the movement was away from them, down the slope, towards Broadgarth. Macdonald remembered his own instructions to Hoggett: "Bolt both doors. Don't open them unless you hear my voice or Reeves'." Hoggett was a reliable chap: he could be counted on to do what he was told. At the conclusion of his five minutes Macdonald nudged Reeves.

"He's gone, down towards Broadgarth."

"Want me to shadow him?"

"No. Our job's here."

"Good! There's a party coming up. I reckon there's three sets of footsteps altogether: two from the west, one from the east. Listen!"

As he listened, Macdonald was aware that Reeves moved a little beside him, loosening up, giving cramped muscles a stretch, drawing up his knees, flexing his fingers. A man is not at his best, physically, after lying prone for an hour or so on cold rock. Reeves had no intention of letting cramp or stiffness incommode him. He was a past-master in the matter of muscular control.

3

Young Walsh was enjoying his "night-out." Having snaked his way through the coppice he reached the road a few hundred yards west of the quarry pool and recovered the cycle which he had hidden in the undergrowth. It was a good cycle, built to a racing model, though professional discretion caused its efficiency to be camouflaged to the likeness of a rusty and muddy antique. Having listened intently for a while, Walsh got his machine on the road and wheeled it along for some yards. It was not until he was clear of the borders of the coppice that he switched on its lights. In the reflected glow, Walsh looked very much like an oil-stained young artisan: he wore old dungarees, an ancient mack and a still more ancient beret, having found on inquiring from Reeves that this type of headgear was now popular among tractor drivers and farm workers in Lunesdale, some years after most young men in the south had discarded this fashion.

Mounting his decrepit-looking bike, Walsh set out on his journey to the coast. On the main road he made great speed, for he was an expert cyclist, but after he had turned right towards Western le Sands, he soon found that he had to "take it steady." He was actually on the same road along which Caroline Bourne had driven to the auction at Carnton, and the abrupt turn and steep hill beyond it startled Walsh by its unexpectedness. He swung over at a perilous angle and for some little distance one foot acted as an improvised brake—whereby he learned that the road which had looked so straightforward on the Ordnance Survey had to be treated with judgment—like most cross-country roads in the hilly Lunesdale district. He rode through a small village, and past a limestone quarry which was startlingly white in the moonlight. Walsh noticed the limestone and was a bit puzzled by it, because it was so different from the rock formation at the quarry pool, a rock which he had plenty of opportunity to study while he was there with Reeves. He knew that he had to keep straight on through Western le Sands and that he could not risk any short-cuts, because he had got to cross the main Lancaster-Carlisle road, the Lancaster-Kendal canal, and the Furness branch of the railway line before he reached the coast. Another mile brought him to the main-road crossing and the first traffic he had met since leaving the quarry: the great arterial road with its stream of lorries and brightly-lit buses seemed in a different world from the remote stillness of that coppice, only four miles away in distance, centuries remote in time. Once across the main road and the canal, silence and darkness closed in on him again, and when he had ridden over the railway crossing he soon found himself on open ground—the saltings, the last pastures which ran down to the sands. There was no one about, but Walsh suddenly became aware of how visible and noticeable he would be in the moonlight if he continued on his bike. He dismounted and hid his machine in the final hedge, after collecting a camouflage cape from the carrier. Then he walked swiftly over the short grass to the sands.

There was a ridge between the saltings and the sands proper and he slid over this and saw the sands stretching out before him in the moonlight. The sight almost made the tough young ex-Commando gasp. He had read about the extent of the sands: he knew that the tide went out for miles, but no reading could have prepared him for that seemingly limitless stretch of sand, white under the moon. Walsh flung himself down by the ridge and considered. Once he set out across these sands, it seemed to him, he must be visible for miles in this moonlight, a black, obvious upright whose presence could not be concealed. He sat and concentrated on the map-reading he had done. He knew that the black bank mussel-bed was due west from the point where he now sat, nearly a mile distant across the sands. The tide was falling, for which he was thankful. He didn't feel so confident about these sands as he had done when he spoke to Macdonald in the coppice. He looked up and got his bearings from the stars, and then got under his camouflage cape—it was sand-coloured and dull in texture. He had done a lot of crawling in the Commandos, complete with tommy-gun and service kit—well, he could crawl now, over the glistening sands of Morecambe Bay, until he had put a sufficient distance between himself and the shore to give him a chance of "slipping into the landscape." As for being observed from the sea, Walsh knew the sea must be somewhere, but it was so far away that observation from that quarter need not be bothered about. Stubbornly and skilfully he crawled on under his cape, making remarkably good progress considering his mode of locomotion: sweating and uncomfortable he crawled on over stranded jellyfish and starfish, over small crabs and slimy weed, only pausing occasionally to take his bearings to ensure that he was still going due west. It was not until he reckoned he had put over a quarter of a mile between himself and the shore that he risked getting on to his feet, and even then he bent double and moved at a shambling trot.

So immense was the space of moonlit sand about him, that Walsh had something almost like a shock when he first caught sight of the man he was searching for: on a rough patch of sand away to the west there was a darker blur, and Walsh decided that this was where he could afford to hurry. Shoving his cape under his arm he ran, an eerie flying figure on that immense expanse. As he drew nearer the mussel-bed he realised that the dark blur which he had decided was a human being had disappeared, and he had a moment of doubt; was he imagining things and rushing to his own doom in the quicksands around the channel which the River Keer ploughed through the sands? But Walsh was a realist at heart: if he believed in anything at all, it was in the objectivity of a map-reading, and he knew he had kept his face due west. It was this conviction that kept him running at speed, that made him risk speaking clearly when he neared the dark line of the mussel-bed and the ridge of sand which might have been a child's fortification on the sands, or else a very lonely grave.

"Bateson!" he said urgently. "Bateson, it's Walsh..."

The "grave" seemed to heave itself up.

"What the hell...?" demanded the gruff voice of a disgruntled C.I.D. man. "If this is your idea of 'identifying yourself with the landscape' I don't think much of it."

"Sorry, sir. Message from the chief inspector. Urgent. I had to hurry."

"And to think I buried myself in this ruddy sand for your benefit. Get down here: nice wet trench, plenty of room for two. What's the trouble?"

"Things have got out of gear, sir. One of the local men's been laid out at that farm-house, and the chief reckons if there's going to be a move it's going to be to-night, probably just before the tide turns."

"Cripes! Have you got the local men out? I had young Lane with me, but I had to send him inshore; there's some sort of activity going on with a mussel-cart and a donkey-man. If you ask me, they're planning to get something buried on these qualified sands."

"We haven't contacted the local men, sir. No time. I came out here at the double to put you wise."

"Thank you for nothing. Two of us here... and the deuce knows how many miles we're supposed to keep under observation. I came out here to reconnoitre, and now you say the balloon's going up... Steady, lad... flat on your face... Hear anything?"

"Motor-boat... far out. Wind's from the west."

Walsh crouched beside the older man on the wet sand. He was enjoying himself again; alone on those vast sands he had felt a feeble thing, now, having made his "point"—and justified his belief in a compass course—he was ready for anything.

He listened. "They've changed course out there; heading south."

"Umps... They've been cruising about this last half-hour... Waiting for the tide to turn? I don't know. It beats me altogether..."

"They've put about... They're nearer inshore," said Walsh.

Bateson grunted, almost inaudibly. "Two of us. Hell. It's plain silly. See here, lad. If there's a landing party they may divide up. We'll have to separate and chance our luck. Use your wits and do what you think's best according to circumstances... What's that? Hear anything?"

"Yes... from the shore... Someone coming out."

"They would," grumbled Bateson resignedly. "Between the devil and the deep sea... Well, if it's a scrap, give 'em hell and don't mind me... once we're seen, they'll have to do one of two things—beat it or scupper us... if we're seen, shine your torch and make all the row you can, the more row the better. This is a mug's game... don't make sense..."

4

Walsh heard the older man's growl with a sense of exhilaration. The position did make sense to Walsh. He had seen so many peculiar happenings during his service career, and been in such fantastic positions, that lying in a wet trench half a mile off shore in Morecambe Bay seemed almost a commonplace. He sympathised with Bateson, because the latter seemed to him to have led rather a stereotyped life. Only two of them? Well, Walsh had often played a lone hand in far more desperate circumstances than these. Walsh had read the report which Macdonald had written in the train, because Macdonald liked his men to use their intelligence on his cases, and Walsh had studied that report as carefully as he had studied the map and charts. He knew all about this case: about Caroline Bourne's purchase of Broadgarth, about Rolph's broken crown and Hoggett's theories concerning David Wynne's death; he knew about Tom Field and his tractor and his association with the dog-racing crowd, about Hauxhead Castle and Sholto Barren's commission to Caroline, and to Walsh it *did* make sense. Although he had no idea what was going to happen in the next few minutes, he knew why he was there and he thought that Macdonald had been pretty spry. If things didn't go according to plan, that'd be just too bad, but he was quite prepared to improvise activities according to developments. The one thing that bothered him was that Macdonald had told him to get back as quickly as he could; but Walsh didn't see how he could leave Bateson alone in the present circumstances.

Bateson, a sturdy, competent C.I.D. man, was feeling none too happy at that moment. He had sent Lane off to investigate movements way back on the saltings, but Bateson hadn't anticipated a "pincer movement." If the motor-boat party landed and came in from the sea and the mussel-cart and donkey-party came out from the shore the two C.I.D. men might find themselves in difficulties. Bateson whispered to his companion:

"They can't land on a falling tide... the motor-boat would be stranded for hours."

"Don't you believe it. I've played that game," Walsh whispered back. "The motor-boat stands in as close as it can—very shallow draught they've got, some of them. Then you launch a rubber dinghy. You can paddle them in in shallow water: they float in a few inches. Drive 'em on to the sand and anchor them, and the tide'll leave you high and dry. I've done it. I know."

"Oh, do you? It's a new one on me," muttered Bateson. "I reckon they've sold too many of these Admiralty spares. Puts ideas into people's heads."

Walsh chuckled silently to himself. He hoped that neither of the parties who might be approaching would make for that spot on the sands where he and Bateson were situated. The mussel-bed was charted: it was even marked on the Ordnance Survey, and there was good hard sand between the mussel-bed and the saltings. He wriggled his camouflage cape clear of his arm. "Might as well get under this, sir. They give good cover."

Bateson grunted and with great care they spread the cloak over their trench.

"I'll watch the land side," whispered Walsh.

For the next ten minutes they lay, soaked and chilly, while Walsh argued out again to himself that if the motor-boat party meant to land it must be on a falling, not a rising, tide. Once the tide turned, it came racing in like galloping horses and turned the solid sand to quicksand faster than a man could run. It wanted only half an hour now until the tide turned... "and then, by gosh, we'd better beat it ourselves," he thought. "Wonder if the old chap can run..." Bateson was only forty-five, but he seemed elderly to the young Commando.

5

Walsh soon picked up the sound of the shore party approaching, and before long he could see the dark grouping on the moonlit sands. There was a cart—that would be one of the mussel-gatherers' carts; gathering mussels by moonlight, why not?—a nice innocent recreation and, as Bateson had said, a donkey. "What's that for—local colour?" queried Walsh. The group came on: two men, a cart pulled by a quiet nag, and a led donkey. They seemed to be making direct for the spot where the two detectives lay concealed, and Walsh had some anxious moments while he watched their progress, but they turned north a little as though to avoid the mussel-bed itself.

Looking shorewards, Walsh could make out two lights. They might be lights in the bedroom windows of some law-abiding fisherman in Western le Sands, but they might also be serving a very useful purpose as signal lights; get them in alignment and you came in "on the beam," an excellent guide across such an expanse as these sands.

Slowly the party with the cart came on, until they halted not much more than twenty yards from the two detectives. Several times Walsh thought that the cart was being driven directly at the trench where he and Bateson lay, and it seemed impossible that they could escape detection, but there was this point in favour of the hidden men: it seemed certain that the party with the cart was to meet the landing party from the motor-boat, and that meant that those with the cart would be intent on looking towards the sea, and would waste little time on scrutinising the sands or the mussel-bed. Wriggling silently—and painfully—in the trench, Walsh managed to turn so that he could get the cart in view. It was halted, and the two men beside it were talking in low voices. "A miss is as good as a mile," thought Walsh. "From our point of view it couldn't be better."

FIFTEEN

I

WALSH HAD CONTRIVED TO WRIGGLE HIMSELF INTO A POSItion from which he could see the cart and the donkey. Bateson was in the more privileged position of being able to scrutinise the vast stretch of sands ahead. The sea was somewhere far away to the west, unseen, unheard on that peaceful night. The moonlight was puzzling: despite the clearness of the white light, it was all too easy to get dazzled and confused simply by staring at the "nothingness" ahead. Bateson found it best to shut his eyes occasionally to rest them. When something did appear at last in the far distance of the wet glimmering sands, it behaved mirage-like, now seen, now unseen, but with every second that passed the half-seen blur became more substantial. Bateson had good eyesight, and he had done a bit of calculating concerning "visibility" on these flat sands in the moonlight. He reckoned that his eyes could recognise an obstruction at a distance of eight hundred yards—recognise, that is to say, that something interrupted the flatness of the sand at a distance of rather under half a mile, but he could not pick out a human figure as such until it was within less than five hundred yards. He began to understand about this rendezvous on the sands. It was calculated to take place at a point where both parties would be made invisible by the distance from observers either at sea or on the shore.

"It's a damned good meeting place," he meditated. "Talk about space to manœuvre in—by heck, it's a winner. If they scatter and run in all directions, most of 'em will get away whatever we do. Maybe this Commando chap can run, but I'm not much good at a long chase these days. And these sands are treacherous, too... they're wet and quaggy and your feet slither. If you go north, you run into that ruddy river channel... real quicksands. It's a qualified picnic..."

The distant blurs, casting confusing shadows on the wet glistening sands, drew gradually nearer. "What in blazes have they got... a sledge... or is it something to carry a corpse on?" Bateson asked himself. "Looks as though those chaps are harnessed to something... Why the heck didn't the cart go right out to meet them?"

He thought of the answer to that one in a moment or so, when he could see the laboured progress of the party from the sea. "The sand beyond the mussel-bed is too soft for the cart... the wheels would bog down. They've got runners on that thing... Who'd have believed it? Takes the blooming biscuit..."

Bateson was so much interested in the outfit approaching that he forgot all his apprehensions about future movements and watched, fascinated, as the party drew nearer, steering towards the group by the mussel-bed. A moment later he was startled by a peremptory voice from the cart. The last thing he had expected was a raised voice—but why not? Who could overhear, either from the sea or the shore? Nobody.

"Look sharp, you chaps. You're behind time. The tide will be turning in a few minutes."

"Look sharp yourself, old cock," retorted a breathless voice. "These sands are hell to-night. Not a hard patch anywhere."

"Get a move on and load the cart. We've got orders to disperse. The usual place is no go, got to be evacuated to-night. O'Maffey there, you've got to take a load for the boss, on the donkey. Usual route, and abandon your load if you're spotted. Careful now, and make it nippy. Report all O.K. this end. Dispersing according to orders."

Bateson heard every word: he heard some vigorous cursing, too, as the men began to unload the long sledge-shaped carrier.

"Here's yours, O'Maffey. Sling it up and get a move on. It'll take us all our time to move this lot."

Bateson made up his mind quickly. He leaned towards Walsh and breathed: "Follow the donkey-man. Lane will help with the others. Got that?"

"Sure."

Bateson felt the other begin to squirm out of the trench: he wasn't worried about Walsh being spotted. The men by the cart were working on the far side of it, and working much too hard to take notice of anything else. They had the tide to reckon with, and they'd cut it pretty fine. The donkey-man was already heading for the shore, leading his quiet little moke. In a moment Walsh was free of the trench and squirming over the wet sand.

2

Walsh took his time. The bloke with the donkey had got to reach the shore… plenty of time to pull up with him when they were closer inshore. Let the chap get ahead, safer that way. As long as he was just in sight, that was near enough. He'd be steering by those signal lights, and he wouldn't bother to look back… Walsh squirmed along, allowing the distance to increase between himself and his quarry. Then a cloud came over the moon and Walsh risked getting on to his feet. The man ahead went steadily, not hurrying, and when he reached the ridge by the shore Walsh was a hundred yards behind but gaining steadily. He made the ridge and felt the close turf of the saltings under his feet, and had a second of panic. Had he lost them?

No—away to the left man and donkey went on steadily. They were heading north, keeping to the coast-line. Walsh followed, beginning to wonder where his chase would end: were they going right round the shore of the bay? It must have been close on a mile they kept to the coast, and then turned abruptly inland by a rough track which led them to another level crossing and eventually to the main road, the Lancaster-Carlisle road. The traffic was much more open than it had been earlier in the evening, and the donkey-man led his moke across the road during a lull when no headlights lighted the roadway—and Walsh followed, over the main road and into a narrow stone-walled track. He was quite sure where he was going now—to the quarry, following a donkey-man and a moke with an unknown load.

As he followed through a maze of narrow roads, Walsh thought back to his map-reading again, and to Macdonald's notes concerning the old bridle tracks and pack-pony bridges. Didn't make sense? By gum it did. A donkey could carry a heavier load than a man, and a donkey was neat-footed. It would take those pack-pony bridges, un-walled and hump-backed, in a way that no horse would take them, unless it had been trained to it. This moke knew its way, too, meditated Walsh. It went on with a sort of calm unconcern, halting at gates and then going ahead on its own while the driver shot the gate. "I bet he carries something like fish manure or seaweed or mussels most nights, so that if he's seen it's all O.K.," thought Walsh. "Of course the only folk who ever *would* see him are the farmers, and they don't go out much after dark. Cripes, I wonder how long this track's been in existence? Centuries—and not used by anybody until some smart alec worked out the possibilities. It's dead north and south, across country. Where in blazes are we now?"

Their sedate progress had brought them to a considerable group of buildings. Walsh was puzzled, because he knew that no town or village of any size was mapped in this area. He dropped flat at one point, sensing that the man ahead was looking round, and he could hear a dog barking somewhere ahead. The donkey went on, and Walsh saw it clearly on the top of the little hump-backed bridge beneath which a beck in spate gurgled merrily. Beyond was a pile of masonry—and some huge arches. Suddenly Walsh connected it up with his map-reading and with Macdonald's notes. This was "Merchant's Corner," one of those strategic points in cross-country communication which have conditioned transport throughout the centuries. "Merchant's Corner" was once a meeting of the pack-pony trails: the rivers, the contours of the ground, the alternating rock and bog had made this point of prime importance when pack-ponies were the only means of transport. What was odd about it was that Merchant's Corner retained its significance in the transport system of to-day. The great mass of masonry which Walsh could see was the abutment of the aqueduct which carried the Lancaster-Kendal canal: the arches carried the railway viaduct. Beside and below these great pieces of engineering the ancient pack-pony bridge was still there, about two feet wide; its humped-back structure still bridged the beck beneath. On the rising ground beyond, the solid block of a farm-house with its barns and outbuildings looked like a fortification in the moonlight. Continuing his cautious pursuit, Walsh yet had time to reflect, and his meditations concerned contour maps and strategy. The nature of the land, the underlying rocks, the outcrops of hill and crag, the drainage which formed the rivers, these did not change. The lie of the land had conditioned the directions which men took when their feet first tramped out the primitive tracks which connected up one settlement with another. It suddenly flashed across Walsh's mind that no matter what surprising situations his career might have in store for him, he would probably never follow a more unexpected trail than this one: the track of the pack-ponies of the Kendal wool trade.

3

The donkey and its drover went serenely on in the quiet moonlight. Over another bridge, through gates, across pastures and between sparse avenues of age-old thorn trees they went on, while Walsh calculated the distance between himself and the quarry pool. He reckoned they must cross the Lancaster-Chapelton Lonsdale road any minute now, not far from "Broadgarth gate." He heard the sound of a lorry not very far away: then its engine was cut out and a moment later came the squeal of brakes. Walsh crouched in the shadows of the hedgerow when he realised how near that lorry was. The donkey had halted, and the drover let out an eerie call, the call of an owl, which was echoed from a short distance away. Then came a gruff voice.

"That you, Tom?"

"No... It's me, Jock. What the heck's up? The old man don't want you around to-night. Orders is—scram. That fool mucked it up. I knew he would."

"Scram be blowed. I've got to get rid of this here. Cap'n told me to come by the old road and I've done it. The sooner I'm rid of this the better. The boss can have it and welcome."

"Well, if you're going to the quarry tell him I'm here. I'll wait till midnight. After that I'm off. Police patrol's due at a quarter past the hour. Tom's got his outfit backed into the coppice."

"See here, Jock. You load this lot into your lorry and you can have my share of the doings. It's easy for you, working in them lime quarries—"

"Not me, mate. I never go asking for trouble. That's the boss's business. You take it along to him—and better beat it. Reckon them cops is on the fair hop to-night."

Before the donkey moved on, Walsh had thought out his next move. He couldn't cross the road in front of the lorry: he'd got to get behind it. Crouching like any fugitive, he slipped back to a field gate he'd noticed, whipped over it, a lithe and silent shadow, and ran parallel with the road for some twenty yards. Then he turned southwards again and made for the road behind the lorry. It had no tail-lights on, and was practically invisible, well off the road. In a trice Walsh had slipped across the road and gained the cover of the coppice. In the shadow of the tree he stood still and listened.

4

For the best part of an hour after Walsh had left them, Macdonald and Reeves lay in their shelter without an event of any kind to enliven their vigil. A period of waiting under such conditions was one of the hardest trials of a detective's life, Macdonald considered. He had leisure to think out all the weak points in his own theories. Although he knew perfectly well that he had been right in sending a warning message to Bateson, he couldn't help worrying about young Walsh. The quicksands of the bay began to assume nightmare proportions in Macdonald's mind—and it wasn't even that he had acted on a certainty. He had made an assumption, and it remained to be proved whether he was right or wrong. He had just come to the conclusion that Walsh, being overdue, had come to a horrible end, when his ear picked up the grumble of a tractor in the distance. It came on until it was within a few hundred yards of them before the engine was stopped.

Reeves' whisper was only just audible against Macdonald's ear. "Parked at the far end of the coppice. There's no fence there."

Silence fell again, for a space of about ten minutes. Then quite audible footsteps sounded on the road and turned in towards the track. They continued up to the ruined cottage, and then somebody whistled, quite blithely.

"Where are you, ducks?" asked an ingratiating voice, quite clear across the still waters of the pool. There was no answer, but Macdonald could hear another cautious movement, somewhere along by the ruined shippon.

"You're right again, Chief. To-night's the night." Reeves' whisper had a quality Macdonald knew well: that of sheer exhilaration. Reeves loved a scrap.

Again Macdonald waited, and the tense silence seemed to have a tingling quality. Then, without any sound preceding it at all, Macdonald saw a movement along the ridge of the pool, not twenty yards away. It was as though a rock had moved in the moonlight. He felt a nudge from Reeves' elbow, and waited again, his eyes fixed on the rock. It moved again all right, a dark, shapeless something. Then for a few seconds a tiny pencil of light was directed down to the still waters of the pool: it quivered on the surface and was then plunged into the water. It had the weirdest effect, creating a tiny patch of green luminous water, growing fainter as it sank. Macdonald was in no doubt about what the light was: a water-tight torch, with a sinker attached. There was the faintest luminousness shining upwards from the water now: it had a quality akin to the moonlight, but it was enough to give shape to the formless hump on the ridge above. Macdonald felt a small quiver run through Reeves' shoulder against his own: Reeves was laughing to himself. He had realised, as Macdonald had, that someone else was using a camouflage cape. That dark hump was a man's head and shoulders, shrouded in a cape, and the man was fishing for something in the water, fishing with a dark-gloved hand, guided by the sunken light. There was no sound, no ripple of water, and then the light was switched off.

Still Macdonald made no move. He was backing his own theory. He believed that the fishing he had seen was only a preliminary: there would be further action to follow: the hauling of a heavy weight to the surface, the lifting of that weight over the ridge. It was during this operation that he and Reeves would be best able to control matters. Waiting had been their policy that evening: they could wait a little longer.

5

Giles Hoggett, left alone with the unconscious Bord, had proceeded to do exactly as he was told. He had made a good fire, with speed and dexterity. There were logs and kindling to hand, and Giles was a pastmaster at making wood fires. He then sought for a brick, as Macdonald had suggested, and found some in the dairy, knowing that bricks are often used to support barrels and other impedimenta. Macdonald's final instruction had been hot water. Giles found the kettle, and then stood with a troubled face, scratching his head. There was a good fire, the brick was heating up nicely, there was a kettle—but no water in the house. The well, as everybody knew, was outside the back door: there was plenty of water in the well, good water, as Emma Brough had said, but it was outside, and Macdonald had told Giles to keep both doors bolted. Giles felt dejected. Now that he realised there was no water in the house, he suddenly felt exceedingly thirsty. He would have liked a cigarette, but he had a vague idea that it was improper to smoke while in charge of a concussion case. Giles sat down by the fire and thought how comforting it would be to have a cup of tea. Caroline had kindly left a tin of tea on the mantelpiece. There was no milk, but tea by itself was refreshing and helped to keep a man awake. With the good fire and nothing to do but to sit in the garden chair and watch Inspector Bord, it was all too easy to get drowsy. Unhappily, Giles studied his "concussion case." Bord might become conscious: if he did, he might moan for water. The water ought to be boiled, of course; Giles was sure Kate would insist on boiling water for an invalid. The well was *very* close to the back door. Giles decided at length to go upstairs and observe all he could from an upper window.

With great caution he went up the stone stairway and knelt down by a window. It was a very small window and it would not open, but since it faced north and the moon was shining from the south, it gave an excellent view of that portion of the garden not shadowed by the house. When Giles first saw something moving beyond the sparse hedge, he assumed that it was a cow, but quite soon he perceived that it was not a cow. Immediately his spirits rose, his sleepiness vanished, and he forgot all about the cup of tea he had wanted so badly.

Crouching by the window, he studied the interloper. Of course it might be one of the C.I.D. men: Giles made this concession to the commonplace because he was a man endowed with common sense, but he did not really believe in the possibility. It was a man's figure: a man dressed in an ordinary raincoat which looked light in the moonlight. It was certainly not Macdonald, his raincoat was darker in hue: besides, it was not so tall as Macdonald. The man made his way along the hedge and began to negotiate the gap which Giles had meant to mend for Caroline, to keep the cattle out of her "garden." Then Giles caught sight of the man's head: it was fair in the moonlight. It was not Macdonald, it was not Reeves. Giles remembered Reeves very well; he was lithe and slim and black-haired.

"It's Tom Field," said Giles to himself. "He's come back here to hide Bord's body."

Giles caught his breath. What was his duty? Below him, in the garden, Tom Field was intent on some nefarious villainy. Was he to be allowed to get away with it?

Giles realised the problem he was faced with. It was his duty to protect Bord, and he admitted that though he felt quite sure that he could deal with Tom Field unaided, there was always the possibility that he might be "dealt with" himself. He remembered Kate's trenchant comment: "If you go getting yourself drowned or knocked over the head, you'll just be being a nuisance to everybody. It isn't heroic to get knocked over the head, it's just silly."

Giles rubbed his head tenderly, partly out of uncertainty as to what to do next, partly because he had conjured up the feeling of an almighty whang on the head, like the one which had laid Bord out.

Then, quite suddenly, the man below turned and looked up at the house: his face was quite clear in the moonlight. It was unmistakable. It was not Tom Field. It was Francis Rolph.

6

Giles Hoggett had rather the same feeling that a child can have when a good card-house collapses suddenly at the addition of the final storey. The thing was so unbelievable… Rolph, an architect of repute, a friend of Caroline's, a man they all liked and trusted. In that tense moment, when he saw Rolph in the moonlight, Giles never doubted that the architect's presence meant that he, Rolph, was involved in the chain of desperate violence which seemed linked to Caroline's purchase of Broadgarth. The whole thing had started with Rolph, and there he was, in the garden below, studying the house with a thoughtful eye.

Giles Hoggett got to his feet. Field was a young man and a powerful one, not easy to down, but Hoggett felt himself perfectly capable of dealing with Rolph. Slipping downstairs, swift and quiet, Giles caught up the good stout blackthorn stick he had brought with him and went into the parlour, whence he could see the garden. Rolph was still there, still gazing at the house, his hands in the pockets of his raincoat. Seeing him there, so placid and unconcerned, Giles had his first moment of shamed doubt. Was he being too precipitate in judgment? The whole affair was crazy; it had a nightmare quality of complete unreason. One thing Giles was convinced of: he was going to see this thing through himself. If Rolph were in this, Rolph was going to answer to him, Hoggett.

His stick ready to hand, his large torch in his right hand, Hoggett shot back the bolt and opened the back door, keeping his foot against it in case of a sudden charge. He switched the torch on and directed its beam full at the architect's face.

"What are you doing here, Rolph?" he growled.

Any one who has had a torch shone suddenly in his eyes, after those same eyes have accommodated themselves to moonlight, must know that the experience is a confusing one. Rolph almost staggered back, and his hand went up instinctively to shield his eyes.

"Keep your hands up," growled Hoggett.

Rolph fairly exploded into speech.

"Hoggett, you fool, it's me, Francis Rolph. What the hell's the matter with you? Are you mad? Am I mad? Is everybody mad? For God's sake put down that ruddy torch."

SIXTEEN

I

GILES HOGGETT WAS ACUTELY AWARE OF THE IMPROPRIETY OF the whole thing. He had been told to black-out the kitchen window so as to give no sign that the farm-house was occupied: he had been told to keep Bord quiet and warm: he had been told to keep both doors bolted: and here he was, with the back door open, while Francis Rolph raised his voice in loud and bitter complaint. Hoggett was horrified: horrified at the situation, at Rolph, and at himself. He did the only thing that seemed possible: gripping his stick in one hand and his torch in the other he growled:

"You can come inside, but keep your hands out of your pockets."

Rolph came unhesitatingly towards the door. "'One cried in 's sleep, and one did say God bless us,'" he quoted, in the voice of one completely bewildered. "What *is* the matter, Hoggett? Have they banged you over the boko? Is that it? Are you hurt?"

"No. It's not I that is hurt," said Giles, unaware how odd his academic phraseology sounded in those particular circumstances.

"Not you? Good God, man, is it Caroline?" demanded Rolph.

"No," began Giles, and Rolph after an audible sigh of relief began to laugh.

"My poor chap... Here, you can't hold all those gadgets and shut the door at the same time. Let me hold the torch. What in the Lord's name are you afraid of?"

"I'm not afraid of anything," said Hoggett, "and don't make so much row. There's a casualty in there."

He managed to bolt the back door and then escorted Rolph to the kitchen door and opened it. Two candles burnt on the mantel, the fire crackled cheerfully, and Bord snored stertorously on the hurdle on the camp-bed. Rolph took a comprehensive glance round and then said:

"Well, you haven't killed him, anyway. I was beginning to wonder if you wanted me to help you hide the corpse."

"Don't be flippant," growled Giles, and Rolph protested:

"I'm not. Have a heart! Do you really expect me to be normally chatty after being treated like a criminal and then shown that... catafalque. Can't you realise the effect of all this on a normal well-behaved bloke like me?"

Giles took a deep breath: he was beginning to realise how odd things *did* look.

"Say if you tell me what you are doing here," he said.

Rolph, his head tilted, surveyed Giles thoughtfully.

"Look here, Hoggett. I don't know what's happened here, but I realise that it's not anything amusing. I wasn't amused, either, when I woke up on those qualified rocks. Did you expect me to forget all about it, and go on with the trivial round and common task as though nothing had happened? Oh, I know you all thought I'd imagined the whole thing. I don't blame you—but it happened that I *knew* I hadn't imagined it. Someone tried to put paid to me, and that poor mutt on your catafalque was just condescending about it. Well, do try to understand a chap's got some feelings. I'm a very ordinary bloke. I resent being batted over the head gratuitously."

"Yes," said Hoggett. "I realise—"

"Well, kindly realise this. I wanted to know *why*. I still do. I want to know what devilment somebody's been up to in this blasted place. So when I'd finished inspecting my Manchester job to-day I came on to Lancaster. And legged it out here. It's the hell of a long way. I went to the quarry pool, because I've got an inkling of an idea what's been going on there. There was nothing doing there at the moment, so I came down here to see who was in this house, since it was obvious that someone was here."

"How did you know there was someone here?" asked Hoggett. "You couldn't see a light."

"Admitted. But I've got a nose."

Hoggett suddenly grinned. "I wonder if Macdonald thought of that," he said. "I didn't. Of course you smelt the wood-smoke."

"Of course I did. I smelt it right up there. The wind's taking it that way. When you first kindle a fire the smell of the wood-smoke travels. I came to the back of the house. It was all dark, but I could see the smoke in the moonlight, and then you did your Lyceum melodrama act, and here we are."

"Yes. Here we are," echoed Giles. "I'm very sorry if I misjudged you; the circumstances—"

"Oh, can it!" interrupted Rolph. "I expect it was quite reasonable on your part, but I couldn't be expected to see that all at once. What I want to know is, what the hell's happened? How did this inspector bloke get his? And what's Macdonald doing here? Oh... Now I get there. My clerk rang through and told me the C.I.D. had paid a call at my digs when I was out. So Macdonald's on to it after all. So it *was* murder?"

Giles Hoggett rubbed his head unhappily. "I'm afraid so, Rolph, but we haven't found Wynne's body yet. Macdonald's up at the quarry pool with his men—"

"Is he, by gad! Are you sure? The place was as silent as the dead when I was up there half an hour or so ago."

"I'm not sure of anything, except that," said Hoggett, indicating the camp-bed. "I found him in the shippon, covered with sacks. I thought he was dead. Have you ever found a corpse, Rolph?"

"Yes. Plenty. In the blitz. Rescue squads. Thank you for nothing for reminding me of it. I'd rather forget it." He paused. "I see. That explains things a bit. You thought you'd found a corpse and you didn't enjoy it. Decent blokes never do enjoy it. That's why some detective novels make me mad. Bloody corpses aren't funny. So when you saw me you thought I was responsible. All right. No offence meant and none taken. It's a pretty sorry set-out, all the same."

Silence fell between the two men. Then Rolph said:

"Where's Caroline?"

"At Hauxhead Castle, drawing and writing. She's enjoying herself."

"She always does," said Rolph gloomily. "She's made that way. It's poor blokes like us that get let in for the doings, like this. When I... good God! What's that?"

He jumped at a sound outside. Hoggett jumped, too. There had been a quiet rat-tat at the door, three knocks, then silence, then three more knocks, and a scratching sound.

"That'll be Macdonald," said Rolph.

"It isn't," groaned Hoggett. "It's Kate."

2

Kate it was. Calm and self-possessed, looking exceedingly vigorous and sensible, with more colour in her cheeks than usual, Kate Hoggett dealt firmly with her husband's horrified disapproval.

"Don't fuss, Giles. I'm sorry if I startled you, but I had to come. I've had a telephone message from Caroline, and Macdonald ought to have the message. Good heavens! What on earth are *you* doing here?" she demanded of Rolph.

"Nothing I oughtn't to be, Mrs. Hoggett," rejoined Rolph. "But your husband has arrested me. At least I suppose he has. He thought

I'd knocked the inspector bloke out. I'm not sure he doesn't still believe it. He thinks I'm the *fons et origo*..."

Kate looked down at the recumbent police inspector. "Poor Bord!" she said. "He offered me a packet of cigarettes. Who found him?"

"I did," said Giles. "In the shippon. Under some sacks. Macdonald told me to keep him quiet and warm."

"Well, it's warm enough, but not so quiet as it might be," she said. "Who attacked him?"

"I don't know," said Giles. "I suppose he was searching the buildings after you left, and Field attacked him."

"I hope he isn't very badly hurt, but it was his own fault because he didn't believe you. I told him he'd made a mistake," said Kate to her husband.

"Well, I've made dozens of mistakes," said Giles, "including believing that Rolph was a desperate criminal. But what about this message from Caroline?"

"It's an extraordinary story," said Kate. "I didn't understand half of it. She was phoning from an A.A. box. Apparently she left a book outside in the garden and didn't remember it until she'd gone to bed. She left it in the middle of the maze and she put a coat on and went out by a back door. She heard two men talking in the maze, and realised they were talking about the quarry pool. She says she heard one say quite distinctly, 'The body's got to be moved to-night. We can't leave it any longer.' So she slipped away and went along the road to an A. A. box—having the A.A. key in her coat pocket—and phoned to me. So I came up here. I thought somehow I should find you here," she added calmly.

"You shouldn't have come, Kate," expostulated Giles.

"It's no use saying that," she retorted. "I should probably have come anyway. I'd been sitting worrying about you until I couldn't sit still any longer. I've brought you a thermos of coffee in the rucksack and some sandwiches. You'd better have them before you start. Where's Macdonald?"

"Up at the quarry pool, at least I suppose he is," said Giles, and Kate went on:

"Well, I suppose you *must* go. I'll look after Bord. It's a good thing Francis is here: he can go with you and you can look after one another."

Rolph began to laugh, silently, his shoulders shaking. "Sorry, Mrs. Hoggett. I know there's nothing to laugh about. It's just the way you women take us in hand. Caroline's just the same. Do this and do that... but, by gad, you had some pluck to come out here by yourself."

"It'd have taken much more pluck to sit by myself and worry," she retorted, opening the thermos. "I came up the gill, by the holy well," she added. "It was perfectly peaceful and the moon's lovely. I'd have been glad to have had someone with me," she added truthfully, "but I thought I should make less noise alone."

"Aren't women wonderful?" grinned Rolph, as he accepted a sandwich, and Kate grinned back.

3

Five minutes later, Hoggett and Rolph set out together. There had been a period of heated argument, when Giles tried to insist that Kate could not be left in the farm-house without "protection," but Kate had said that it was not indoors that protection was needed, and that she could keep the doors bolted and would be perfectly safe. Rolph had grinned and put in, "And even if she sees me howling at the moon she still won't unbar the doors. I'm a desperate fellow, I am. Have you got a second stick, Hoggett? I rather fancy that cudgel of yours. I've got a pistol—"

Kate gave a horrified exclamation. "Then you can leave it here. I'm not going to have you shooting, you might hit Giles."

"I couldn't," he grinned. "It's not loaded. It's the look of the thing that's useful."

Hoggett looked very solemn. "We've got to be absolutely quiet, Francis. If we make a sound—"

"I know, I know," responded the other. "You might remember I've crawled all round that pool once this evening, and nobody spotted me. I know the way by this time. When we reach the coppice, you'd better bear right and I'll bear left."

Hoggett agreed, and they set out, leaving by the back door and slinking round the farm-house in the black shadows of the buildings.

It was a marvellous night. The moon rode high at this hour, and the world was white. As he walked, Giles Hoggett thought sorrowfully how his peaceful world seemed all upside down. He had had so many jolts that evening: he remembered the grim sight of Bord's sprawling body in the shippon: his own suspicion that Rolph was guilty, and then remembered, too, that message of Caroline's... moving the body. Plodding on, using all his skill to move silently and to utilise the shadow as cover, Giles felt the whole thing was a nightmare, and he wished he could wake up and find that he had been suffering from a bad dream.

At the edge of the coppice he bore left, testing every piece of ground before he put his weight on it. He was moving towards the old shippon and it was dark under the trees. He stood still for a breather and found his heart was pounding, not with physical exertion but with excitement. Suddenly a bird flew past him: then another, and there was a twitter in the branches: a wren gave its alarm call, a little whirring, chattering note, and a jay spoke harshly and angrily. Somewhere, close to the quarry pool, something was happening to disturb all the birds. Giles went on towards the ridge. He could hear movements now, a creak and a faint plash of water. He realised then; something was being hauled up from the quarry pool, something heavy and resistant.

4

When the white swathe of light cut across the darkness, Giles had a momentary sense of dizziness and fear. The light shone in his face, dazzling him: he put up a hand to shade his eyes and suddenly saw a wild vision of struggling men. On the bank of the pool, two men had been hauling in a rope, while a third coiled the slack on the ground behind them. So much he saw in a split second, and then another figure leaped across his vision, a swift, lithe, dark form, springing not at the men but at the rope. He jumped for the rope just behind the two men who were hauling, lifted it, hurled himself sideways with it, and in a flash the whole group were involved, tied up, tripped up. The rope was still held taut by the weight of something in the pool, and when the slack was caught up by that springing figure the men who were hauling let go their hold, only to find the rope impeding them in every way. The third man, who had been hauling in the slack, turned away from the light to spring into the shadows. Giles saw him, and sprang almost involuntarily, gripped cloth and arm, shoved his knee up, heaved forward for a wrestling grip, while Macdonald's voice urged, "Sit on his head, Hoggett, sit on it. Here, Reeves, quickly..."

Another voice yelled: "I've got him. Walsh, here... oh, you would, would you. Take that..."

Giles, panting but triumphant, had pinned down his own captive and was fully occupied "consolidating" his position. Between his own breathless heavings he heard a high sing-song voice: "I'll put you in the pool, indeed. I've waited for this... in the pool you go, you dirty twister..."

"He's a Welshman," thought Giles bemusedly. "Who's he drowning?"

"The damned Taffy—haven't we got enough to do without any life-saving," grumbled a familiar Cockney voice, and then Francis Rolph's voice spoke:

"I'll keep my knee in his back, chum, then you can chuck a rope-end to the guy who's drowning."

At that moment, quite suitably, a donkey brayed with all its might. A donkey giving voice at close-quarters is a startling sound. When Giles Hoggett had had time to think about things, he told Kate that the "asinine epilogue" was most appropriate, but at the moment that it occurred he was too busy to think of epigrams.

5

Giles Hoggett, very fully occupied in dealing with the man he had straddled, heard Macdonald's voice close behind him.

"Handcuffs for this chap. If you kick, my bonny lad, you'll get kicked back. We haven't time for conventions this evening. That's got it. Well played, Hoggett—tie his ankles. He's a slippery customer. How many have we collected? Three, plus the lad in the pool. Walsh has laid his man out. Who's the chap who came up with you?"

Giles sat back on his heels, panting. "It's Rolph," he said. "He insisted on coming."

"Well, I'm not saying he wasn't useful," called Macdonald over his shoulder. "All right, Mr. Rolph, we'll make this one fast. He's an old friend of mine, too fat for parties like this one. Knocked silly at the moment, but he's coming round. Now who's the chap Walsh has just collected? Oh, the Welshman. You shouldn't go heaving your old pals in quarry pools, you've only yourself to blame. Got him, Reeves? He can't swim, ought to be grateful he's not drowned."

Giles sat and blinked in the merciless white glare: it was a sort of portable searchlight, and his eyes weren't used to it yet, but he could recognise at least one of the motley group who were being so firmly dealt with by the three C.I.D. men. That one was Tom Field. He had been hurled into the dark waters of the quarry pool: he had sunk twice, and the second time he had come up he had grabbed the rope-end which Reeves had thrown him, grabbed it as any drowning man will snatch at a support. He stood now, swaying and spluttering, too bemused to resist, while Macdonald put handcuffs on him. For the first time Hoggett heard the formal words of arrest spoken... "for assaulting a man unknown to you... may be taken down and used in evidence..."

"But David Wynne wasn't unknown to him," muttered Hoggett. He was completely bewildered.

Francis Rolph was being very helpful. While Reeves had thrown the slack end of the rope out to Tom Field, Rolph had gripped the same rope just above the ridge of the pool. When Macdonald ceased speaking, Rolph yelled out: "I can't hold on for ever... this thing's damned heavy."

In a second Reeves and Walsh were behind him, hauling for dear life. Hoggett felt miserably that he ought to help, but he hadn't the heart to move. He knew exactly what to expect at the end of that rope. He saw Macdonald leaning over the ridge, queerly silhouetted against the glare of white light. He heard his voice: "Here, Hoggett, lend a hand—it's awkward over this ridge."

Giles went as he was bid: he gripped a thin hawser as he was told to do. It was wet and cold and slimy, and he hauled on it, sick at heart. His shoulder muscles ached with the strain, until, with a sudden jerk, the weight came over the ridge and rested on the rock. Giles went ignominiously backwards and was fielded neatly by Reeves. Sitting up again, he stared at the object they had hauled from the pool. Anything less like a corpse he had never seen.

"It's not David Wynne," he gasped weakly.

"No, it's not David Wynne. It's Irish whisky or French brandy," said Macdonald. "David Wynne's behind you. It was he who chucked Tom Field in the pool just now. I told you that preconceived notions play the deuce with a man's judgment."

Reeves was leaning thoughtfully over the pool. "There's plenty more where that came from," he said.

"I always supposed there would be," rejoined Macdonald. "They wouldn't have run an organisation like this for a couple of cases of whisky."

"Whisky…" breathed Hoggett… "only whisky…"

SEVENTEEN

I

"I WAS THE MUG ALL THROUGH THIS CASE," DECLARED MR. Hoggett. He spoke quite cheerfully, without any rancour at all, but Macdonald promptly contradicted him.

"Oh, no, you weren't, Hoggett. It was you who laid the foundations of this case. Without you, there might never have been a case."

"If you want a mug, choose me," said Caroline Bourne.

They were sitting by the Hoggetts' fireside at Wenningby: Giles and Kate, Francis Rolph, Caroline Bourne and Macdonald himself.

"I really *was* a mug, because I insisted that Francis had tripped over a bramble," Caroline continued. "I suppose it was wishful thinking, because I was so anxious not to have any 'orrors on my new land. I admit that I began to feel uneasy at Hauxhead when that Stern man first talked to me about Broadgarth, but when I heard those voices in the maze, talking about 'moving the body from the quarry pool' I was really in despair."

"I haven't heard about that part of the story," put in Macdonald, but she replied:

"Oh, it was all over in a few seconds. After I'd gone up to bed and had my bath I looked for my book and couldn't find it. Then I remembered that I'd left it in the maze. I slipped a topcoat over my pyjamas and went down to a side door into the garden, as I didn't want to go through the front hall looking such a guy. I got outside and found my way to the maze quite easily. I'd learnt the key of it—first right, second left, all the way, and I was nearly at the centre when I heard voices. I was annoyed, because I knew I'd left the book on the bench in the very middle. The first voice said: 'Well, the whole thing's an infernal nuisance, but they'll pull it off if they hustle. That quarry pool was a marvellous find, but someone was bound to rumble it,' and then a second voice said: 'Are they moving the body to-night?' I thought of Francis and how he'd been attacked, and of Giles, being so suspicious, and I just didn't wait for any more. I hurried back and I found that A.A. box in the road and phoned Kate... And the body *wasn't* a body after all!" she ended joyfully. "They were just using that expression, instead of saying 'the goods' or 'operation alcohol,' or some jargon like that. It simply gave me the horrors. When I'd telephoned, I crept back into the hotel and up to my room in a state of perfect dither. Then Kate phoned about midnight and the night porter put the call through to my room and I heard everything was all right. *What* a story!"

Macdonald chuckled. "Quite a story. I didn't realise you'd be let in for anything so sensational at Hauxhead, though I did wonder if that five-starred establishment could have any connection with the other events which were so confusing at the time."

"I'm still feeling confused," said Kate. "I want Macdonald to tell us the whole story and sort it all out. We've all been guessing wildly, but we never got anywhere near the truth. Giles and Francis both guessed there was a body in the pool, and Inspector Bord thought there was a body in the well, and I thought there must be buried treasure on Broadgarth land; and then Macdonald made sense of the whole thing while we were still floundering."

"In short, we were all mugs," said Rolph gloomily, but again Macdonald contradicted.

"Nothing of the kind," he said. "Every one of you present, Mr. and Mrs. Hoggett, Miss Bourne and Mr. Rolph, contributed something towards the sum-total in this case, and I am in the best position to appreciate that fact. Mrs. Hoggett said that 'dementia prevailed' here. For once she was wrong. From the point of view of pure detection this was an unusually interesting case. It really did involve detection, the mental process of arguing from observation, and interpreting facts which might have had various meanings. Say if we get back to the beginning, to Miss Bourne's contribution."

"My only contribution was wishful thinking," said Caroline contritely, and again Macdonald contradicted.

"No, it wasn't. Your contribution was in speaking up loud and clear when an unknown auctioneer tried to ignore your bid. The auctioneer *did* try to ignore your bid: we have Mrs. Brough's evidence to that effect. You spoke up so clearly that it wasn't possible to ignore you. That was your first contribution."

"But why had that any bearing on the case?" demanded Caroline.

"It had a great deal, as I will explain later," said Macdonald. "Mr. Rolph's first contribution was more involuntary, getting batted over the head. It was perhaps the most valuable contribution of all, because it provided Mr. Hoggett with a basis for detection. But previous to that incident, Mrs. Hoggett provided one of those pieces of detailed observation which can always, from her, be relied on as accurate. She said that the track from the old cottage to the quarry pool must have been used regularly by a number of people because the track was hard. If it hadn't been used regularly, the track would have been covered in soft leaf-mould, and she was able to prove that the track had been used since the bluebells had come up, because some of the bluebells had been trampled shortly after they had appeared above ground."

Macdonald paused a moment, and then added: "Having stated those preliminaries, I want you to consider the matter purely from my point of view when I first arrived here. I came up north for the straightforward duty of arresting a man for smuggling offences. The man was named William Maredeth, and it had been proved that certain cases consigned to him contained contraband. As you know, I failed to arrest him because he was not on the boat he was reported to have travelled on. Now you must all of you be aware that if the Excise officers ask for help from Scotland Yard it is not on account of small evasions of Customs duties. While it's no part of my business to give away the methods of detection used by the Excise men, I can say this: they often become aware that smuggling is taking place on a large scale when certain dutiable commodities are more plentiful in some areas than they should be. That was the case in the northwestern division, and my department was called in to trace one proved offender, the man known as William Maredeth, a man with large business interests, known to have control of considerable capital."

"But we didn't know all that to begin with," observed Giles Hoggett, and Macdonald replied:

"Not in so many words. I told you that I had come north on duty, for the purpose of arresting a man who had been evading Customs duties. From that statement you could have argued a good deal, but evasion of Customs duties did not interest you at all. I knew that and perhaps I took advantage of it as far as you were concerned. I will enlarge on that later. For the moment I want you to consider my own point of view at the outset of the case. I came up here on the trail of a man who had been evading the law very ingeniously for a long time. In order to evade Customs duties a man has to be ingenious these days; he also has to be pretty smart to evade arrest once our department is really out after him. Now I have always found it a sound argument that if peculiar things happen in an area where a known law-breaker is at large, then those peculiar things are worth investigating. There is always a possibility that they are germane to the case."

Kate Hoggett spoke here. "You're really telling us that we might have argued quite a lot from the casual remarks you let drop. You told us that you had been expecting your man on the Heysham boat, and that you had been up to Ulverston, where you thought he had a house. That is, you were investigating the area between Heysham and Ulverston, around Morecambe Bay. Because our interests are concentrated on the land, we tend to forget how close we are to the sands."

"If I'd heard about evasion of Customs duties, I should only have thought of one thing," put in Rolph. "To wit, whisky. Considering the stuff used to be sold somewhere round three bob a bottle, you don't need great arithmetical powers to see what a profit you can make out of it if you *do* evade Customs duty."

"Agreed," said Macdonald, "but let us get back to my own point of view, which was what I was trying to expound. Mrs. Hoggett told me her husband was out 'detecting' at the quarry pool, and she gave me a very succinct account of the events which had caused his outing. On arrival at the quarry pool, I was bound to admit the suitability of the spot for hiding anything, whether it was a corpse or whether it was smuggled whisky. It had occurred to me that if smuggling were going on on a large scale, it was highly unlikely that most of the stuff came over concealed in consignments of legitimate imports. Some of it might come that way, but a larger proportion might well be smuggled in by private transport, and if that were so, some safe place for dumping it might be very useful. Now I want to make it clear that any theory I held on this matter was as hypothetical as the corpse which Mr. Hoggett believed to be concealed in the pool. He had perfectly sound reasons for his suspicions, and he believed that Rolph was knocked over the head because he was a possible witness to the concealment of the corpse."

"There must have been *some* reason for the attack on Rolph," argued Hoggett. "It's no use telling me that a man who's played rugger doesn't know when he's been tackled. All this argument about brambles and briars seemed just foolish to me."

"And there you were perfectly right," said Macdonald. "I think your only error in reasoning was to omit considering any odd things which had happened *before* Rolph was attacked. When you list the unusual happenings which preceded the attack you find they are quite numerous. In the first case, when Mrs. Hoggett and Miss Bourne went together to see the quarry pool, they found a hard track, worn by use, and evidence that folk had passed when the bluebells first came up: next, the timber from the cottage had been looted. At the auction, where there was a stranger as auctioneer, a 'townee,' to use Miss Bourne's description, bid against her and later tried to buy the property from her—"

"Yes," said Giles thoughtfully, "I did say that was unusual—"

"—and Emma Brough said that the auctioneer tried to ignore Caroline," put in Kate.

"—and someone else tried to buy the coppice when I wanted it," murmured Caroline."

"That's it," said Macdonald. "From these items of evidence, I argued that someone was taking an active interest in this property before Rolph *was* attacked at all. Now, examining Hoggett's theory in the light of these facts, while it seemed quite conceivable to me that Tom Field might have tried to hide the body of a man he had murdered in the quarry pool, I argued that such a proceeding would have been made necessary by the sudden emergency of the postulated murder. I could not believe that the using of the track, and the oddities connected with the auction, were a logical prelude to this hypothetical murder. I did not deny that there was a possibility of murder, but if Field had murdered Wynne in the circumstances which Hoggett postulated, then the murder had taken place on the impulse of a moment, after a sudden quarrel. It could not be linked up with the facts concerning the previous use of the quarry pool track, nor with the odd behaviour of the auctioneer, nor with the attempt to buy the coppice and the unexpectedly vigorous bidding for a remote smallholding."

Giles Hoggett rubbed his head: he was evidently thinking hard. "I argued like this," he said. "I always thought that Field had had some business which took him to the quarry pool: he knew the place well, and he knew that folks around here seldom went near it, so it seemed a reasonably safe place to hide the body."

"Yes, that's all sound enough up to a point," agreed Macdonald, "but in my experience a murderer does not hide a body in a place which he has been known to visit. The condition of the track suggested that more than one person had used it, from which one could argue that somebody else, an associate or associates, knew that Field was in the habit of using it, and if Wynne's body had been discovered in the pool, Field's associate could have given damning evidence against Field. However, I kept an open mind on the matter. While there was no proof at all that a murder *had* taken place, I admitted that Hoggett's reasoning might be valid. Since I was aware that his knowledge of the locality and its inhabitants was more comprehensive than that of any of the local police force, I asked him to pursue his own investigations to see if he arrived at any definite result—"

Giles Hoggett chuckled: "'To follow my own hare' was the way you put it, Macdonald. Isn't it true to say that I had started one hare and you had started another, and that you used me as a cover to your own investigations?"

"Perfectly true, Hoggett," agreed Macdonald. "I argued thus: if your suspicions about Wynne's death were true, you were quite capable of bringing facts to light which would justify a full police investigation. Remember that you had very little—if any—proof that a murder had been committed. For myself, if it turned out that the activities at the quarry pool were concerned with smuggling on a large scale, it was useful to me to have a ready-made explanation in this locality for any interest which was being taken in the quarry pool and the coppice. 'Mr. Hoggett was seeing to it'; not the police, mark you."

"So you *were* useful after all, Giles," said Kate. "You were Macdonald's 'cover story.'"

"All right. I'm glad if I was useful," said Giles, "but what I want to know is this. What did Macdonald think had *really* happened when Rolph was attacked?"

"Yes. I chewed over that for a long time," said Macdonald. "I told you that I believed that *if* the quarry pool were being used by smugglers, the organisation was on a large scale. I saw at once that a man like Tom Field could be very useful to that organisation. His tractor and trailer outfit provided a most valuable type of transport: its great value was that a farm tractor, of all vehicles, is the least likely to attract the attention of the police. Agricultural contractors cover considerable distances: they are on the road at all hours, because their speed is so low that their journeys take a long time, and they fit into the picture."

"That's a very good point," said Giles. "We're so used to them we never notice them; and so you believed that Field was about to dump a consignment in the pool when he saw Rolph?"

"No. I didn't think that," said Macdonald. "If that *had* been so, Rolph must have heard the tractor approaching. One thing tractors can't do is to move silently. Rolph heard nothing. Therefore I argued that Field—if it *was* Field—had come to the pool to meet somebody or to inspect arrangements. Perhaps to make sure there was nothing for the inquisitive Miss Bourne to notice."

"Then why should he have bothered to lay *me* out?" asked Rolph plaintively.

"You may well ask. So did I," said Macdonald. "I had ruled out the idea of a consignment being dumped, because Rolph heard no tractor. It wasn't likely that the stuff would have been manhandled for any considerable distance—"

"Here, wait a minute," said Kate. "That argument applies still more strongly to Giles's corpse. He said Field would have moved the body on his tractor, and we never thought of asking Francis if he had heard a tractor."

"I should have said so if I *had* heard one," said Rolph, and Macdonald nodded.

"Of course you would, but you stressed the absolute silence. Very well. Here was one man, possibly Field, attacking another man for no reason that I could see: but remember Mr. Hoggett's evidence. After being associated together for some time, Field and Wynne had quarrelled. We knew that. We knew that Wynne had tried to get rid of Field, only Mrs. Wynne had insisted that the ploughing and planting must be finished. Wasn't there a possibility that Wynne had realised he was being involved in something illicit and dangerous? After that row with Field, might not Wynne have said: 'I'm going to find out what he's really up to, and give him away to the police'? Now, following that argument, isn't it reasonable to postulate that when Field saw Rolph in the moonlight, Field suddenly thought that it was David Wynne he saw, and attacked him on impulse? It seemed much more reasonable to me that Field should attack a man he knew and feared than one who was quite unknown to him."

"Well," said Giles, "I must say that never occurred to me... of course, it's reasonable enough when you think it out. But wait a minute, didn't Rolph say he thought he heard two men approaching... breathing heavily."

"He said he *thought* there were two men," said Macdonald, and Rolph nodded. "Actually there was only one man: the other noises were the owls, as Mrs. Hoggett suggested," said Macdonald. "If my idea were anywhere near the truth, I was willing to hazard a guess that the aggressor was pretty badly frightened when he had time to think. Rolph was knocked out so completely that he made a very good effect as a corpse, face downwards in the moonlight. You've got to remember that Field is only a country lad, for all that he got in with this smuggling gang. When a country lad is frightened, he runs away, just like any other lad. That's what Field did. He ran away, not knowing if he'd committed murder or not."

Kate Hoggett spoke again here. "Then it was Field who sent the money and that note to Alice Wynne?" she asked, and Macdonald nodded.

"That's it. Field sent it to prevent her making awkward inquiries about her husband. You see, he was so frightened that he made the same mistake as Hoggett did in the shippon: he believed he'd seen the man he expected to see. A body lying face downwards in the moonlight isn't so easy to recognise, as Hoggett found."

2

"Well, that's all right as far as it goes," said Rolph. "Field thought I was Wynne and that I was snooping, so he batted me one and bolted, but that doesn't explain why you were so convinced that Field was mixed up with your racketeers."

"No, but between you you'd provided me with lots more evidence," went on Macdonald. "We've mentioned the fact that the track had been frequently used, and we've gone into the Field-Wynne quarrel. We've also mentioned the auctioneer, a very fat chap who tried to freeze Miss Bourne out of the bidding. He didn't succeed, and shortly afterwards Miss Bourne was offered a handsome commission to write up Hauxhead Hotel. Now you must remember that the Maredeth group did not know that I was at Wenningby. If they had, they would never have drawn attention to Hauxhead. It seemed highly relevant to me: a newly opened, very luxurious hotel, which needed to make a lot of money to justify its purchase and upkeep. The sale of drinks is always profitable to a luxury hotel, but how much more profitable it would be on duty-free liquor. The mention of Hauxhead sent me up to town, but I had also got another promising side-line—Judge Warrender."

Giles looked unhappy. "Don't tell me he's in it too," he said.

"Not a bit of it!" replied Macdonald. "He's honest to his fingertips, but I had been wondering how on earth Maredeth and Co. ever heard of the quarry pool. Judge Warrender gave the answer. He had described it to one of Maredeth's associates on his voyage home, and they came to inspect it as a possible hidey-hole. Of course I didn't learn this until after we had collected the gang, but it's an interesting sidelight. Well, during my brief stay in town I set inquiries going about Judge Warrender's fellow passengers and about the syndicate which owned Hauxhead. On my journey back north, in company with Reeves and Walsh, I was pondering over the possibilities of landing contraband on Morecambe sands, and Walsh was very helpful in making suggestions. It seemed probable to me that Maredeth had his own methods of getting to and from Ireland without recourse to the usual shipping lines. The more I thought about the sands, the more I saw the possibilities."

"Yes," agreed Rolph, "and the quarry pool is within convenient distance of the sands; I see all that. What beats me is why you didn't search the ruddy pool and have done with it."

"Not on your life!" said Macdonald. "I wasn't in the least interested in collecting a few hundred cases of whisky. What I wanted was the men who brought it in. The one thing I was afraid of was that Hoggett would go diving again and find it. It wouldn't have suited me at all.

No. I was prepared to play a waiting game—only poor Bord rattled the whole lot up. They knew that once a policeman on duty had been wounded it was time to quit."

"I suppose it was Field who attacked Bord, too?" asked Rolph, and Macdonald chuckled.

"No. It wasn't Field who attacked him. Field had been sleeping at Broadgarth, and Mrs. Hoggett's friend Wilson visited him there. Bord found them both, up in the hayloft in the barn. Nobody attacked Bord. He was just telling them they must come with him to the station to be interrogated when he forgot where he was, and took a step backwards. He turned a somersault as he fell and hit his head on the threshing-floor. A pretty kettle of fish for the other two. They made the best of a bad job: Wilson sent the phone message to explain Bord's absence, Field got busy informing the boss what had happened, and there were orders for a general evacuation, 'scram' as they put it, clear the pool, disperse the fresh cargo. They dared not wait any longer. Things had got too hot for them. Fortunately, with Hoggett and Rolph to assist, and with David Wynne behaving like the crazy Welshman he is, the thing worked out very satisfactorily for us."

3

"But who *is* William Maredeth, and where was he while this was going on?" demanded Caroline.

Macdonald began to laugh. "You're the only one who has really had the chance to study him," he replied. "You've seen him twice."

Caroline looked blank. "You mean he was at Hauxhead?"

"Certainly; but you saw him before that, only you didn't recognise him the second time, or rather you didn't place him. I think you did recognise him. Now then, Hoggett: apart from Mr. Wilson, on what occasion has a stranger appeared in this neighbourhood when no stranger was expected?"

Giles looked blank, and suddenly Caroline gave a yell.

"Why, he means the auctioneer!" she yelled. "Fool that I was! I *knew* I'd seen the wine-waiter before. It was obvious he knew me by sight, because he knew I went to the Café Napoleon, and I thought he was a waiter there, but now I realise where I'd seen him. The wine-waiter at Hauxhead *was* the auctioneer at the Broadgarth sale, only he wore a wig and he looked quite different at the auction."

"That's it," said Macdonald. "I was pretty certain that Maredeth had several aliases and doubtless some occupation which would serve as a cover story if things got too hot for him. There's nothing unexpected in a business man having started as an auctioneer. When I heard about the auction it struck me that the auctioneer had behaved very oddly. Of course he might have been trying to get a private commission through, or he might have been playing his own little game. Actually it was the small townee who was bidding for Maredeth."

"But why didn't he go on bidding?" asked Caroline.

"Because he didn't want to focus attention on the property publicly," said Macdonald. "He thought he could probably buy from you later without rousing too much comment. Maredeth, under the name of Robert Sharp, bought a partnership in that auctioneering firm, partly as an alternative identity, partly to be able to have a large finger in the pie when likely properties came into the market. I have no doubt that Miss Bourne's vigorous and audible bidding annoyed him a very great deal, especially as Wilson had failed to materialise at the sale."

Mr. Hoggett rubbed his head thoughtfully, and Macdonald said: "Look here, Hoggett. Try your hand at a recapitulation, just to see if you're clear about it. Give us 'a logical exposition of things'—to quote your own phrase."

"Right," said Giles, fumbling for another cigarette.

"Here you are," said Macdonald. "I've still got plenty and it's a small return for all the help you and Mrs. Hoggett have given me."

Puffing happily at a perfectly good cigarette, not one reconstructed from fag-ends, Giles began:

"As I see it, this case begins when an associate of Maredeth's travelled home from the East with Judge Warrender. The latter, talking over old times, gave a detailed account of the quarry, the coppice and the old cottage. The operative parts of this description, if I may lapse into modern jargon, were the secluded position of the quarry, hidden just off a main road, and its proximity to the bay and the sands. When this description was repeated to Maredeth, he said, 'By gad, it's the goods. Bring me an Ordnance Survey map.'" As was usual with him, once he was well launched into his narrative, Giles Hoggett's sense of the dramatic expressed itself in both speech and gesture.

"'By gad, my boy, it's just what we've been looking for,'" improvised Giles with relish: "'A coupla' miles from the Carlisle-Liverpool-Manchester main road, right plumb in the middle of a network of by-roads and footpaths, easy access to the bay, yet as secluded as though it were in the heart of the jungle. Let's go and look, old boy. Seeing's believing.' So they went and looked, and it was even better than their wildest hopes," continued Hoggett. "Moreover, the nearest farm, being Broadgarth, was owned by a bedridden man and the land farmed from Bromsgrove, so that the track to Broadgarth was hardly ever used. Of course it meant a lot of work, arranging transport and personnel: mussel-gatherers for the landing, a donkey team for special work—"

Kate snorted indignantly here: "Donkey team indeed. When Walsh told me about the donkey-man and the old bridle path, you said you didn't believe it—"

"I know better now," said Giles placidly. "Where was I? A donkey team for special work and road transport. Very important that. 'A farm tractor, old boy, the very thing.' I must say this auctioneer was a good organiser. Well, they'd landed several good cargoes by motor-boat and rubber dinghy and got quite a nice store secreted in the quarry pool, ready for 'direct transmission' as the B.B.C. says, when the owner of Broadgarth died and it was decided to auction the property. 'Leave that to me, dear boy,' says the boss, 'I'll fix it'—only our Caroline spoilt that little game. The auctioneer didn't worry too much. He said all along that they must be careful not to draw attention to the place by a sensational sale. 'She'll sell all right, we'll find some good reasons to induce her to take a good offer,' said the boss (of course Wilson's story about the well was one of the good reasons). Then the boss said: 'Meantime, let's get her away from the place *pro tem*. Offer her a commission to write up Hauxhead. She's quite bright, we can probably use her stuff.'" Ignoring Caroline's indignant sniff, Giles lowered his voice to stress his most dramatic point: "And *then*," he said, "just as everything was working beautifully, Tom Field threw a spanner in the works by attacking Rolph and getting that busybody Hoggett interested in the quarry pool. They'd had a bit of trouble with Field before," said Giles conversationally, "and they must have been very angry when he showed signs of going behind their backs and trying to buy Broadgarth himself, but he'd been very useful with his tractor: he'd got a job in the neighbourhood with the Wynnes, a cover story again. Is that too steep?" he inquired of Macdonald abruptly.

"Not at all. A very sound deduction," said the C.I.D. man.

"Good... Cover story. Oh, yes. Apropos of cover, Field had looted the timber from the cottage to conceal his illicit cargoes. He dealt in wood, and if he'd felled trees without permission he'd have got into trouble, but no one noticed the cottage was stripped, and a trailer full of firewood and old junk looked natural enough—"

"Hoggett," said Macdonald, "I congratulate you. That showed the real detective spirit."

"I can often see the details, after you've told me the main facts," said Giles modestly, "only I can never see the wood for the trees. However, about Field. They'd decided to sack him, of course, only they had to wait until they'd cleared the pool, because his tractor was so useful. Things were going pretty well: that fool Hoggett was out looking for corpses, but the police weren't really interested: Miss Bourne was safely at Hauxhead, enchanted with her noble bedroom, and the boss had given the C.I.D. the slip and was doing his stuff as wine-waiter—that chap has initiative," said Giles. "He really used his brains… yes, everything was going nicely and Wilson was told to contact Field to arrange for evacuating the pool, when Inspector Bord found the pair of them in the shippon and the final disaster was when Bord fell off the edge of the loft—really he ought to have been more careful," said Giles. "Those lofts are quite safe if you're sensible. But it put the cap on it for the miscreants. They did their best in a great hurry, and we all know the consequences. Have I included everything?" he wound up.

"It was a very fine effort," said Macdonald gravely. "Any questions from anybody?"

"Yes," said Kate. "Where was David Wynne all this time?"

"Never very far away," said Macdonald. "He was out to down Field, you must remember. Wynne left his home in a rage and in a hurry, with hardly any money in his pockets. The first few nights he slept in the hay in Broadgarth shippon: he went to Strand once or twice to see if he could get a line on Field's activities. Then he saw Field get into Broadgarth farm-house one night. Wynne knew that there had been some queer business connected with the quarry pool and he decided to watch it at night: he slept during the day in one of his own outhouses at Ashdale. He's a queer, brooding sort of fellow, by no means particularly bright, but he was convinced the quarry pool would give him the key to Field's secret, and in that he was perfectly right. He had been watching there for twelve solid hours before the showdown, hidden in the undergrowth. It's not surprising he went a bit crazy when the excitement started—he's given to these moods of alternate exaltation and depression."

"Was it Tom Field who monkeyed with Judge Warrender's car outside the Preston garage?" asked Giles.

Macdonald nodded. "Yes. That was a queer coincidence. Warrender actually asked Field for directions to the quarry pool. Field was determined that Warrender shouldn't get there, so he lifted the bonnet unobserved and loosened the lead from the battery. Humorously enough, the lead didn't work loose until Warrender was almost at the Broadgarth turning."

"And I suppose it was Tom Field whom Caroline and I met when we first went to the quarry pool," said Kate, "and Field who made the big footprints?"

"Yes," said Macdonald, "and he *was* carrying a heavy load. It was actually a sack of logs, wood he'd cut without permission. We found it later, at Broadgarth. In fact Hoggett used some of the logs."

"Well, that's about the lot," said Macdonald after a short pause. "Maredeth organised the racket, and Wilson was in with him, knowing all the details. There were a number of smaller fry, including lorry-drivers, mussel-gatherers and the donkey-man, who followed the old pack-horse tracks when he had a private consignment for the boss."

"What was the load on the donkey which Walsh trailed?" asked Kate.

"Liqueur brandy, Mrs. Hoggett. A very valuable private consignment for Maredeth, which he wanted for his own particular use. You see, the rest of the cargo that night was to be 'dispersed,' as they said, but Maredeth wanted his own precious tipple to be brought direct to him. Well, he won't have the pleasure of savouring the aroma of that little consignment—nor any of his friends, either. We've got the whole gang, and the principals, at least, were caught actually on the job. So a hearty vote of thanks to all of you who assisted, particularly to my private 'cover story.'" Macdonald turned to Giles with the friendly grin which made his long lean face look youthful again.

"You won't hold it against me, Hoggett? You see, you were very useful to me, because while everybody in the neighbourhood was watching *you*, they hadn't time to be interested in *me*."

"I'm very glad if I helped, in however small a way," said Giles cheerfully, "but *next* time, Macdonald, I'll think out first principles more carefully. I slipped up because I didn't examine all the prefacing of the attack, so to speak."

4

"And now all the excitement's over, can I have peaceful possession of my brakes and brackendales, peats and mosses, to say nothing of my still waters?" asked Caroline plaintively.

Macdonald laughed. "Yes, you can have peaceful possession, Miss Bourne. Had you realised how apt was your own favourite description of the quarry pool?"

Caroline looked blank, and Mr. Hoggett chuckled. "Still waters, meaning potable alcohols," he interpreted solemnly. Glancing at the clock, his jaw fell. "I'm late for milking," he said in consternation.

Macdonald got up, too. "I learned to milk once, when I was a lad," he said. "I've never dared to mention it here."

Giles Hoggett seized him by the arm. "It's a thing you never forget, Macdonald. There's a nice quiet Ayrshire I've got…"

Macdonald threw a glance at Mrs. Hoggett.

"Go and try," she encouraged him. "You've no idea what a compliment you're being paid. It's akin to a vote of confidence on a comprehensive scale. And you see, no matter what happens in the outside world, the cows have still got to be milked. And milking's such a nice chatty occupation. The cows like to hear your voices, you know, and they'll enjoy hearing you and Giles talk over all the details you forgot to mention just now…"

"Aye," said Mr. Hoggett, as Macdonald followed him through the kitchen, "a cow's company like."

Caroline Bourne, sitting by the fire, had taken out her notebook and fountain pen.

"Still waters," she murmured… "How did it all begin… 'Giles, is that the place'?"

ALSO AVAILABLE BY THE AUTHOR

Yet for him the city had a charm all of its own... After all, under its gaiety and brilliance Vienna has always been a centre of intrigue.

On a bright autumn morning, Superintendent Macdonald boards the plane bound for Vienna to visit his old friend Dr. Natzler. His detective's eye notes some unusual passengers including Elizabeth Le Vendre, new secretary to the diplomat Sir Walter Vanbrugh—but this is supposed to be a holiday. After arriving with the Natzlers and crossing paths with Elizabeth again, Macdonald settles into the trip as best he can, determined to relax for once.

But when Elizabeth is reported missing and a string of violence and murder encircles Vanbrugh and Natzler's social set, Macdonald's short-lived stint as a tourist comes to an end—and the race to stop a killer on the loose begins.

First published in 1956 and steeped in the turbulent history of post-war Vienna, this edition ushers E.C.R. Lorac's characteristically atmospheric classic mystery back into print for the first time in over 65 years.

ALSO AVAILABLE BY THE AUTHOR

While hot on the heels of serial coupon-racketeer Gordon Ginner, Chief Inspector MacDonald of Scotland Yard receives word of a peculiar incident up in Lancashire—the fishing cottage of a local farmer has been broken into, with an assortment of seemingly random items missing which include a reel of salmon line, a large sack and two iron dogs (or andirons) from his fireplace. This incident becomes all the more enticing to MacDonald when a body washes up on the banks of the River Lune not far from the cottage in question; the body of Gordon Ginner.

First published in 1946 and set in the fell country of Lunesdale over the course of a rainy September, *The Theft of the Iron Dogs* is the very picture of a cosy crime mystery and showcases Lorac's masterful attention to detail and deep affection for both Lunesdale and its residents.

ALSO AVAILABLE
IN THE BRITISH LIBRARY
CRIME CLASSICS SERIES

Big Ben Strikes Eleven	DAVID MAGARSHACK
Death of an Author	E. C. R. LORAC
The Black Spectacles	JOHN DICKSON CARR
Death of a Bookseller	BERNARD J. FARMER
The Wheel Spins	ETHEL LINA WHITE
Someone from the Past	MARGOT BENNETT
Who Killed Father Christmas?	ED. MARTIN EDWARDS
Twice Round the Clock	BILLIE HOUSTON
The White Priory Murders	CARTER DICKSON
The Port of London Murders	JOSEPHINE BELL
Murder in the Basement	ANTHONY BERKELEY
Fear Stalks the Village	ETHEL LINA WHITE
The Cornish Coast Murder	JOHN BUDE
Suddenly at His Residence	CHRISTIANNA BRAND
The Edinburgh Mystery	ED. MARTIN EDWARDS
Checkmate to Murder	E. C. R. LORAC
The Spoilt Kill	MARY KELLY
Smallbone Deceased	MICHAEL GILBERT
The Story of Classic Crime in 100 Books	MARTIN EDWARDS
The Pocket Detective: 100+ Puzzles	KATE JACKSON
The Pocket Detective 2: 100+ More Puzzles	KATE JACKSON

Many of our titles are also available
in eBook, large print and audio editions